THE
REGULATORS
DEAD LINE

WWW.BENBRUCE.CO.UK

By the same author

The Regulators

The Regulators: Shadow of Malice

First published in Great Britain on Amazon Kindle Direct in 2024
by Ben Bruce

Cover design by Sean Strong

Edited by Sophie Bristow

ISBN 9781999846947

For the kids, Jack and Eliza

1

Nathan Nelmes always wanted to be a journalist. From an early age, writing stories for the school newspaper, Nelmes had enjoyed the buzz of being the one in the know. Sometimes that had got him in trouble. He had a nose for a story, as the old cliché went. He didn't care who he upset either, and if there was a tale of a teacher being unfair or crossing a supposed line, Nathan was always more than happy to put it down in black and white. Often, those stories never made it to print. Staff would intercept them, Nathan would end up in the headteacher's office, and the world would be none the wiser. For some people, that would be a lesson learned. Not for Nathan. That became his fuel.

Nelmes's passion for breaking stories upset as many editors as it had teachers. His first jobs had been for local newspapers. They were far more used to telling stories about school fetes than scurrilous exposés of corrupt local councillors, especially without always being able to back up the accusations he made in the surest sense. There were other publishers, however, that loved him. The rise of the internet meant that his specific brand of investigative journalism found a home online. His reputation grew. Stories were broken. Scandals were exposed. Nathan Nelmes became the scourge of those who had something to hide. The *Daily Inquirer* offered him a role as their chief investigative journalist, and his reputation was cemented.

That had brought him to the attention of David Warner. David was the head of an underground vigilante group, the Regulators, an organisation that targeted those who skirted the law and avoided punishment for the crimes they committed. The same sort of people Nelmes targeted. Venal politicians, people in power who abused their position. Both sides could offer the other information. Nelmes often filled in blanks in David Warner's investigations and, in turn, when it was decided the best punishment was publicly exposing these people, Nelmes would get a huge scoop. It was a profitable relationship for both. Warner had moved upstairs in the Regulators, so contact with Nathan Nelmes had been passed to Jack Quinn, then Adam Morgan. It was Morgan who, two years ago, had brought Nelmes his biggest story.

The Regulators had stumbled upon a honeypot operation, run by an aristocrat called Lord Briar. Young children were used to entice and entrap politicians and other people of influence with the purpose of compromising and controlling them. Morgan had brought a dossier to Nelmes, and Nelmes had broken the story. It had nearly cost him his life.

Unbeknownst to Nelmes or Morgan, their plan to reveal the story had been uncovered, and Nelmes's computer had been doused in a nerve agent that left him in a coma for seven weeks. He had survived, but at cost. Both his forearms had been amputated, and he had been confined to a wheelchair for the most part, struggling to move more than a few painful steps at a time. It had barely been a life.

Now Nathan Nelmes was dead.

His name had cropped up in a police bulletin. The Regulators monitored all the usual methods of communication for the emergency services. Their job meant they had to move fast, keeping their actions covert, which was why Nelmes's name had been listed as soon as he became an informant. The sad reality was that it had to be. Sooner or later, someone was going to catch him out.

The alarm had been raised by a neighbour who hadn't seen Nelmes for a week. Police had entered and found the scene. Forensics had been called, and the alarm had been tripped. Adam Morgan and his partner Emmie Weston had made it to the scene just before the circus had arrived.

"ID." The officer at the front of the house put his arm out to halt Adam and Emmie as they approached. Both reached confidently for their badges, handing them to the officer. He scanned them, never noticing for one second that the Security Service IDs he was looking at were fake, before handing them back. "Didn't realise it was this big, sir." He looked a little taken aback.

"It might not be, but we need to be sure," Emmie reassured him.

"Uh, yes, of course, ma'am." The officer turned his attention to her, his face flushing as he realised he'd forgotten to address her. "In you go."

The overwhelming smell of decay hit Adam the moment they stepped through the door.

"Fucking hell," he groaned, looking at Emmie who was also pulling a face. There was no doubt there was a dead body in there. The smell lingered so heavily in the air, Adam half expected to see signs of it floating past. They walked through the flat towards the sound of officers talking, along a narrow corridor and into a bedroom. Now there was no doubt.

Two officers stood just inside a dirty and untidy bedroom. The window was closed to preserve the scene, but Morgan was sure that the officers must have debated opening it. The smell in here was even more intense. The room was in disarray. Bedsheets were twisted and stained, falling half off the bed to the floor like a linen waterfall. They were soaked with sweat, blood and God knew what else. Not just the sheets. The bed, the cupboards, the bedside table, even handprints on the wall. Then finally, the centrepiece: the word "Judas" scrawled in what Morgan presumed was Nelmes's blood. Under the morbid motif was Nelmes, tied by his ankles and the stumps of his amputated arms at each end, stripped naked, electrical tape over his mouth. Dried bloodstains marked the cream bedsheet on which he lay. There was a hell of a lot of blood. His body was a mess. Even given the broken state his assailant would have found it in. Hundreds of little cuts littered his body where his torturer had taken their time picking him apart. His toenails were gone. One testicle missing. Both eyelids removed. A massive slice carved up the middle of his abdomen, like a surgeon had been preparing to go in for open heart surgery.

Adam stepped forward, pulling on some blue protective gloves.

"Anyone checked?" Adam asked the two officers, who shrugged back.

Adam pulled the tape back, confirming something he already knew.

"You think he talked?" asked Emmie, who was still staring at the room, looking at the blood and guts mural that had been created.

"He couldn't," Adam grimaced. "No tongue. They didn't come here for information. They already knew who he was talking to and what he'd said. He'd have given up anything a long time before they got this far with him. They just wanted to leave a message."

"To us?" Emmie looked at Adam.

"Probably," Adam sighed. "But it could be to anyone else who was thinking of doing the same. Jesus, we need to get a copy of the forensics report quickly."

"I'll get Raf to forward it on. You think we might get lucky?" Emmie peered down at Nelmes who was staring at the ceiling. Raf Hoban was their deputy director. He was a by-the-book guy, something Adam had feared would make him an obstruction in a position of power, but he had found Raf's guidance to be far more constructive than he'd expected.

Adam followed Emmie's gaze down to Nelmes. His face still looked scared. Petrified, Adam thought.

"No. This was a professional job," Adam lamented. "But sometimes you get lucky, and sometimes they get sloppy. Whoever did this revelled in it; they might have taken their eye off the ball for just one moment. All we need is a print or a hair."

"There's a number of CCTV cameras in the area as well. We can get the footage and see if we've got anyone entering the property in the last week." Emmie walked through the process.

"It's a shared property so we might not have much success." Adam knew that it would be impossible for him and Emmie to canvass the neighbours without raising suspicion. If they overstayed their welcome, someone with more authority and clout would begin asking questions.

"I'm going to guess that there're no computers left," Emmie surmised. It was a fair assumption. Adam knew that whoever had done this had all the time in the world to carry out a full and thorough search. If they were looking for something, they would have found it and taken it with them. A power lead sat forlornly on a desk in the far corner of the room as if to highlight the fact. "It looks like they cleaned up."

"Well, looks like we're starting from scratch. You think this is to do with the dossier?"

"I don't know." Adam paused looking at the room. "The Judas thing makes me think that it wasn't. It doesn't fit. This suggests more as if he was betraying some sort of trust."

"Or it could be a red herring?"

"Like you said," Adam looked at her, "we're starting from scratch." He looked down at Nelmes once more. He couldn't help but feel guilt. He hadn't brought Nelmes into this world, he doubted anyone could have stopped him, but he'd certainly put him in harm's way more than once. No one deserved to be subject to this level of brutality in their final moments. He took one last look at the tortured look on Nelmes's face. "I promise you, though, we're going to find out who did this, if it's the last thing I do."

2

Thea Watts hated it when it was this hot. Summer was only a couple of weeks old, technically speaking, but already London sweltered under an oppressive heat that had lingered for what felt like months. It was making the whole city angry and on edge, which in turn put Thea on edge. She didn't need anything to make her angry.

Right now, the object of her anger was the officer in charge of securing the scene of Nathan Nelmes's murder. Thea had turned up with her boss, Jane Astley. That had caused a stir. It always did. Thea remembered her days in the police. Never once had MI5 turned up to one of her crime scenes, so it was hard for Thea to guess how she would have reacted. As she'd progressed up the ladder, through CID, the NCA and back to CID again, her contact with spooks had been limited. Even in those moments, she hadn't really been the point of contact. Her superiors, probably using their better judgement, had always stepped in.

That said, she knew that the sergeant they'd introduced themselves to today hadn't acted the way she would have done. The moment they'd flashed their identification at him, he'd become flustered, stammering his words, scrambling to try and do anything he could for them, only to reveal, ultimately, the shocking level of his incompetence.

"I'm really, really sorry." He'd repeated this more times than Thea could remember now. She even knew what he was going to say next. "I didn't know they weren't real. I'd never seen MI5 badges before." There it was.

The whole shit show had kicked off in seconds. Thea and Jane had come over more as a formality. Thea had insisted. Too much of the old cop inside of her. Jane had been happy to wait for the police to do the dirty work for them, before reading through reams of reports, but there were things that you couldn't ascertain about a crime scene from a report. You had to see it in person. Thea had made her case as forcefully as she could the moment the news of Nelmes's death had filtered through to them. She knew they wouldn't have long to get there. Jane had quickly agreed, either because she thought that Thea was making a great point, or that, ultimately, she knew that if Thea didn't get her own way, she wouldn't let her forget it for the rest of the day. Or week. Depending on how pissed off she was.

It was entirely plausible that another team from MI5 had visited the scene. Nelmes was a man of interest on many levels, not just for the reasons that had put him in Thea and Jane's crosshairs. But any thoughts of other agents were quickly extinguished when the sergeant, whose name Thea had forgotten by now, had asked for a second look at the identification, before asking if they were real, or if there were other types of MI5 ID. That was at least to his credit. He may not have spotted it at first, but he'd seen enough differences between what Thea and Jane were presenting to him and what he'd seen earlier to be able to spot that at least one set of identifications were fake. The ability to do that in just a couple of seconds was impressive. Perhaps when his police career was in tatters, he could find work as a bouncer at a night club.

Thea had sworn. Quietly at first and then loudly when that didn't do the trick. Jane had provided the proof that the sergeant needed to be happy that they were legitimate Security Services operatives. Thea had then got to work, finding a selection of photographs of people who she assumed would have been behind the fake identifications. The sergeant didn't make it to the third photograph. He quickly identified Adam Morgan and Emmie Weston, which made Thea even angrier. She swore again, even louder this time, before admonishing him.

"Adam Morgan's had his face plastered all over bulletins in police stations for the last year. Emmie Weston too," she ranted. "Do you not pay any attention to what you're being told?"

The sergeant could only shrug, unable to offer either an excuse or genuine reason for his failure to spot one of the most prominent vigilantes in the country. Adam Morgan wasn't yet at the top of any agency's most-wanted list, but that was only because there was no solid evidence of him committing a crime. At least until now. Impersonating an officer was a crime, be it a police officer or a member of the Security Service. It wasn't likely to see him do any serious time, but it was something that they might be able to use at some point. So, there was that. It did little to diminish Thea's anger.

"Look, if there's anything I can do," the sergeant began as a hundred options flashed through Thea's mind, most of them painful or humiliating for the sergeant.

"You can fuck off," Thea snapped. "And trust me, that's me being constructive."

The sergeant dropped his head and turned, retreating to safety.

"Think you could have left a little of his dignity intact?" Jane Astley had been watching the whole time and she stepped next to her subordinate.

"I did," Thea replied.

"Remind me never to piss you off then."

"You're a big girl, you can take it."

They turned to face each other, ready to get down to work.

"The whole room is a mess," Jane explained. "I've just had a quick look. Whoever it was did a number on him. Doesn't immediately scream assassination."

"Maybe that's the point." Thea hadn't seen the crime scene yet, but the two of them had been briefed on the way to the address and she could easily imagine the brutality that awaited her. "We can't ignore it, not with the stakes as high as they are."

"You really think there's a link?"

"Nathan Nelmes was in deep with the Regulators. If they're really looking to take out the prime minister, then there's every possibility he could have known and this isn't playing hunches or anything here, I'm just covering all the bases."

Jane Astley nodded her agreement. "Let's get to work then."

* * * *

His first operation in charge of the team had been a complete success. He could barely believe it. Any of it. They had broken into the house, found the traitor, then they'd made him suffer. It had been glorious. He'd watched his team do their work, then he'd joined in himself, delivering the final blow. Those who worked for him had insisted. It had felt electric. No remorse. No feeling guilty for the pathetic specimen they'd ripped apart, even as his twisted, stumps had reached towards him, begging him for mercy. In fact, mercy was what he had delivered. How could anyone live like that? He wouldn't want to. He couldn't. He knew that now. He knew what he was. He was the sum of all his parts and he was just getting started.

3

From the outside, the Regulators' London field office was nothing much to look at. Another shabby office block out in the east of London. All drab grey concrete and windows that were covered in plastic film that made it hard for anyone outside to peer in. But appearances can always be deceptive. For Adam, every time he saw the building, he felt pride that this was the place where he worked.

Adam and Emmie had entered through the car park that lay underneath the building. Two floors for cars, either belonging to the people who worked there, or fleet cars that often carried modifications including armour plating, highly tuned engines and built-in communications systems that rivalled anything the Security Service had. To the front of the building was another, more unassuming entrance. A narrow staircase, with cheap-looking linoleum flooring, leading to a sparse waiting area. It was manned by a lone receptionist. Another part of the front of the Regulators. Anyone entering would see what they were expecting to see. The reception area of Bonaparte International, an import and export company. They would have no idea that as they walked up those stairs, they were being scanned for metal objects, explosives and more.

Both routes led to the office floor. This was where the majority of the Regulators' staff did their work. A huge open-plan space, capable of hosting two hundred people at any one time, with desks arranged in clusters to promote collaboration within teams. Beneath that floor were interrogation rooms, holding cells and the armoury, whilst above served as a buffer to attacks both physical and electrical. Concrete and steel meshed together to absorb any direct hit from above by a missile, whilst the whole building was encased in a Faraday cage, both of which protected the Kernel, the Regulators' supercomputer that lay underneath everything.

The office was full as Adam and Emmie entered. People worked at their desks, others mingled, discussing work or their home lives. They would be working on a range of cases, including the Nelmes murder. Adam and Emmie were the leads for that, but there would be different teams working below them, often independently, all feeding back through Adam, Emmie and Raf, the Deputy Director, who had been assigned to oversee the case. His office was situated adjacent to a gantry that ran above head height along the entire span of one wall of the office floor. It wasn't just his office either. The Director's office, currently occupied by Eammon Grant, was next door, whilst meeting rooms made up the rest of the space. Somewhere for people to get together away from the hubbub of the office floor and chew over what they found.

"Raf's called a meeting." Karen Small didn't look up from her computer to greet Adam and Emmie as they approached their shared workstation.

"Morning, Karen," Adam replied, taking no offence from her curt welcome. Work was work with Karen and niceties and small talk simply got in the way. In a tactical officer, it was an excellent trait. Disseminating information efficiently and clearly was key to what she did.

Emmie was stooped over her keyboard, bringing up the details of the meeting. "Fifteen minutes. Room A."

"Time to grab a quick drink," Adam replied. "Anything come in we need to know?"

"Nothing of note. Met's still pulling it all together. Looking at the chatter there are plenty of other agencies circling, waiting for the police to do the grunt work for them."

"We'd be one of them. Come on, let's get a brew."

Drinks in hand, they joined the other department heads in the conference room. Raf was already there, scanning through a tablet he had brought in with him, ignoring those around him until he was ready to start. The meeting began with an overview of the crime scene. The Regulators had back doors into most of the police's systems and had been able to pull the crime scene photographs. Adam and Emmie's 360 shot had also been used and already an advanced AI algorithm was parsing together all the data to create a virtual representation of the crime scene that would be accessible via VR.

"Bottom line, though, whoever did this was a sadist," Raf finished his opening statement. He'd laid out all the basic facts, as they knew them: when Nelmes had been found; when he had last been seen; the initial findings of the pathologist. Nothing had been surprising. Now it was time for those in the room to add their findings.

"One thing that might be of interest is a possible DNA sample." The voice came from Sean Campbell. Sean headed up the analytics team assigned to the case. Their job was to trawl through the paperwork and look for links or leads that might otherwise be missed. It was a painstaking job at the best of times, one Adam was glad was being farmed out. He was also glad that they'd seemingly found something.

"DNA sample? I didn't see that on the original pathology report?" Raf's finger traced quickly across the screen of the tablet he had in front of him. Raf always had it with him. It contained anything pertinent to the case, and he kept it close to hand at all times.

"Late addition, sir," Sean explained. "It wasn't found in the bedroom, but the bathroom."

"Someone stopped to spend a penny?" Adam smiled as he said it, enjoying the laughter his comment brought. It was always important to have a little levity in these cases, otherwise everyone would lose their minds.

"Thankfully, no. Urine's not great for extracting DNA," Sean replied, making Adam feel a little silly, but nothing he couldn't shrug off. "A small speck of blood. Quite probably the person who left it didn't even know they'd bled in there, or it was missed in a clean-up operation. According to the report we intercepted, it looked relatively fresh."

"Any news on a result yet?" Raf asked.

"Not yet. We're hoping to be able to get hold of the relevant information to run it against our own database as well. As you know, chances are we'll be a little bit faster and a little bit broader than our colleagues at the Met."

Sean was right. The Met had access to the records held on the Police National Computer, which belonged to people who had been arrested for what were termed recordable offences. There was little doubt given who the victim was and his links to cases concerning national security in the past, that the database would be widened once MI5 got involved in the case, but even so, the Regulators' records went further. Their reach was global.

"Be nice to know when you do," Adam nodded at Sean.

"Goes without saying," the analyst replied confidently.

"How about cameras in the area? Have we been able to tap into those yet?" Emmie was asking the questions now and it was a good one. Cameras were becoming an invaluable tool in all forms of law enforcement. The Regulators, of course, had far more freedom to do what they wanted when it came to accessing footage. They didn't need warrants. Where cameras were wireless, they could hack the system to see if there was anything stored on the cloud. There were some limitations. Older systems, where the cameras recorded to a drive or physical media, were outside of their reach and they had to wait and hope that the police would acquire it promptly.

"Lots of footage in so far." This was Sean's area again. "Sadly, there's nothing we've located yet that has an angle on the entrance to the flat and the cameras in Nelmes's flat were removed. We're running what we've got through facial recognition, see what we can come up with. Couple of the team are watching manually as well, to see if we can find anything that stands out. So far, nothing. Again, when that changes, you'll be on my speed dial."

"There's a lot to be said for hoping we get lucky with a face on a camera or something that looks amiss." Raf's voice was always a little louder when he wanted to assert his authority on a conversation. He wasn't shouting, nowhere near. But he was louder than he needed to be and it served to make sure all eyes went on him. "We're going to have far more luck if we focus on what Nathan Nelmes was involved in. That means we need our people going through his online history, his phone records. We need to follow up on every IP address he's ever contacted, then spread the web out further. Cross-reference it with our databases, look for the links that start to stand out. Let the Kernel do its thing. In the meantime, Adam, Emmie, go play cops. I'll arrange for you to interview Nelmes's old boss. He knows who you are, he knows what you are, but we know he's sympathetic to our cause. It's one of the reasons he kept Nelmes around. I'm sure we can come up with some kind of arrangement that suits him as much as it does us."

Adam had never met Aidan Marshall, the editor of the *Daily Inquirer*. He knew his reputation, however. A passionate journalist with an old-fashioned nose for a story. He had a knack for exposing corruption. Adam assumed that just meant he had a lot of sources and learnt a lot of dirt. It didn't matter. His success had seen him rise to one of the top jobs in the country. Now, one of his journalists was dead, maybe for doing the sort of thing that Marshall had made his name doing. Adam hoped that would motivate him, either out of a desire for justice or revenge, or through fear it might happen to him.

"Look forward to it," he said.

"Good. I'll get it scheduled for tomorrow if possible. For now, let's comb through the police statements, see if there's anything in that and find who did this."

4

Security at Thames House was beyond anything Thea had experienced in any of her other workplaces. Even now, three months into her role here, she still felt the eyes of every guard piercing into her as she entered, as if she didn't belong. Clearly, they knew she did. She wouldn't have got very far otherwise. Armed Response Officers loitered in the reception area. Should they think she was an intruder, they'd let her know. Verbally, then lethally.

Her working space, when she finally reached it, was far quieter and more intimate than the spaces she was used to when working for the police. The teams at MI5 were far smaller, meaning that there was less need for shared desks, or crammed office floors. Here, there was room to breathe. Probably a far higher budget as well. But that wasn't something that concerned Thea. That sort of politics could be left to the bureaucrats.

Thea had driven them back to Thames House from the crime scene. Astley had spent the journey scrolling through her phone as new information came in from the scene of the crime. It was what she did. Rarely was she without some sort of device feeding her the latest information. Jane Astley prided herself on being 'in the know'.

"This DNA evidence. I don't like it," she said as they both returned to their desks.

"What about it?" Thea hadn't really had time to process things as deeply.

"I don't like convenience. Convenience is for stores. Or toilets. Not for crime scenes."

"You think it was planted?"

"We'll have a better idea when we see who it belongs to."

That was one thing that Thea had been thinking about. Who was behind the crime? Nathan Nelmes had a long list of enemies. Not exhaustive but certainly enough to keep them guessing for now. But like Jane, Thea wasn't a huge fan of coincidence. That Nelmes had been murdered when there was a credible threat to the prime minister from an organisation he'd had dealings with was a red flag. That was where her focus had to lie. In her police days, getting the collar for the murder would have been the most important thing in the world. Not now. Now there was a far bigger picture to think of. If she didn't solve Nathan Nelmes's murder, but her investigation uncovered something that let her stop an assassination attempt, then that was what counted.

"The list of Regulators that we know Nathan Nelmes had dealings with is pretty short," she said. "It'd be great to link it to one of them. Then we'd know we were onto something."

"Jack Quinn, Adam Morgan, Emmie Weston," Jane was reeling off the names. "We've got DNA for two of them –

Quinn and Morgan. Weston is a different matter. She didn't come through any of the normal routes."

"I'd love to know how she did get in." Thea had pondered that for a long time. Most Regulators field operatives were recruited from the police, the Secret Service or the armed forces. Emmie Weston hadn't been on the books of any organisation. It appeared she'd never worked a day in her life. "I didn't see them advertising any graduate schemes."

"Given the chance, we'll make sure to ask her," Jane said. Interrogating any vigilante that they could get their hands on was something Jane had long been advocating for. She'd requested picking them up off the street on more than one occasion, but at the moment, without any probable cause, the higher-ups were digging their heels in. They wanted to see something more concrete than the current rumour and supposition. There were some parts of being a spook that weren't too dissimilar to being a police officer. "In the meantime, I'm going to seek authority to get a sample ourselves. For reference purposes."

That meant sending in a field operative to Emmie Weston's house and removing something that contained her DNA. It wasn't without risk. The Regulators were a cautious group. Their homes were protected as best they could be, covered by electronic surveillance measures that put any regular home security setup to shame. "Sounds good. I'm requesting an electronic tap on Nelmes's work computer. Hopefully he wasn't just using his personal devices. I'll contact his network providers as well, see what they've got stored on him."

Thea knew that wouldn't be much. Whilst they might uncover some web domain names, or the addresses of computers that Nelmes's device had communicated with, the exact contents of any conversation would remain hidden unless they could find one of his devices. Even that wouldn't necessarily yield results. Nelmes would have encrypted any device he was using. It was going to be a slow and laborious process, like a playing a huge game of connect-the-dots, but you weren't allowed to connect more than two dots at a time and you were only allowed one go a day.

Thea stretched out in her chair, her arms raising up over her head, fingers intertwined so that her knuckles cracked.

"Fun, isn't it?" Jane said, as if reading Thea's mind.

"Good and clean and honest," Thea replied. Jane was a good boss and an excellent mentor. The transition between police work and her new job had been a lot easier than Thea had expected and she knew that a part of the reason for that was Jane Astley. She was easy to like and didn't patronise those who worked for her. The people around them were different as well. Whilst Thea knew that most police officers were in it for the right reasons, there were plenty who were there for the pay cheque only. It didn't matter if they had become jaded through the job or if they were simply bone-idle shits, they sucked the energy from the teams they worked on. Five didn't have room for people

26

like that. Thea couldn't imagine how any of her former colleagues would have passed the rigorous recruiting process she'd been through. She was often surprised she had. A part of her still wondered if she was only here because of her history with the Regulators. There were very few members of the law enforcement community who had ever met a Regulator and were willing to admit it. Most who did were in their employ. Thea had been different. She'd worked against them, alongside them, but never for them. She'd asked for their help when she'd needed it and she'd stopped them from carrying out their own brand of justice, even if ultimately, she'd found out she'd been wrong to do so.

"The cards will fall for us," Jane continued her positivity. "They bloody well have to."

* * * *

They were all sitting in the hotel room now. Five of them. He and four other men that he'd never met before. They were all older. All looked battle-hardened. But they were all his men. That was the order and so far, there had been no sign of dissent. They'd greeted him with smiles and strong claps on the back, like old friends convening for a night out. They'd all eaten together in the hotel restaurant. The idea was to look as normal as possible. Five blokes in town for a meeting with a security company. Close protection. If anyone asked. No one asked. No one came over to them. As happy and laid back as they had seemed to be at dinner, he knew that they all looked intimidating. There was just something about them all that spoke of violence. Even him, now, with what he'd done with the other team. He was just as dangerous. Just as deadly. And in a day from now, his kill count would be even higher.

5

Adam had picked Emmie up on the way to the *Daily Inquirer*, rather than heading to the office first. Raf had been good to his word and arranged the meeting for a little after nine in the morning. So far, all other lines of enquiry had drawn a blank, although the promise of the DNA results kept Adam excited that a breakthrough could be coming at any second. Their talk with Aidan Marshall was also intriguing, although Adam wasn't certain it was about to offer anything quite as dramatic as a potential name for their suspect.

The Daily Inquirer had recently moved to new purpose-built offices in South Kensington. The building's modernity stood out around the Georgian architecture in the area. It was too obvious. Too in-your-face. Whilst efforts had been made to match the colour of the stone to the light beige and tan of that around it, it was all too pristine. There was no character to the building yet and that was made all the more stark when set in the Victorian citadel, as it was known. Just flat, smooth stone and shiny glass that reflected the beauty of the buildings around it, rather than sitting alongside them.

"Isn't there supposed to be a car park with this thing?" Adam grumbled as they rolled slowly past the front door of the building, seeing nothing that suggested where they should be going.

"Around to the right," Emmie said, pointing to a turning onto a small side street that ran up the east edge of the building.

"Remind me that I hate driving in London next time I can't be bothered to take the tube."

"And listen to you moan about how crowded it is? Or the fact that the tube map is misleading? Or watch you pacing the carriage when we stop in a tunnel? Nah, I'll pass."

"Are you suggesting I'm grumpy about a lot of things?"

"Me? No."

Adam chuckled as he spotted the narrow entrance to the car park, entering slowly and halting by a barrier that blocked their progress beneath the building. A security guard took a slow amble towards them, asking if they had an appointment before scrolling through his phone to confirm that they were there to see Aidan Marshall.

"Park on the first level. Plenty of room," he said, waving them through as the barrier lifted.

"See, no one drives, we should get the tube," Adam said as they moved off.

"You get the tube. I'll drive and feel sorry for the poor sods sitting next to you."

* * * *

Aidan Marshall met them at the reception desk, striding over to them purposefully, his slight frame belying the strength of the handshake he offered. "Welcome to the *Inquirer*. I'm sorry it's under such circumstances," he greeted them, his smile sitting at odds with the sentiment. Clearly a man who was used to presenting a certain way to visitors to his empire.

"Mr Marshall. Thank you for taking the time today," Adam replied, feeling the most like a police officer he had in a long time. It wasn't often he could be so open and candid with someone he was looking to interview, who wasn't a suspect.

"It's not a problem. We need to ensure that we find out what happened to Nathan. His death has caused quite the ripple around here. I mean, Nathan was his own man and all, but he was still liked. Still loved by his colleagues. There've been a lot of tears this last twenty-four hours."

"I can only imagine," Emmie said. "We only met him a couple of times, but he certainly made an impression."

"Well, yes. If my recollection is correct, you two were there when the first attempt on his life was made. I'd say that was an impression." The smile was still on his face as he said it and Adam couldn't help but think that he was showing off. Letting them know that he knew a lot about them.

"We were very lucky that day," Adam tried to keep the story short.

"You all were. Nathan as well. And I think he knew that, by the end. He had his struggles afterwards, but he still had his life and that was what mattered the most. He didn't believe in anything after that, you know. I don't think he felt he was in any rush to meet his maker or lack thereof. A shame." Once again, Aidan was oversharing. Reinforcing that he was a man who knew things.

They made their way through the building to the elevators and onto the third floor, where Aidan showed them to his office. He opened the door for them, letting them into a corner room with frosted glass walls and a door that sat next to the main open-plan work space. It thronged with journalists typing out stories, calling sources, or just generally enjoying the camaraderie that the space created. It felt like a happy place to work.

"Had you and Nathan talked about the projects he was working on before he was killed?" Adam asked, as they sat around Aidan's desk.

"Of course," Aidan said, crossing one leg over the other and pushing back into his chair, fingers coming together in a triangle in front of his chest. He could easily have been a motivational speaker. Or a leader of a cult. "Well, I assume we had. There is always the possibility he held some things back from me, but we have access to his computer."

"We'd really love to take it with us." Adam knew he was pushing his luck, but he had to ask.

Aidan raised a hand dismissively, bowing his head and closing his eyes, some approximation of what he clearly felt *sad* looked like. "I can't do that. You know I can't do that. I've done you a great courtesy by letting you in as soon as I could, but I have the Met Police coming over. I'm sure they won't be the only ones either. And I can't say no to their requests. Nor would I. But I can to yours."

"I had to ask. Do you know when you're expecting the Met?"

"Sometime today, I would hope. It would be a damning indictment of their process if they were any slower."

"If we can't take it with us, would you object to us making a copy of the data on his system?" Emmie asked.

"I've already had the drives backed up and you're free to take a copy."

"I'm afraid we'd need to make our own," she explained and for good reason. As much as they were happy to believe that Aidan Marshall wanted to help them, there was never a bad time to wonder if you might be having the wool pulled over your eyes. Taking their own copy was as close as they could get to ensuring that what they were getting was everything from Nathan Nelmes's computer.

Aidan shrugged. "Not a problem at all. I would imagine, then, that you'd like to get started soon. No one wants to get flummoxed by a stalled status bar, do they?"

"It's the sort of thing that keeps me up almost every night," Adam quipped. "So, what was it he was working on?"

"He had a couple of small things going on. A cocaine dealer in the Houses, of course. Some civil servant who was happy to make a little on the side. Quite a good market to get yourself into, it seems. But the main one, he hadn't spoken much about, although I got the feeling it went back to what you were doing before."

"What we were doing?" That got Adam's attention and he leaned forward.

"Yes. There was a cautiousness about Nathan ever since his attack. He wasn't keen on leaving the house too much. And he insisted that people knew where he was at all times. But the last couple of months, that changed."

"He got worse?"

"Quite the opposite. He was hardly ever where we expected him to be. It was like he had a new lease of life, a new confidence in himself again. I'll be honest with you, it was quite inspiring to see. The old Nathan was back, whatever his physical limitations might have been. His mind was at its best when Nathan had a story cooking. I asked him, of course, but he wouldn't say much. He was worried where the fallout might land. I guess you could say he was protecting me."

"Did he say what from?"

"Exposure, I assumed. Politically, legally."

"Not physically?"

"It's never the first thing that crosses my mind. In this job, regardless of what some pulpy, popcorn thriller-writing wannabe might try and suggest, you're far more likely to be sued than shot. It's a shame that whoever wrote Nathan Nelmes's lot in life was so bloody overdramatic." He smiled at his own joke.

"He never mentioned names?" Emmie asked.

"He didn't, although I must admit, I assumed it was you two he was working with."

"Why?"

"Call it intuition. It felt like he was back into his old habits. I assumed that meant running with his old crowd."

A thought crossed Adam's mind, but he dismissed it quickly. It was more hope than expectation.

"It would be great as well to talk to anyone who had any interactions with Nathan. The more people we can get stories from…"

"Of course. And what cover am I to give to you two?"

Adam was a little bit surprised to hear that Aidan wouldn't automatically just announce who the two visitors asking questions about Nathan Nelmes were. He didn't strike him as someone who helped authority. Perhaps the Regulators were counterculture enough for him.

"Just the truth," Adam said, feeling strangely liberated by doing so. "A lot of your staff here know who we both are anyway." It was a price of the notoriety that had followed the Regulators since they uncovered a huge plot that had seen politicians and other powerful members of society blackmailed and used for the vested interests of a small group. Adam, Emmie and a few others had exposed it, with Nathan Nelmes's help. In doing so, it had placed a spotlight on their work. Life hadn't quite been the same since.

"I'm sure they'll all very much enjoy that. Although it will mean that they ask as many questions of you, if not more. They are journalists after all."

Aidan showed them through to another room on the floor above, where they found Nathan's computer, already working and being looked after by a technician, who quickly made way so that they could look at it themselves and start the process of backing up the hard drive, whilst waiting for the first of the journalists to be sent up to talk to them.

"What do you think?" Emmie asked when they were alone.

"He's everything I thought he'd be and then some," Adam said. "Imagine spending a weekend on a corporate retreat with him. That's some kind of intense going on there."

"I guess you don't do what he's done in your life without some sort of bee in your bonnet."

"Ain't that the truth."

"What about the stuff about Nelmes being like he was back in the old days?"

"What about it?"

"Well, it wasn't us, was it?"

"No." Adam knew what she was getting at. It was the same thing he'd stopped himself from thinking earlier. It appeared he wasn't going to be able to avoid it any longer.

"Well?" Emmie clearly wanted him to say it.

"Is it Jack?" he said for her.

"It could be."

"It could." Jack Quinn was his former partner. An ex-soldier who had been instrumental in bringing down the plot that he, Emmie and Nelmes had also worked on. He was also one of Adam's best friends. In the aftermath of their operation, their boss, Eammon Grant, had attempted to apprehend Jack. Jack had escaped and gone to ground but not before warning Adam. Adam had never been able to ask Grant about why he had orders to take Jack in, even though it had been eating at him since that day. All he'd been able to do was make sure he kept one eye on Grant at all times.

"Is it?"

"Damned if I know. I've not heard from him in over a year. You know that."

"Do I?"

Adam shot her an annoyed look. He trusted her. She should be able to trust him.

"What?" she replied to his look. "Don't pretend that you and Jack didn't have more of a relationship than we do."

The words stung him. Even if they were true. It wasn't a slight on Emmie. She was a good partner and a great friend. He'd put his life in her hands without thinking about it. But for all Emmie was, she wasn't Jack. Jack was his best friend.

He was about to respond when there was a sharp rattle. At first, he assumed it was someone knocking at their door, but the sound was too far away. Too quick.

Emmie looked at him, her eyes wide.

"Gunshots."

6

"Do you believe in miracles?" Jane Astley stepped over to Thea's desk, sliding the keyboard from her computer away and typing.

"What's going on?" Thea asked, bemused. She was slowly getting used to Jane's quirks and idiosyncrasies.

"We got a result on the DNA. Not a full result, admittedly. It's not Christmas. Far too hot out there. But maybe it's time to start making our list and checking it twice."

Thea checked the urge to laugh and turned to the screen, scanning through the information. Then she fought the urge to laugh again. "This can't be right."

"It's a preliminary result, admittedly. But it is what it is."

Thea re-read the report. It explained about the science behind the process. Then it got to the nitty gritty. The result. There had been no close match in the system. Whoever had left the DNA was a clean skin, at least as far as their bodily fluids were concerned. But someone related to them wasn't.

The DNA testing had found a 53% match between the sample they had taken and a person on its database. That person hadn't committed a criminal act. At least not one that they had been arrested and processed for. Thea knew for a fact that they'd crossed that line on many an occasion.

She'd been there for some of them. Encouraged some of them.

The person sharing a 53% DNA match with the sample found at the scene of Nathan Nelmes's murder was Jack Quinn.

"Puts the cat among the pigeons, doesn't it?" Jane said again.

"It does that," Thea agreed, before adding, "How does this play into your disdain for conveniences?"

"It really puts my back out," Jane agreed. "But what can I do? I can't ignore it. Nor can you. Right now, Jack Quinn is implicated in the murder of Nathan Nelmes, directly or indirectly. There's a link we can't ignore and we have to find him. What's more, it's another link to the assassination chatter. There's something happening with the Regulators."

"Jack Quinn isn't a Regulator," Thea objected.

"Are you sure about that?"

Thea knew she couldn't be a hundred per cent sure. She hadn't heard from Jack in a long time. But if she was going to have to pick a side... "I'm as sure as I can be."

"It's not enough. And even if he's not a Regulator, it still looks like there's something going on around them. I still want Weston's DNA. On that note..." She opened up a video link on her tablet and waited for the person at the other end to answer.

"Hill." Thea could see the screen. The man answering had short dark curly hair and the sort of stubble you expected to see on someone who'd been out of the house for a couple of days.

"Where are we at on the sample I requested?"

"Got it myself yesterday. It's going in the system as we work."

"Top man, Hill. Thank you." Astley closed the connection.

"I don't like it," Thea said, deciding that there was no point being coy about it.

"Neither do I. So, eyes and ears open, let's make sure we're not being strung along, but we follow this thread and see where it leads."

Thea was about to agree when they were interrupted by Jane's phone.

"Astley." She answered the phone and listened as whoever was on the other end spoke. It clearly wasn't information that needed to be questioned, because Jane simply said, "Understood," and hung up. "Chatter about an impending attack, somewhere in London."

"When?" Thea felt the hairs on the back of her neck stand to attention. Was this it? The assassination?

"Today."

"Shit. Anything else?"

Jane was back at her desk now, loading up the report that she'd been told about, reading the information on her screen as she spoke. "I can't see how it could be. No mention of a political target in anything coming through. Highly visual though. And well-funded."

Thea had the same data on her screen now. She always found it amazing how much people talked. In her head, if you knew something was about to go down, you kept your mouth shut. But that wasn't the real world. If people knew things, they told people. Not people that they trusted. People they wanted or needed to impress. Knowledge was a currency. It bought you status. Bought you opportunities to impress in other ways. Years of experience taught them when to speak and when to hold back. Too loose a tongue and who knows what might happen. But when it was something that was happening that didn't involve you, your cell, your people, what was the harm in telling that something was about to happen before it did? Who wouldn't want to look as if they had their finger on the pulse? It was an asset to intelligence-gathering organisations all over the world. But it didn't mean that they could find out what was happening in time to stop it.

"There's not a lot more to go on," Thea cautioned, hoping Jane had spotted something she hadn't.

"Suppose this is linked to Nelmes and the assassination. Where are we thinking?"

"We still don't know why they killed Nelmes. We're guessing it's because he found something out or he was about to."

"What if they don't know either?"

"What do you mean?" Thea looked at Jane. She sounded as if she had the beginnings of an idea forming.

"What if they weren't sure if he'd found something out? I mean, they tortured him. I think it's safe to say that when they went to see him, they needed to find something out from him. What if they didn't find out before his body gave up? Or if they weren't sure what he did tell them was legit?"

"They took his computers," Thea carried on, guessing where Jane was going with this. "They either knew something was on them or were worried it was. Stands to reason he would have made a backup. Stands to reason they would have known that."

Jane was typing as Thea spoke. "Met Police are sending a team over to the *Inquirer* in the next hour to secure his computer."

"Which means if any attack was to be successful, it would need to happen now."

Jane already had her phone to her ear. "Put me through to whichever inspector is on duty at MO12."

Thea was up and out of the door as Jane followed, still barking down the phone. "Jane Astley, MI5. We've got a credible threat to the *Daily Inquirer*. You need to send armed response and you need to send it now."

7

The fire alarm blared across the building seconds later as Adam and Emmie both hunched down next to the door. They'd abandoned the transfer of the files. At least for now. Adam had safely put the drive into his inside pocket. If anyone did get to it, it meant they'd got to him. At which point, he'd probably have bigger problems to deal with.

"Elevators will be shut down." Adam was working through what he knew of the building in his head. They'd come up in the elevator, but there would be stairways that would be used for fire exits. It was common practice for the elevators to be automatically switched off in the event of the fire alarm being triggered, which meant one thing. "They've come up the stairs. Trying to pin people in."

"They" was a very fluid concept at that moment. Shots were still ringing out. It sounded as if they were coming from the floor below them, where the majority of the staff were congregated. Adam was certain there were multiple attackers. The sounds of gunfire overlapped and he could feel the vibrations coming from different parts of the building. But he wasn't sure if that meant two, three or more people firing. That in itself was a problem. A bigger problem was that he didn't know if someone was coming up the stairs to them. "We need to get eyes on this."

Emmie was already slipping in her Bluetooth earpiece. "Karen," she said as the call connected. Adam patched himself into it so he could hear both sides and feed in if necessary.

"Go ahead," came the reply.

"We've got shooters at the *Daily Inquirer*. We need eyes."

"I'm tapping into the camera system now," she replied. "Calls are coming in from their switchboard to the emergency services."

"No shit," Adam replied.

"There was also a blue light request made before the calls came in. MO12 scrambled armed response. Looks like a tip-off from Five."

"How the fuck did they know?" Adam growled.

Karen ignored the question. "Okay, I've got the system. Where are you?"

"Fourth floor."

Terrified shouts rang out from the floor below as the assault continued. The sound of death being dealt came almost incessantly. Automatic weapons then.

"I have you. You're clear for now. I'll guide you to them."

Adam and Emmie moved into the corridor towards the door to the fire exit. Their whole floor seemed deserted. Whether people were sheltering in place or had already made their escape, they didn't know. Adam put his hand on the door, wishing that he'd armed himself. The Regulators had access to firearms, but as a rule, they didn't carry them everywhere. They were safely secured in a locked compartment in the boot of the car. A whole four floors below them. Past the massacre taking place just yards away.

Adam eased the door open. Even with the din reaching up to them from just below and Karen's input, they both moved carefully. Every footstep was considered as they edged first towards the stairs, then down them, creeping ever closer to the door. As they reached it, Adam wondered what he should do. Head downstairs for the car and his weapons or make a stand here? He looked at Emmie for inspiration. Her face was focused, completely removed of fear. He knew it would be.

His hand reached out for the door. "Clear," came the confirmation from Karen. He opened it. No need to hesitate. Every second he waited now was a life lost. The sounds of bullet fire had eased. To some, that might sound like a good thing. All it really meant was fewer targets. It could mean people had escaped. It could mean people were hiding safely. It could mean everyone was dead.

Grey carpet stretched out in front of them, glass-walled offices on either side. At least they were once glass-walled. Now all that was left were shards scattered on the floor. People had been in those rooms. Adam wondered if they had even had time to realise what was going on when the attack began. He turned to Emmie, nodded, then they were both moving into the corridor. He didn't want to look, but he knew he had to. To be certain. To his left, one body was slumped forward over a desk; another, partially obscured, lay on the floor. He fought the instinct to go and check on them. They didn't have time. If they were going to survive this and get other people out safely, they had to move fast.

The end of the corridor split into a T-junction. "You've got a hostile approaching you from the east," Karen warned.

"How far?" Adam tensed, ready for action.

"Ten yards to the corner."

Adam moved fast to get there first, Emmie right there with him. As they reached it, so did a man dressed all in black combat fatigues, a bandana around his head and gun clutched into his shoulder and against his chest. He turned the corner, straight into Adam. It would have been comedic if the stakes hadn't been life or death.

Their eyes locked for a moment. Adam saw the man processing the information. Working out what to do. Making a decision. The man went to push Adam away, but Adam gripped on to him, realising that the rifle he was carrying was pinned between the two of them. He grasped at the barrel with his other hand, trying to push it down toward the ground and safety. The two of them struggled, neither daring to release what they had a grip on, lest it give an advantage to their opponent.

The gun went off, a quick ripple of bullets into the floor. It recoiled and Adam felt the body of the weapon bounce off his chest. He staggered, a slight separation between the two of them. A fraction of a moment, but one that the man in the combat fatigues tried to make the most of.

This time he pushed, using Adam's sudden unsteadiness against him. Adam grabbed at the gun once more, his other hand clasping at the man's back, but it was no good. The purchase he'd had was gone. They were coming apart and with it, the man was gaining control of his weapon. Adam was losing.

Then Emmie struck. A powerful blow to the man's neck. Adam hadn't seen her coming. Neither, it appeared, had the man in the combat fatigues. It was his turn to stumble backwards, grabbing at his neck as he did so, fighting for breath. Adam saw Emmie's hand darting towards the man's hip, but he didn't have time to think about what she was doing. He lunged forward, pressing his whole body against the side of the gun, knocking the two of them into a wall. He was about to aim a headbutt at the man's spluttering face when it exploded in front of him.

"Jesus!" He released his grip, falling to the floor and landing on his rear as the body of the man in combat fatigues slumped across from him. He turned to see Emmie holding a pistol in her hand. It took him a moment to realise that the motion she'd made to the man's hip had been to remove his side arm from his holster.

"You okay?" she asked.

Adam shook his head to clear it. "I'll live."

"You got a little something on your face." Emmie said, offering a hand to haul him up.

"Yeah. Thanks for that." Adam was no sooner on his feet than he was bending down, unhooking the automatic rifle from where it was strapped to the man in black. "Least we're on a more level playing field now. These boys didn't come to play either." He looked down at the rifle. It was a Sig Sauer MCX Spear. The civilian version of the US Army's XM7. A semi-automatic that packed enough punch, even at range to get through the Kevlar body armour that the man was wearing. He looked down to the floor and saw where the bullets had hit. There were no ricochets. Just holes. He hoped no one had been under them.

"I have Raf on the line," Karen announced. "Immediate area clear."

"Are you okay?" Raf got straight to the point.

"We're one-nil up," Adam brought Raf up to speed.

"What's happening?"

"Not sure yet. Multiple shooters. Well-armed. Well equipped. Not a disgruntled employee in sight."

"Are they there for you?"

"I didn't get the chance to ask. Any news on backup?"

"Met's on the way. They'll set up a perimeter first before making any decisions on going in. You're going to have to survive on your own for now."

"Fine. Shooting has calmed down. Guess they're getting to the crux of why they're here. Reckon we should go throw a spanner in the works on that."

"Stay safe."

Then Raf was gone. "Met will be playing it by the book. Expect the phones to start ringing." Adam knew the procedure. Establish contact. Talk your way out of it.

"We planning to render that moot?"

"It seems the civically minded thing to do."

They moved through the corridor towards the open-plan section of the office. Another door hung open to their left. Behind it was a store cupboard. Emmie stepped across the doorway, gun levelled at the space, then Adam went in to clear it. There was a noise from somewhere down low. Something scrabbling. He looked down and saw a foot pulling itself away, behind a dust cloth draped over a collection of buckets.

"It's all right," he said in a low tone. "We're the good guys. I need you to stay here and stay quiet until the police arrive."

He waited a second. Finally, there was a reply. "O-okay," a nervous voice replied. Adam couldn't see the woman, but he could tell from her tone that she was absolutely terrified.

"It's going to be all right. You're going to survive. Just don't move until you know it's the police. And I mean *know*."

"Okay." The voice was quicker to respond this time. But no less scared. Then it added. "If you're not the police, who are you?"

"The next best thing," Adam replied, stepping out of the cupboard and closing the door.

* * * *

He stalked across the office floor, looking at the people below him. Some were dead. Some were dying. Others were left to watch. There had to be witnesses. That was critical to the success of the operation. There had to be no doubt who had done this. There had to be no doubt that he had done this. Even if he barely believed it himself.

He smiled and looked to his subordinates, nodding. Time for the final part of the plan. They knew what they had to do and moved off to secure their objectives.

8

The sound of shooting had finished now. Whatever plan was unfolding had moved into its next phase. Adam and Emmie were still moving slowly and methodically through the office, towards the open-plan area where they assumed the main action was taking place. They were alert, ready. The next attacker they saw wasn't.

Karen had warned them of his approach. They'd lain in wait. He came around the corner, strolling easily, gun hanging loosely down by his side. He barely had time to register what was happening before Adam and Emmie both opened fire. Emmie's rounds didn't do much. They struck the Kevlar body armour the man wore and stopped. Held back by the fibres that caught the bullet. But the assault rifle Adam had liberated was far more powerful. It had done enough to put the man down. He writhed on the floor, injured. How badly, they didn't stop to ask. There wasn't room for clemency. There was no way to restrain him. No way to ensure that he didn't get back up. Emmie stepped over him, firing a bullet into his head. It was an execution. But it was either that or run the risk that he got himself back into the fight.

"We should try and keep at least one of them alive. If we can," Emmie said as she relieved the man of his side arm, tossing it to Adam, then taking his MCX for herself.

"If we can," Adam said softly, hating the violence that they had been forced into. Selfishly, he was glad it was Emmie pulling the trigger in that final moment and not him. He hadn't been a soldier. A killer. He'd been a police officer. A career he'd chosen because he wanted to help people. To save them where possible. This part of being a Regulator still jarred with him. He didn't look at the man's face in case he saw it again, later, when he tried to sleep that night. He'd learned that lesson before.

"You need to move." There was an urgency in Karen's voice on the comms that snapped him out of his malaise. "They all heard that."

They didn't get the chance to go far before Karen reported more incoming. Two of them. Adam and Emmie had to take cover as shots rang out. They responded with quick bursts of their own, sending their attackers scampering behind the corner they'd appeared from.

"We're going to get pinned down here if we're not careful," Adam shouted to Emmie as they each took up cover in adjacent doorways. It wasn't going to shield them for long. The glass-walled offices offered very little compared to the corners their adversaries were behind. Adam had once heard someone say to beware of doors and corners when entering a space. Clearly, they'd never seen these doors, or they'd have never put the two together.

"They've cut the cameras. I've got no eyes." Karen's voice was emotionless. No apology. Just the facts. More glass shattered around him and he ducked down as shards scattered over his back, forcing him to swear to himself. He heard Emmie returning fire up the corridor. He knew that this couldn't go on. They would die here and he didn't want to die. Not here. Not today.

He turned and fired himself. One quick burst at the corner diagonally across from him before stepping into the middle of the corridor, opening the angle and firing at the other corner. He timed it perfectly. Or maybe he was just lucky. The assailant on that side stepped out of cover to take a shot himself, just momentarily and only a fraction. Enough to put a fleshy chunk of arm into the path of a bullet. There was a shout of pain and the clatter of a gun being dropped and striking the wall as it swung from its strap.

Now was the time to act. Emmie knew it too, instinctively. She stepped out behind him, firing at the other corner, keeping the uninjured attacker pinned. Now they were in a race. How far up the corridor could they get before the wounded man regained his composure just enough to be able to fire again?

Adam let off another burst at the corner where the unhurt attacker lurked. He would know what was coming. At some point he'd be making the calculation about when it was best to try one last attempt to save himself or, at the very least, go out in a blaze of glory. There was going to be a reckoning and it was going to come in seconds.

Emmie fired again. Two bursts this time. One at each corner. To be certain. Adam did the same. Maybe he'd get lucky. One of the bullets might punch through some gap in the corner. The metal they used to frame these rooms couldn't be that thick. It couldn't be everywhere.

He saw movement, the twitch of a barrel coming around the corner. His finger was already resting on the trigger. Another burst of gunfire. They were nearly on the corner now. They were out of room and out of time. Something had to give. Someone had to die.

It happened without Adam realising. Just as he supposed it always would. It was the moments that you didn't see coming that would ultimately end you. He had been so fixated on the guns that he hadn't thought about anything else. Least of all a stun grenade. He didn't even know what it was as it dropped around the corner in front of him. His brain was still processing the information, part of it trying to fight the urge to turn and look at it, urging him to keep focused on where he knew his target was. Another part was screaming internally that this was another threat. That he had to take action. By the time he realised that side was right and he began to take cover, it was too late. The stun grenade erupted. It wasn't a detonation. It was called a deflagration. A moment of subsonic combustion. Enough to create a large bang, a blinding flash, but without the compression that caused the damage from a grenade, as the magnesium inside the device caught light. Adam tumbled to the floor, his senses overloaded. He gagged as the smell of burning chemicals washed over him, spitting on the floor as he struggled onto all fours. Then he felt the barrel of the gun pressed into the base of his neck.

It should have ended there and then, but it didn't. Adam hadn't expected mercy. In those first split seconds he said a quiet goodbye to his wife Laura and his kids. But split seconds passed into full seconds and he was still alive. The darkness didn't envelop him. He heard a firm voice saying something that he couldn't understand. Then someone kicked him, hard, in the ribs, driving all the air out of him and dropping him to the floor completely. He sprawled on the floor before he was hauled up. His ears rang and colours and shapes danced in front of his eyes as his vision battled the effects of the stun grenade. He saw Emmie, hands on her head, gun being taken from her by a man in black who had blood pouring from his arm. The one that they had shot. With the gun removed, he delivered a sharp punch to the side of Emmie's ribs and she gasped, wobbling down onto one knee. He raised his gun, but the man securing Adam stopped him.

"No. The mission said we bring them both back."

The other man grunted. Adam had regained enough of his senses now to tell that the hole in the man's arm was making him want to forget all about the mission. He didn't, though. He hauled Emmie to her feet. The man with Adam frisked him, finding the drive and taking it. Adam said nothing. Then they were both being frogmarched through the building and into the open-plan office.

"Holy shit!"

Adam couldn't have said it better himself. Nothing could have prepared him for what he was seeing now; for *who* he was seeing now. He wondered if he was concussed. Or drugged. But then the owner of the voice that had just exclaimed excitedly at his arrival was walking forward, standing next to him, eye to eye in a way that the last time he'd seen him, he'd not been able to. He'd changed a lot in that time. He was taller. He'd filled out. He was obviously older. But he was still barely a man. And he was still Calum Quinn, Jack Quinn's son. Adam had no idea what to say.

"Not like you to be so quiet, Adam." Calum was smiling. Something he'd never seen the boy do much in his adolescence. Admittedly, he'd not spent too much time with Jack's family. The nature of their job meant that fraternising together wasn't something they liked to do. But they had become friends and, as such, they'd shared their lives. Jack's youngest son Calum had been a part of that life. One that Jack had spoken to Adam about a lot, especially in the latter days of their working together, as the father–son relationship became more and more fractured. Calum and Jack had grown apart. Calum hadn't shared his father's physique or his mentality. Jack had told him that his son had been the victim of bullies. The bullies would have thought twice now if they'd seen the young man, dressed in a black T-shirt, half hidden under a Kevlar vest. He was clutching an MCX like the rest of his team and his arms bulged from his sleeves. They were round bodybuilder's arms, though. More for show than borne out of years of actual use. His neck had thickened considerably and wispy facial hair stood in place of where a beard and moustache might one day take root.

"Calum," Adam gasped, not sure what else he could say.

"Good to see you again," Calum replied jovially, sounding completely detached from what was happening. Adam could tell he was proud. Like a kid showing off his A level results.

"What are you doing?"

"We're carrying out our mission."

"What mission?"

"That would be telling." The smile on his face was broader and slightly unhinged, like he was on something. Adam thought that was a distinct possibility. He'd heard plenty of tales of soldiers who pepped themselves up before battle. It had been the policy of a number of governments, past and present. It also meant it was probably prudent to watch what he was saying.

"Why?"

"Why what?"

"These people. Why kill them?"

"Collateral damage. Sorry." Calum's voice sounded far from sorry. More disinterested.

Adam thought for a moment of talking about Isobel, Calum's mum. He'd always been a mummy's boy. But something about the way he was acting told him that it could have made things worse.

"Can I help you?" he offered hoarsely, almost dreading the answer.

"You can tell them we were here. You can tell them who did this." Calum turned and walked away back into the middle of the room, addressing the last handful of cowering workers. "You can all tell them who did this. That Calum Quinn, son of Jack Quinn, the Regulator, came into your office, killed your colleagues. Butchered them. That he took what he wanted and he left. But that he will be back because this is only the beginning."

It sounded like lunacy. His voice barely had the maturity to make it sound credible. It was only the wasteland that was around them that emphasised that it was.

There was movement from the back of the room. Another man in black combat fatigues came in, his hand locked around the forearm of Aidan Marshall. Adam felt another *Holy Shit* moment coming on when he saw who the soldier was.

Nick Poole.

Poole was a former Regulator turned traitor. He had betrayed their boss, Lowri Graves. Sold her out to a splinter group within the Security Service. She hadn't been seen since. No one knew if she was still alive. She'd been completely disappeared.

He looked at Adam and Emmie but gave no sign of recognition. He looked at Calum. "We have it," he reported.

Adam still couldn't wrap his head around what was happening. Was Calum Quinn giving orders to Nick Poole? That's what it looked like, but how could that be?

"Excellent," Calum asked, without asking to see it, whatever it was.

"What're our orders?" Poole asked.

"Proceed to objective Foxtrot Four," Calum replied, smiling.

"Foxtrot Four?" Poole replied calmly.

"That's what they said."

Adam began to wonder who *they* were. It remained an unformed thought. Poole released Marshall, drew his weapon and fired. Three times. Each bullet struck Calum, who crashed backwards across a desk.

"No!" Adam felt a surge of panic rush through him. Regardless of what Calum had just done, he was his friend's kid. He lunged at the man guarding him, who was slow to react. He grabbed at his rifle and the two of them tussled for the weapon. There was a commotion next to him as Emmie and the other man got into it.

The man holding the rifle aimed a headbutt at him, catching him on the nose. Lights flashed before his eyes, but the survival instinct in him refused to let go of the gun, holding on tightly even as tears flowed from his eyes and his vision blurred. He heard a gunshot to his left where Emmie and the other man were fighting. Then he was being shoved backwards, a powerful push by the man holding the gun. He couldn't hold on as he spilled onto the floor waiting for the inevitable. There was the echo of semi-automatic gunfire. Then silence.

"You all right?" Emmie was crouching over him, holding out her hand.

"I'll live," Adam gasped, wondering quite how that was possible and if Emmie had saved his life for a second time. Then he remembered. "Calum."

9

Outside of the offices of the *Daily Inquirer*, it was chaos. Emergency vehicles from every possible department were jammed into the narrow roads which had been closed in a quarter-mile radius from the building. Traffic had already snarled to a halt making the final couple of minutes of Thea and Jane's journey to the scene torturous. Their radios were on, bringing them real-time updates as first, the police moved in to secure the scene, then paramedics rushed to aid those who were fighting for their lives. The preliminary body count was twenty-six. Thea was certain that would rise as more of the building was searched, or people succumbed to their injuries. Four attackers were down. Three dead, one barely clinging on. There was confusion over the number remaining, other than at least one had escaped. The police had found no sign of him so far, but the search was widening with every second.

When they finally reached the scene, they walked past the entrance to the building's underground car park. A forensic team was already at work, photographing a burnt-out MPV. Its blackened shell had merged with the tarmac below it as fire had ripped through it. On the floor, a blue body bag marked where someone had fallen. If Thea was a betting woman, she would have guessed at it being a security guard. A small hut stood next to the barrier of the car park. In her head she saw the MPV arriving and the guard stepping forward to ask the routine question of who they were there to see that day. It would have been the last thing he did. She knew that the autopsy would report that he was shot at point-blank range.

They were escorted through the cordon and made their way in through the main reception of the *Inquirer*. Already, a command centre had been created and the inspector on scene was giving out instructions.

Jane went to check in with the inspector and let them know of their arrival. A courtesy as much as it was a chance to glean as much information as possible. Thea carried on up the stairs. The lifts were still off limits.

There was no mistaking that it had been the third floor where the attack had taken place. The smell of gunpowder lurked in the air. Countless bullet holes and casings were scattered on the floor, slowly being identified and marked by the forensics team who were already beginning the process of putting together the pieces of what had happened, even whilst, for those who had been involved, the drama was still unfolding.

The office was a large open-plan area that looked out over the main road in front of the building. A handful of uniformed police officers stood by watching as witnesses and people of interest received the medical attention they required to clear them from the scene. Among them were the two people that Thea was desperate to get to first.

When Adam Morgan's name had cropped up on the radio reports, Thea hadn't been surprised. She knew there would be a Regulator angle to this somehow. Now she needed to work out just why he had been there at the time of the attack and how he'd come to survive it. As she looked at him being checked over by the paramedics, she could tell he'd had to earn that survival. His nose had been bloodied and he had a bruise forming around his right eye already. His shoulders were slumped and his face was glum.

"You're not going to fucking believe this." Jane crept over to Thea, making her jump. "The injured shooter. Take a pop at his name?"

Thea shrugged. She hadn't seen any sign of the shooter since they arrived. She assumed he'd either been whisked away, or he'd not made it and she'd just missed the update. "Jack Quinn?" she said, half as a joke.

"Nearly. Calum Quinn."

"Who?" Thea asked, before she remembered. "Oh my god."

"Right. The partial DNA."

"His son? His fucking son?"

"Apparently so."

Thea thought back to what she knew of Calum Quinn. It wasn't much. He had been a kid the first time that Jack Quinn had come to her attention. Beyond that, she knew precious little about him.

"How old is he?"

"Eighteen."

"Eighteen years old. Were they all kids?"

"No," Jane shook her head. "We've not been able to identify any of the deceased yet. But they're not kids. They look professional."

"Why the hell would professionals be working with an eighteen-year-old nobody?"

"We'd best hope we get the chance to ask him. He's barely hanging on by a thread is the word."

"Jesus Christ," Thea sighed and looked at Adam. Now his face made sense. "We really need to be the first people to talk to them."

"Already cleared with the inspector."

"Brilliant."

"They're finding a room they can free up and we'll speak to them before they take them down the station for a full debrief."

"Great work, boss."

* * * *

Ten minutes later, Adam Morgan sat opposite Thea and Jane. Emmie Weston waited outside for her turn, but Thea knew that the really good stuff was going to come from Adam.

"What were you doing here today?" Jane asked. She and Thea had agreed that it was best if Jane led the interview, given Adam and Thea's previous history. If and when it was prudent for Thea's expert knowledge to come into play, then she would.

They'd explained their position before they started the interview. They weren't interested in the fact that Adam Morgan was a vigilante and therefore breaking a whole host of laws by interfering in a criminal investigation. That was secondary right now. Thea's being there seemed to go some way to convince Adam that he could be candid. Or maybe it was some code of conduct of the Regulators. They were a strange organisation in that way. Their rules forbade them from resisting law enforcement. Maybe that extended to providing them with witness statements. Even when it was incriminating.

"We were following up after the murder of Nathan Nelmes. His place of work seemed as good a place as any," Adam replied. Honestly, Thea thought.

"You were here before, with Nathan Nelmes, weren't you?" Jane pressed on.

"Not here. No. His old offices," Adam corrected her. "Over at Canary Wharf. I can understand, after that, why they'd want to move. Horrible business. But I spoke to some of your boys about it at the time."

"My boys?" Jane asked.

"Five. Not sure if they were your department or not. But they came out and spoke to us. Right before they helped Nick Poole in renditioning Lowri Graves."

This was news. They'd already been informed that Adam believed that the shooter who escaped was Poole. He'd been a Five agent, placed in the Regulators' system as a mole. But he'd gone rogue and disappeared off the face of the earth and now sat near the top of pretty much every most-wanted list in Thames House.

"Tell me about Poole."

"What do you want to know? Other than that he's a massive fucking prick?"

"What do you think he was here for today?"

"You'd have to ask Aidan Marshall that, I guess. It was him he frogmarched back in here, right before he shot my mate's son."

"After your mate's son shot countless civilians. He might well have shot you too, had Poole not done what he did."

Adam's eyes narrowed. "Don't even go there. What Poole did wasn't for me."

"Who was it for then?"

"Himself. Everything he's ever done has been for his own arse. That's what double agents do. They learn to lie and cheat and save their own hides in whatever way possible. The way you're talking about him, I'm guessing he's done the dirty on you lot as well. Who'd have thought it?"

Adam sounded pissed off now. It was time for Thea to come in and try to bring him back on track.

"What about Calum then? Tell us about him. We're trying to understand why he'd be involved in something like this."

"I can't tell you that either. Last time I saw Calum he was a skinny teenager whose biggest issue was playground bullies and why he couldn't get a girlfriend. The kid in there today… that wasn't Calum."

"What do you mean?"

"If I had to guess, I'd say he's been groomed."

"Groomed?"

"Is that so hard to believe? Or is it only something that happens to impressionable Muslim kids?"

Jane snorted derisively at that dig. "Don't start looking for moral high ground here. Legally, you have none."

"Well, the law's always been an arse, hasn't it?"

Thea could sense that the two of them weren't going to be friends and she needed to act, even if peacemaker was hardly her default setting. She did it the only way she knew how.

"Look, can you two stop playing silly fuckers and get on board here. You've both got one ball bigger than the other. You can tell by the way you stand." Jane and Adam both settled backwards a little. There was even a wry smile on each of their faces. Maybe they did have some common ground. "The big question we need to ask is, was this attack linked to Nathan Nelmes's death?"

"It's a rather big fucking coincidence if it isn't," Adam replied.

"Agreed," Jane nodded. "So, if that's the case, what's it all about?"

"I've no idea." Adam shook his head.

"Would you tell us if you did?"

"What have I got to hide?" Adam asked. Thea noticed he sounded curious now rather than defensive. As if he'd picked up on something. She wondered how much of her hand Jane was about to show.

"I'm just wondering if you're protecting someone."

"Like who?"

"A friend. In hiding."

"Jack?"

"Crossed my mind."

"Why would I be protecting Jack?"

"It's no secret that Jack and Nathan had a professional history. And now his son is implicated for the murder of Nathan Nelmes and is guilty as fucking sin for the shootings here."

"Implicated? Circumstantial evidence, sure. But implicated?" Adam didn't know about the DNA yet then. In fairness to him and the Regulators' system, he had been a bit busy this afternoon. Thea waited to see if Jane would tell him.

She did. "We found DNA at the murder scene. Again, no doubt you know. We made a partial match on it earlier today, which I'm guessing you don't know, or you want us to believe you don't know. Doesn't really matter which. It had a familial link to one person on our database. Jack Quinn. Chances are, when we check it with his son's DNA, we're going to get a much firmer match."

"Fuck." Adam ran his head through his dark curly hair and turned to gaze out of the window. Thea could see how much that news was hitting him. She wondered what questions were racing through his mind. She knew that the most urgent one would be what this all had to do with Jack Quinn.

"Anything you want to say on that?"

Adam swallowed then turned to face them, fighting back the emotion. "I don't know what's happening here. But I do know this. Jack Quinn wouldn't have his son killing people he used to work with. Wouldn't have him killing anyone. That's not who he is."

"Who he is? When was the last time you saw him?"

"About the same time as her," Adam nodded in Thea's direction. "But that changes nothing. That's not who Jack Quinn was. He protected his kids. From everything. Definitely from this world. If I had to guess, I'd say that's why he disappeared. He wanted to protect them from what he was."

Thea had a horrible thought forming in her head. She knew Adam was thinking it too. She could see the emotion on his face. The distress of what was being played out on Jack's family. The fear that someone could do something to his family as well. She could see the fear in his eyes, no matter how much he tried to hide it.

"Shit," Adam spoke again, biting his lip, forcing back tears. "Why the fuck are they going after his family?"

"You want us to believe that they're doing this to him? To hurt Jack?" Jane asked. It was a harsh question and though she sounded as if she didn't believe him, Thea knew she wouldn't be discounting it.

"It's the only thing that makes sense. Jack made a lot of enemies. So did Nathan Nelmes. Someone wanted Nathan dead. They got it. Then they wanted to hurt Jack. They've got that too."

"Who though?"

"If I knew, I swear, I'd tell you," Adam said. Thea believed him.

10

They took Adam from the *Daily Inquirer* to a police station on the other side of the river. He had travelled alone. Whether Emmie had been taken to the same station, he didn't know. He doubted it though. The standard play in these situations was to keep everyone separate. Although he was technically a witness, he'd be classed as a hostile one. Hostile enough to not be afforded the usual luxuries. Even the offer of a drink only came after he'd been sitting unattended in an interview room for the best part of an hour. The sergeant who finally came to him was hardly a conversationalist.

"Tea?" he half-barked. When Adam smiled and said he'd love one, all he got back was a grunt. Monosyllabic was his conversation style then.

It took another fifteen minutes for the tea to arrive. It was lukewarm by the time it got to him. Adam drank it anyway. He didn't know how long he'd be waiting for another one.

The rest of his day had been spent replaying the events of that morning for different people from different organisations. He told them all the same story. The truth. Almost. There were a few moments he left out. Like Emmie shooting the man at point-blank range. He couldn't bring himself to talk about it. For fear of the trouble it might bring her. And for the fact that it made him feel ashamed that he hadn't been able to stop it.

Eventually, they must have run out of different branches of law enforcement because no one else wanted to talk to him. His personal belongings were returned and he was told he was free to go, although he had to keep himself available if they needed him. He was sure they would.

When he was clear of the station and certain he wasn't being followed, at least not physically, he took out his phone and dialled the office.

"Morgan, checking in," he said as he heard the voice of the operator asking where to direct his call. A couple of seconds later he was talking to Eamonn Grant.

"Wondered when I'd hear from you. How are you?" Grant's voice managed to sound both condescending and caring at the same time. It was quite the trait.

"It's been a long day." Adam knew that, for all he said, Grant didn't care about how Adam felt. He was here to talk business.

"Calum Quinn?" Eamonn would know most of the details of the day, so it made sense to cut to the chase. This was always going to be the biggest talking point. Especially given the history between Jack Quinn and Eamonn. The day Jack disappeared, Eamonn had attempted to arrest him, for reasons that he had never disclosed and Adam had never asked. Now Adam heard the echoes of that moment in the way Eamonn brought up the name Quinn. Whatever bad blood existed between the two of them, it had Eamonn Grant worried.

"I can't even begin to get my head around it." Adam had tried to make sense of what he'd seen all day. With every new person asking him about his thoughts on why Calum Quinn had been one of the attackers, he'd hoped he'd find some moment of inspiration. Each and every time, he had drawn a blank. He just didn't see how the skinny and scared teenager he'd known could have been turned into a mass murderer.

"You're going to need to," Eamonn pressured him and Adam knew in that moment that it was out of self-preservation. There were only two ways that they were going to find out why Calum Quinn had been part of this: if Calum Quinn told him, or they found the people he worked with. Neither seemed likely to be happening soon. If at all. But Adam was too tired for the argument that pointing out the obvious was going to bring from Eamonn.

"I'll do my best. Have we got any leads?"

"Not yet."

"Then I think I'm going to head home. See Laura and the kids." Adam had managed to phone his wife after the attack and tell her he was going to be out of contact for most of the day, but that he was fine and would be home soon. She understood. Accepting his secret life as a Regulator had been hard, but it was in the past and they'd managed to move on from it, although something in her tone when they'd spoken earlier told him that they would be rehashing some of her fears about it when he saw her.

"I need you to do one more thing for me."

Adam sighed. "What?"

* * * *

Isobel Quinn was asleep, curled up across three plastic chairs. Behind her, Adam could see an armed police officer standing by the door to the room where Calum Quinn was currently deep in a coma. He had survived an eight-hour operation to repair the most immediate of the damage, but his prognosis was still unclear. The fact that he had even so much as an outside chance felt miraculous to Adam. The story was that whilst the Kevlar hadn't stopped the rounds, it had done enough to slow them so that the damage wasn't catastrophic. He'd still suffered a punctured lung and there were lingering questions about whether or not he'd suffered any nerve damage. Aside from his lungs, his heart and other major organs had escaped injury. Again, miraculous, Adam thought.

Eamonn had told Adam to go to the hospital to talk to Isobel. He was after all, something of a friendly face. Probably the closest she'd come to seeing one. Right now, though, she needed sleep more than she needed to speak to him. Adam couldn't even begin to imagine what she was going through. He'd been lucky that his kids had escaped so much as a broken bone. If he could keep it that way, he'd be happy. He didn't know if he'd even have the strength to be able to sleep were he in Isobel's shoes.

The thought of his own family made him want to get home. Eamonn Grant had told him to come to the hospital to sit with Isobel and try and get something from her. At first it had seemed like the right thing to do. Now, as he looked at her, he knew it wasn't. She needed space and he needed to leave.

He turned and made his way through the hospital. It was quiet in the intensive care unit. Probably even more quiet than normal here. The police had locked down the area around the ward and Adam had only managed to get as far as he had thanks to yet another false piece of identification. He wondered how much longer he would be able to get away with that. His face was going to be one known by more and more police officers with every passing day.

A coffee machine beckoned to his lagging body, enticing him over with the promise of a kick of caffeine that should sustain him on the drive home. He typed in the number of the drink he wanted on the keypad, before tapping his phone on the reader and waiting for the drink to be dispensed.

"Getting the round in?"

The voice made Adam jump. He had no idea that anyone was standing behind him. Let alone a ghost.

"Jack." He turned to see his old partner, all six foot five of him. He wore a black leather jacket over a grey hoodie. The hood was pulled up over his head in some effort to disguise himself. Not that any of it worked. As tall and as broad as he was, he always stood out. His attempts to look less conspicuous had the opposite effect.

"Should have known I'd find you here." Jack's voice was neutral, which unnerved Adam somewhat. Warm was what he'd been hoping for when the two of them finally reunited. Then again, given the circumstances, perhaps warm was a bit too much to ask.

"Likewise," he replied, mimicking Jack's tone. "I'm sorry."

"Thank you," Jack replied. "You were there?"

"I was. I don't know what he was doing there. It doesn't make any sense."

"It will to him, so it will to me. Eventually. Then we'll see."

"See what?"

Jack just shrugged and Adam quickly felt uncomfortable. He had seen Jack like this before. Aloof. On edge. He was angry. And he was ready to fight. The last thing Adam wanted to do was fight Jack. He couldn't even flatter himself to say it was because he was his friend and he wanted to spare him. Jack Quinn had a gift for violence that Adam Morgan didn't want to ape.

The coffee machine beeped to break the silence and announce that Adam's drink was ready. He took it and passed it to Jack. He didn't offer his thanks, just kept his eyes fixed firmly on Adam. It left him wary about turning around and ordering himself another drink. He didn't want to leave his back to Jack, not when he was acting like this. But he also wanted to convey some sense of normality.

"Where have you been?" He asked a question designed to take Jack out of the room. Out of the moment. He hoped he was taking him to a place where his mind could be that little bit happier.

Jack sighed. No answer was immediately forthcoming. Eventually he spoke. Not that it was an answer. "Don't ask the questions they want you to ask. Ask what you want."

"I am." Adam didn't even bother to question who *they* were. If he had to guess, Eamonn Grant would have been one of them.

"It doesn't matter. Not now anyway. How was he?"

"He's fighting," Adam said as it dawned on him that Jack hadn't actually been to see his son. He couldn't. That must have been eating away at him. He began to understand just why it was that Jack was acting the way he was. The coffee machine beeped again and he took his drink and they started walking to nowhere in particular.

"Will he live?" This time there was emotion. Just a hint of something he couldn't hide behind whatever macho front he was trying to play.

Adam wanted to be able to tell him it would all be fine, but there was no point in lying. "I don't know."

"Someone put him up to this," Jack said as they walked.

"That was my first thought. Do you know who?"

"No. Working on some theories though."

"I can help you."

Jack brushed the suggestion off. "You know they did all this just to bring me here?"

"Why are you here? You could have stayed hidden. Stayed safe. There's nothing you can do here."

"I'm here because I'm angrier than I am scared."

"But what good does that do you or Calum?"

"It brings them to me."

"To you?"

"Why are you here, Adam?"

"I came to check in on Calum. On Isobel. She's down there, you know. Sleeping outside his room."

"I'm sure she is. And I'm sure the last person on earth she wants to see is me."

"You never know, mate. I bet she could use someone right now."

"Reconciliation wasn't top of my agenda when I came here."

"So what was?"

"I waited for them to come."

"Waited? For who?"

"For them. For whoever they sent. For you."

"For me?"

"Looks that way, doesn't it?"

"Jack, mate. I'm not here for you. I had no idea you were even in the city, never mind the building."

"Then why did two vanloads of what I assume are armed men encircle the building five minutes after you arrived?"

"What?" Adam should have known that Jack hadn't just stumbled across him at the coffee machine. He'd seen him coming. The pretext that he was here to see his son fell apart. Jack had made himself the bait for a trap and he thought that Adam had triggered it. "I didn't know anything about it."

"Who told you to come here?"

"Eamonn Grant." Which explained a lot to Adam and, so it seemed, to Jack. He nodded.

"You learned to fight while I've been away or has that partner of yours been pulling your arse out of the fire?"

Adam thought back to this morning. "The latter."

"Fuck's sake. Well, time to see which way your bread is buttered these days. Come on, we're getting some answers."

Jack clasped a firm hand on Adam's shoulder. It felt like acceptance again. Then they were moving. Quickly now. Towards the lifts.

"If this is Grant, then they'll be seeing everything we're doing," Adam reminded Jack. The Regulators had access to most of the security cameras in hospitals up and down the country. It was just another part of their omnipresence.

"Gives them half a chance," Jack said as they reached the elevators.

11

The elevator was on it's way up. A couple of floors away. There was always the chance that one of the men that had been sent for him might be lurking in there, but Jack felt pretty comfortable in taking on however many people were trying to step out through a small elevator opening. Numbers didn't matter much when you had a bottleneck and the enemy knew you were coming. When the doors opened and the elevator was empty, he was a little disappointed.

Adam still seemed nervy. Jack knew he was a part of that. He was trying not to be an arsehole, but it was hard. He had a lot going on in his mind right now. His son was fighting for his life and he couldn't be there. Not that he'd been there much recently anyway. And Calum might argue he hadn't been around in the right way before. All of that was serving to mash around in his head, twisting his thoughts between guilt, resentment and anger. Adam wasn't the person he needed to take it out on though, despite his initial concerns, which he knew he had to have. He'd wanted to welcome Adam back as his old friend from the get-go. But he knew he had to make him an enemy first and let him prove himself. Who knew what had happened in the time he'd been gone? And the next few minutes were going to a perfect opportunity for both of them to build that trust again. It was just a shame for the men that Eamonn Grant had sent his way.

They got into the lift. Adam warned him again that they'd be being watched and that someone would be waiting for them as they got out. Jack ignored him. He knew he was right. He just couldn't tell him in case they were listening as well.

The lift began its descent. There were only a few floors. He figured he'd be putting a few of Grant's men above them. No doubt they'd be circling around and heading downstairs, so they'd have to watch their backs, but he hoped they'd be out the door before too many made it down.

They reached the third floor, then the second. Jack hit the button for the first and the lift stopped seconds later. The doors slipped open. The hallway in front was quiet. As he'd hoped, they'd seen them heading for the ground floor and scrambled to be there.

"Come on," he said to Adam.

He looked at the signs pointing out which wards were on this floor, trying to get an idea of what to expect and what he could use to his advantage. An orthopaedics department seemed to have the majority of the floor. Fracture clinics and blood tests and a few wards named after people he'd never heard of. That was good. These were the sorts of places that dealt with appointments. There would be a few inpatients convalescing on those named wards, but a lot of the space would be empty at this time. It also made it quiet. A chance to hear anyone coming. Now it was time to get out.

"You armed?" Adam asked as they surveyed the new floor.

"Nope."

"But you knew you were walking into a trap."

"Couple of reasons. First up, if the trap involved armed police, I didn't want to give them a reason to put me down. Second of all, I'm a little out of practice when it comes to hand-to-hand combat. I figured I could do with a warm-up."

Adam grumbled something to himself, audible enough to let Jack know he thought he was at least a little bit crazy. Then there was another noise. Footsteps. Too quick and heavy for a doctor or nurse. Even if there was an emergency going on, they wouldn't be wearing the sort of heavy tactical boots that Jack could hear stomping towards them. He raised a hand up to Adam, although there was no way Adam hadn't heard them too.

The footsteps echoed from the stairwell next to the elevator. People coming down. Or up. Maybe both. But they were coming their way and there was no time to hide. Jack always believed that the best form of defence was attack. He pressed himself to the wall by the door, hoping he was out of sight. Adam followed suit, lining up opposite. As good a plan as any.

The doors burst open and Jack turned his body to let his shoulder take the blow. Then there were men in front of him. Three of them, all with their backs turned, looking for Jack and Adam, no doubt hearing a voice in their ear screaming at them to turn around, because their targets were right behind them.

The first of the men didn't get that far. Jack snapped a punch into the back of his head, just behind the ear. It wasn't something he liked doing and he knew he was holding back a little as he did it. It felt like a coward's way to strike someone. Hit the right place with the right speed and you could kill someone easily. The head wasn't designed to take blows from the back. Humans had evolved into facing danger head on. One of the downsides of being a predator. The spinal column could easily become damaged, even severed, without extending too much force on a blow to the back of the head. Whether he'd killed the guy or not, he couldn't tell. All he knew was that he flopped forward, face finding the floor. He didn't get back up.

The other two men were wheeling around now. Adam was engaging one. Jack left them to it. If needs be, he could step in. He figured, even at his worst, Adam could hold his own for ten to fifteen seconds. There was no way he was planning on taking that long to get to him. If you were still fighting after that long, things were going very wrong.

The next guy had time to process what was happening. He had his gun drawn, but it was clear he wasn't going to use it. The nozzle stayed down. No point even bluffing at these close quarters. Jack could see the man's mind going through his alternatives. In the end he settled on the one Jack would have picked, which he had to give him credit for. He let the grip of the gun slip out of his hand, grasping the barrel and swinging it as a weapon towards the side of Jack's head. It might have worked, had Jack not been cut from the same cloth as his attacker. He knew that the blow was coming even before the swing. He took a quick step to the side, far too graceful for a man of his size. The gun missed not only his head, but his whole body as he continued his dance around to the side. By the time the arc had finished, Jack was a good forty-five degrees round from where he'd started. His attacker was facing an empty space. Not Jack. He saw opportunity. Planting his left foot firmly into the ground, he let his hips continue to arc around counterclockwise, rotating his shoulders and propelling his right fist into the man's face. This time there was no holding back. Jack had given this guy every chance. It was as fair a fight as they were going to get. Only now, it was over. The man's head snapped back and he collapsed to the floor, his body crumpling over his legs. Two down.

Adam was ducking a punch when he looked over. Adam might not be the fighter Jack was, but he was more than capable. He still had the same speed that Jack remembered, dodging back the other way to miss the second punch of the combination that his opponent had unleashed. Jack could have let them fight it out. In another situation, he would have. But time was the biggest issue here. He wrapped one thick arm around the neck of Adam's opponent, gripping onto his left arm, wrapping that around the man's head and squeezing hard, lifting him off the floor.

The man struggled, trying to break free. Adam landed a punch in the man's gut, winding him, taking the fight away. Jack squeezed his arms tighter, restricting the man's airway more and more. The man scratched and grabbed at Jack. But with each move, he used more and more oxygen and quickly his efforts weakened as his body gave up.

"He's out," Adam said eventually, breathing a little harder than he had before the action.

Jack dropped the man, picking up one of the pistols that now lay on the floor. "Let's keep moving."

They entered the stairwell and raced for the ground floor. Jack had counted eight men getting out of the vans when they arrived. That meant five more still in the building. He couldn't rule out the possibility some remained in the vans, ready for a quick getaway. Ten was a round number after all and experience had told him that was how people operated. But it was the five inside that he was most worried about. Three had reached the first floor. If he were a betting man, he'd have said two had come from the second, whilst the first had come from the ground floor. He probably hadn't been the only one down there. Which meant that there was someone waiting for them.

The sound of gunfire echoed through the hospital as they crashed through the doors of the stairwell. It shocked Jack at first. He had been so convinced that they wanted to take him alive that they wouldn't resort to using their weapons. But as he ducked, he heard the sound of plaster and masonry being struck above him. They were warning shots.

Designed to bring them to a halt. To convince them that the game was up.

The problem with that was that Jack knew the shooter was bluffing.

Adam took cover, but Jack didn't. He straightened up and marched towards the man. That clearly hadn't been the reaction he was expecting. His face dropped and he gasped as Jack approached, floundering in his inability to have a plan B.

"Move," Jack barked as he zeroed in on him.

The man didn't move. He froze, caught between knowing he had a duty to carry out and simply not knowing how the hell he was supposed to do it.

"Fine," Jack grunted as he reached the man.

He grabbed him by the jacket, lifting him off his feet, barely breaking stride as he went. The man's legs kicked at the air beneath him as they carried on towards the exit. The man tried to blurt out some sort of plea to Jack but he wasn't listening.

"Would you get the door for me, mate?" he asked. Then he was launching the man through the air, his arms flailing as he crashed back-first into the glass sliding doors that led to the outside world. Alarms blared and Jack heard another voice shouting as the glass fell and the man bounced off the concrete. This voice wasn't someone he needed to worry about. It was a security guard, hollering at him to *Stop right there* or some other instruction he was about to ignore. He looked around to see Adam catching up with him. He could see from his face that he wanted to ask him something along the lines of "What the fuck just happened?" but both of them knew it could wait.

"You got a car?" Jack asked.

"Company one," Adam replied.

"That'll do for now," Jack said. "Let's get out of here."

They ran for the car park, Jack on alert at all times for more armed men chasing them down, or vans to pull up and try and take them quickly, but no one came. They were in the car and driving away in seconds.

Slowly, Jack allowed himself to relax. To let the soldier side of his body relinquish control. To let Jack Quinn take over again.

He turned and looked at Adam driving. He looked tired and bewildered. There was one thing that remained unsaid, which Jack knew he had to be the first to say.

"It's fucking good to see you, mate."

12

"Well, that's a turn-up for the books." Jane Astley had a knack of underselling things. There was no way that what she had just seen could only elicit that low-key a reaction. Thea herself could barely believe it. Even though something along these lines had felt inevitable since Calum had been identified as one of the shooters at the *Daily Inquirer*.

"This is insane, boss," Thea pointed out as she sat watching Jack throwing a man through a plate glass door. He had always been a man of action rather than words, but even for him, this was something new. The violence seemed to have gone up a notch.

"What do you reckon he bench-presses?" Jane laughed as she replayed the video again. "I mean, look at that. He's sent him a good old distance there. It's impressive stuff."

"It's hardly subtle, is it?" Thea said, which was the bit that was puzzling her. If there was one thing that the Regulators did, it was keep things out of the spotlight.

"With a bit of luck, he'll keep it up. Leave us a nice trail of bodies that takes us straight to him."

Jack Quinn had made good his escape. Traffic cameras had followed them for a while. Then the car had disappeared. When it next appeared, only Adam was in it. Met Police officers had gone to talk to him this morning. Thea and

Jane were awaiting their report. Thea didn't hold out much hope of it offering anything of substance. The four men that Jack had despatched of had all been helped from the scene before police had arrived. They too had disappeared into the night, their trails covered. Facial recognition had failed to give them names. Thea assumed that even if they had once been in their database, they would have been purged by now. What she wanted to know was, by whom? Were these more Regulators after Jack, or was this something else?

"It certainly looks like he was checking up on his son, doesn't it?" Jane said, walking from where she'd been standing next to Thea back to her own desk and reclining in her chair.

"I think that goes without saying."

"I guess the question we need to ask ourselves is whether he's a concerned parent, or if he went there for operational reasons."

"Operational reasons?"

"Look at it this way. We've got a man in the field who's been captured. If you're on the bad guys' side, you want to make sure he doesn't talk. So far, no one has come knocking at his door, save his dear old dad."

"Jack didn't go knocking at the door. You saw what Jack Quinn does to doors. If he wanted to get through to Calum, we'd be having a very different conversation right about now."

"Maybe so. Or maybe he got there and the enormity of what he knew he had to do got to him. I mean, I know he's got this reputation as a cold, hard killer, but offing your own son? That's got to take it to the next level. I don't know many people who could pull that off without at least a little hesitation."

"You're also forgetting we had a team of other likely lads turn up in the hospital that night. Who's to say they weren't tasked with that and Jack just put the skids on their mission?"

"There were eight men who entered the building. Using your logic for Jack, stands to reason they could have made a move easily. Half of them had a free run at Calum, if they wanted it, but they all bugged out when Jack made his escape. No, they were there for Jack Quinn."

Thea knew that, at the very least, that last assessment was right. But she didn't buy the rest of it. Not yet anyway.

"Absence of other suspects doesn't mean that Jack Quinn is the one behind all of this. It's a lot of supposition and you and I know we're both well above that."

"We're both well above letting personal opinions get in the way of what's in front of us. We've got a plot that, if it comes off, will be the single biggest fuck-up this agency will have ever let happen. No pressure and all that. And we've got a thread here that we need to start pulling at. Maybe Jack Quinn isn't the big bad in all this. Maybe he's not even on the wrong side. His past suggests he wouldn't be, but with all we've seen, the amount of time he's been off on his jollies, or hiding in a cave, or whatever he's been up to, it's at the least prudent to look at him as a person of interest. And that means asking the awkward question."

"Like did you send your son out to become a mass murderer, then betray him and let him get shot, only to turn up when that didn't kill him, so you could finish the job yourself?"

"Exactly like that."

"If this was Jack Quinn, don't you think he'd have wanted to keep his son safe? Maybe not keep him off the front line, but at the very least not have someone, I dunno, shoot him at point blank range?"

"Maybe he didn't do the dishes?" Jane shrugged and Thea had to laugh. "Look. Whatever he did or didn't do, we don't take it all off the table until we do know what happened. It's just the way we have to do this. I don't want a dead PM on my CV. It'll look shit."

"Yeah, I've tasted the drinks you make. You're not getting a job as a barista if you get fired from here."

"I thought I might go into childcare. Hunting down threats to the state sounds on a par with a room full of toddlers."

"Couldn't convince me to do that, boss."

"What would you do?"

Thea shrugged. Truth was, she was only ever good at one thing. "Guess I'd have to become a Regulator, wouldn't I? I'd have burnt all my official bridges by then."

"Yeah, Jesus. Childcare it is. I'm not being the one chasing you. You make my life hard enough when you're on my side."

Thea laughed. "Thanks, boss."

* * * *

It was the phone call that Eammon Grant had been dreading since he heard back from his team last night. He tried half-heartedly to convince himself that he could ignore it. But he knew that if he did, he was signing his death warrant. At least answering it might buy him another chance. He wondered how many more he would get.

"Grant," he tried to sound as gruff and angry as possible. Better to sound as if he was annoyed, rather than fearful.

"I'm extremely disappointed to hear that last night didn't go to plan. After all the efforts that went into setting the trap, I would have thought eight of your best men could have pulled it off."

"They bloody should have done," Grant replied, hoping to shift the blame from him to those who carried out the operation. In truth, he was right. This should have been a cakewalk.

"I'm intrigued to hear what your new plan is."

"We're putting it in place now."

"That's not telling me what it is."

Grant paused. At this point he didn't have a plan, so to speak. He'd hoped he would be able to bluff his way through this call without having to reveal that. Now he would have to come up with something workable on the hop.

"I've got people following Adam Morgan. He'll lead us straight to him."

"And if he doesn't?"

"He will."

"Very well. Keep me posted."

The line went dead and Grant felt the tightness in his body release. He didn't have to think too hard to imagine what would happen if he failed again. He'd seen what had happened to others.

13

Dodging surveillance wasn't something Adam was used to doing. Normally the boot was on the other foot. But this morning demanded it. Jack had asked to be dropped off the night before, with the promise he would explain everything he could the next day. Adam hadn't got the energy to argue nor had he the inclination to sleep anywhere but his own bed. He'd expected the Met to be waiting when he got back, but they hadn't turned up till half past eight that morning.

His wife Laura hadn't said much about the whole thing. She had acclimatised to being the wife of a Regulator very quickly. It had come as a surprise to Adam. His whole life since joining them had been predicated on secrecy, even to those closest to him. It was seen as the best way of keeping them safe. But as the story had broken over his involvement in exposing the paedophile ring that brought down a government, that all had to come to an end. Laura was brought into the fold by the front pages of the tabloids. At first, she'd seemed irritated. But once the doorstepping had come to an end and a sliver of normality had returned to their lives, she'd been extremely laid back about the whole situation. It had made Adam ask the question whether she'd suspected he was involved in it all before it had come to a head. That had drawn a derisory laugh and the response that, no, she had never contemplated for one moment that her husband led a double life fighting crime for a shadowy underground global network who took the law into their own hands. That, funnily enough, had never crossed her mind. If anything, she had been relieved to find out he wasn't moonlighting as a heavy for some dodgy two-bit gangster.

The last twenty-four hours had been the first time since the revelation that their lives had really been affected by his job. Laura had been in bed when he got home. They had a sparse conversation that extended only so far as: was he okay and was he going to keep being okay? Then she made teas and coffees for Adam and the police officers who came to visit, before taking the kids out to the park. It was another glorious day after all and the temperatures were set to soar. Best to get out and about with the little ones before it got too hot.

Adam had given his statement about what had happened at the hospital. The brief he'd had from Raf that night after reporting in had told him to be as truthful as possible. Adam hadn't told Raf about Jack's suspicions about Eamonn being the person behind the attempt. Nor had he recognised the men involved. His statement taken and with no reasonable cause to take things any further, they left.

Adam had waited half an hour before leaving, spending the time packing a bag with things that were about to come in useful. He knew he would be being watched when he left. He set off on foot, avoiding his car. That could be tracked from the Regulators' office and if Grant really was in on it, he didn't want to lead him straight to Jack. He caught the tube into London, stopping at a couple of quieter stations to reverse his route and show up anyone who might be physically following him. He was pretty certain he had picked them out. A young couple, male and female, in their early thirties. They got on with him and disembarked at his first stop. They hovered cautiously when he moved to the opposite platform, looking at the map. They could have been tourists, day trippers, whatever, but if they were tailing him, the fear of being made held them back from getting on the second train.

He rode it back and changed lines, getting onto a Bakerloo Line train and heading west. Bakerloo Lines trains didn't have CCTV in their carriages. It wouldn't be long before they did. Numerous lines now had it installed. Stations were a different matter. That was something he would have to deal with at the time. He stood at the end of his carriage and took a jacket and pair of jogging bottoms out of his backpack and put them on, folding the backpack down as flat as it would go and placing it underneath his jacket. It drew a couple of looks from his fellow passengers, but no one seemed perturbed enough to make a big deal out of it. Certainly no one got up from their seats.

The first stop was Marylebone, which would be busy. He figured with his change of clothing that would be his best bet. He got off the train, head down, and made his way quickly out of the station, finding himself back out in central London. He quickly grabbed a taxi from the rank outside the station, telling the driver to take him to the outskirts of the city to an industrial estate near Ruislip.

As Adam got out of the car he looked for the telltale signs of someone following him. There were none. But he knew it would only be a matter of time before his trail was picked up again. People would no doubt be working through the footage now, using different AI algorithms to hunt him out of the crowd and retrace his steps. He and Jack probably only had minutes.

Jack had told him the exact spot to wait in. It was secluded, away from the road, underneath a plastic corrugated roof that ran alongside a warehouse in the middle of the industrial estate and probably made up a smoking area. The factory looked as if it hadn't been in use for a couple of years now. The windows and doors were boarded. The chances of someone coming to join them for a smoke seemed slim.

Adam didn't have to wait long. Jack was with him within minutes. He had probably been on station nearby, watching for Adam and then for anyone who might be tailing him. Clearly, he too was satisfied.

"Adam," he said in that emotionless, dull tone again.

"Jack," Adam tried not to sound guarded but he knew he did.

There was a moment of silence between the two of them before Jack moved. "Fucking hell," he said, then he embraced Adam firmly. "It's good to see you, mate," he said as Adam returned the hug.

"You too, pal," Adam agreed, tension evaporating as he saw Jack smiling as the hug ended. "What the hell is going on?"

"It's a long story and I don't think I know the whole of it. I'll do my best though. After I disappeared, I did what I said I was going to and lay low for a while."

"You did a good job. Trust me, we were looking for you."

"And you were never going to find me," Jack smiled.

"What brought you back out of hiding?"

"I felt bad," Jack shrugged. "About Nelmes. I wanted to apologise for what I got him into and what it had cost him. People like us, we know the risks. Nelmes didn't. So I popped round to see him. Only I was wrong. He knew the risks and he was still going."

"What do you mean still going?"

"He had a hunch that whatever we did would have repercussions. It was going to create a power vacuum. I mean, how could it not? We cleared out half the cabinet, a good chunk of the opposition and all sorts of other assorted bad eggs with more clout than they deserved. You make a hole in a pile of shit, there's only one thing that's going to fall in it."

"What did he find?" Adam felt a shiver down his spine. He knew what those people had done before. He didn't want to think of it happening again.

"In Statera."

"In what?"

"It's Latin for 'The Balance'. Some sort of underground organisation that apparently has been running around for centuries, prodding and poking at our political systems trying to keep everything in check. In balance."

"I don't understand."

"What we did created a vacuum. You've seen how things have been in this country. No one trusts politicians anymore. And not like the old times, when no one trusted politicians. Now they really don't. They want something different. Problem is, that doesn't work out for those who are in power. They need to assert control again. Remind the people who the rulers are."

"How are they planning to do that?"

"That's the bit we were trying to work out. I guess we stepped on some toes. Probably more than that in Nelmes's case. He must have got close to uncovering what was happening. Close enough to lose his life. I guess I just pissed them off enough to want to punish me."

"What's the plan now? Are you coming in?"

"To the Regulators? No. If I'm right, Grant's answering the call of someone in or linked to this group. That's why he wants me so badly. It's the only thing that makes sense. I mean, I didn't shag his wife or anything. Not that I'm aware of, anyway."

"I've met his wife. She would not go for that."

"And yet she went for Grant?"

Adam shrugged.

"Harsh," Jack laughed. "Whatever, though. He keeps coming for me. And he has no reason I can think of to do so."

"You've made a lot of enemies," Adam pointed out. It was true. There was a lot of debris in Jack's wake.

"Maybe so. But I don't like coincidences. Never have."

"That doesn't answer how we're going to deal with this, though. I mean, do you want me to be working through the Regulators?"

"That'd be a help. But I'm not doing this alone. It wasn't just me and Nelmes."

"Who else do you have?"

14

Jack's ex-wife lived in a new-build estate, in a smart, red-brick home with a tidy, well-manicured garden bordered by a small white picket fence. She had moved here with the kids a little over six months ago, finally moving out of the old family home that they had shared with Jack. Thea wondered if it had been part of Isobel's process of moving on from her ex-husband, or if it had been as much for Kat and Calum. Jack's disappearance and the absence in their lives must have been hard. The damage it had done she couldn't even begin to imagine. Her parents may have had their faults, but at least they were there. They didn't just cease to play a part in her life without so much as a goodbye. She wondered how much that had played into whatever reasoning had been going on in Calum's head as he built up to what had happened the day before.

The house had already been thoroughly searched by the Met and other agencies the day before. Computers and mobile phones had been seized, but at this point, as far as Thea knew, there was little evidence to suggest that any of Calum's preparations had taken place at home. No sign of weapons being brought into the property. No leftover kit. Nothing that would suggest he had done anything in the vicinity of his family that might have alerted their suspicions. Still, she was going to have to ask. Even if she hated herself for it.

Isobel had agreed to come and do the interview at the family home. It was a chance for her to escape the hospital, shower and change clothes. In the meantime, Calum's sister, Kat, was keeping vigil over her brother. His condition remained unchanged. Thea had arrived at the house just as Isobel had. She'd made her a drink and left her downstairs whilst she showered and changed. It gave Thea a chance to look around the house and get a better feel for the family. She'd only ever briefly heard of them through Jack. He and Isobel had parted by the time she worked with him and Jack was hardly the sort to share stories of his romantic past. Most of what she knew had come from reports on Jack. Information gathering on his wider circle. It hadn't amounted to much.

Now she was getting the first-hand account of it all. From inside Isobel's spotless kitchen in her immaculately ordered house. It was hard to believe that police teams had been searching through here the previous day. It spoke more of the complete lack of clutter in the house than any clean-up. Isobel simply hadn't had the time. Even the garden, where white-suited forensics experts had looked for signs of anything being buried under the lawn, looked like it was from a showhouse. The only sign that it was a home to someone was the mass of family portraits arranged on the walls. Looking at them told Thea far more about the life of the Quinn family than anything Jack had ever shared with her. There were no pictures of the four of them. Those had been consigned either to the bin or to albums that would probably only be opened by the children when they moved out of the house.

For the most part they told the story of family life post-Jack. There were some that clearly went beyond. Jack was always absent. Maybe he was the one taking the photograph. Maybe he wasn't there. Off on a job in some far-flung hellhole. Who knew? As Thea looked at the later ones, she tried to spot the signs of the change in Calum. At first, she saw a gangly and miserable-looking teenager. There were precious few shots of him smiling and where he was, Thea felt that it looked coaxed. Kat had more of her father in her. She stood taller, straighter. Her smile was always there. Set into her face. Replicated to the same proportions each and every time with almost military precision. Isobel was often placed in between them. The bridge between the two kids. She was shorter than her daughter in all of the later photographs. Calum caught up after. Maybe a couple of years or so if Thea had to guess.

Isobel looked happy in the pictures. There was a lot of love there. You could see what being with her children meant to her. What being part of a family meant to her. She smiled in every picture. It wasn't like Kat's smile. There were differences each time. Where Calum looked happier, Thea couldn't help but notice that Isobel looked more relaxed. Where his face failed to meet the occasion, there was something else there. Almost a desperation. Or a hurt. Something that wasn't right. But she was trying her best. Yet no matter what, the three of them always looked incomplete. Something was missing. Or someone. That final piece of the puzzle of the Quinn family that took the three of them and made them one whole.

"It's funny how they change right under your eyes and you never really notice." Isobel had appeared in the doorway, drying her hair. Thea wondered if she meant in general, or specifically in the case of Calum. What must she be going through, knowing what her son had become? What he'd done.

"I don't suppose you can know everything that's going on in their head," Thea said, waiting to see if it was the right approach. "I don't think any parent knows everything that goes on in their kids' lives."

"Do you have kids?" Isobel asked making her way to the kettle.

"No," Thea replied.

"Do you wish you did?"

Normally, such candid conversation was something Thea would avoid, but there were moments she had to embrace it. This felt like one of them. "Never came up."

"Work?"

"Yeah," Thea replied truthfully.

Isobel offered her a drink and they exchanged more small talk whilst the kettle boiled. When they had their drinks in hand, they sat either side of a slate-topped kitchen island and began to talk.

"I met your ex-husband. More than once." Thea had deliberated for a long time over when was the right time to let Isobel know she knew Jack.

"Through what you do?"

"Did," Thea corrected her. "I was NCA and police before this."

"You'll have to forgive me if I ask whether you were arresting him or working with him. I have no idea how all this vigilante nonsense works and he's not been around to ask."

"Nonsense is a good word for it. And it was a bit of both. When I first came across him, I very nearly arrested him. Ultimately, he helped me out. Whether that was because it was the right thing to do, or to stick it to the people he was working for, I never could tell."

"Knowing Jack, it was probably a bit of each."

"I never got my head around that, what with him being ex-forces."

"That was the problem. Neither did he." Isobel sighed and took a swig of her drink before she continued. "When he left the army, it was because he felt it had betrayed him. They weren't doing what was right and too many people wanted to look the other way. It hurt him, not that he'd ever admit it. Which ultimately hurt us because he couldn't work out where to direct those negative feelings. In the end they just became a part of him."

"He does strike me as someone who's lost."

"Not lost," Isobel replied. "He knows where he is. I just don't think he likes it very much. I think life hasn't ever been what he thought it would be."

"Tell me about him and Calum."

Isobel looked away through the window to the back garden. "They loved each other, but could they tell each other?" She let the end of the sentence drift off, signifying that question was very much rhetorical. "Everything would be different if Jack was still around. I'm convinced of that."

Thea didn't feel she wanted to disagree on that. "How was Calum in the run-up? How was he acting?"

Isobel shook her head and blinked away the tears that were forming in the corners of her eyes, before looking back to Thea. "He was the happiest I'd ever seen him." As she said the words, her lip trembled and Thea could see it was breaking her heart.

"You weren't to know."

"I know," Isobel whispered. "I know. You see these moments on the TV. You wonder about what the parents were doing when their children were turning into killers. How could they never know? Then in an instant you are them and you have all the answers just a day too late. But even if I could go back and warn myself, I wonder if I would listen? Would I look at my son, finally happy, finally confident. Turning into a man, or so I thought. Would I see that and believe that, beneath it all, he was plotting to kill innocent people? To throw his whole life away? And for what? That's what I can't get my head around. He didn't believe in anything. Even when he was younger. He didn't care about any cause or buy into any conspiracies. He wasn't an 'incel' or a God-knows-what. He was just a happy kid. For once in his life, he was happy. And it felt incredible to see that. It made me feel like it was all going to be okay. Like we were complete. Now we'll never feel that ever again."

Thea had heard countless people get emotional in interviews before. It was part and parcel of the job. She dealt with people as they lived through their lowest moments. She'd become quite good at placating them. At knowing the right words to say, even if she couldn't truly empathise with how they were feeling. This time she didn't know what to say. She knew Jack and this was his family. She'd been one of the last people to see him before he'd disappeared. She was partly responsible for that. It was her call that had brought him onto the case. "I'm sorry," she said, meaning it.

Thea moved the conversation on to talk about facts rather than feelings. When Isobel had last seen Calum. Their last conversation. His mood. None of it was eye-opening. In fact, it was all rather mundane. Calum had kept everything hidden from her. Just as Thea expected he would. When people were radicalised, no matter the cause, they hid their intentions. They never talked about what mattered to them, lest they slip up. She tried her best to explain to Isobel that she couldn't let herself take the blame for not seeing it. But something inside Isobel wouldn't budge. Some maternal instinct that Thea had yet to ever feel. It was clear Isobel saw Calum as her responsibility, even as an adult. Even as a mass murderer. Thea began to believe that Isobel felt she had in part pulled the trigger.

"You're not the first mother to not understand why their child has done something like this," Thea pointed out as Isobel dabbed at more tears.

"I'll just never understand why. What brought him to that point? It makes no sense. And then for Jack to be back. After all this time he just shows up. No one knew where he was, they say. I mean, does he blame me? He couldn't even bring himself to come and talk to me."

Thea realised she didn't know how much Isobel knew about Jack's being at the hospital. Did she know about the attack on him? About the carnage he had caused? She'd been told that alarms had sounded at the hospital and that police had descended on the scene, but how much had been brought to Isobel?

"What did they tell you about Jack being there?"

Isobel sniffed. "Not much. That there was some sort of altercation. They didn't say who with. I assumed it was with security or something."

"It was worse than that. We believe whoever it was went there to target Jack."

"Target? As in kill him?" Isobel couldn't hide the shock from her voice or her face. Her mouth hung open. The tears she had been shedding for her son and herself stopped in that moment as she struggled with the concept.

"We don't think so. From the footage we've seen, it looks like they were trying to use non-lethal force."

"What happened?"

"Jack's non-lethal force was more forceful." Thea didn't want to go too far into the specifics.

"Were they waiting for him?"

"We think so." Thea paused, trying to think of a way to explain that they were beginning to wonder if Calum had only ever been bait to bring Jack out into the open. Isobel's expression changed, telling Thea she wasn't going to be the one to have to say it.

"Oh my God. Calum. They used him, didn't they?"

"We're not sure yet. We're not even sure who they are. That's what we need to work out. With your help."

"I don't know how to help." Isobel was starting to panic now. Thea could hear it in her voice. It had gone up an octave. Her eyes had widened, looking directly at Thea now, as if pleading for help. "I don't know how to do any of this. I didn't ask for it. This isn't what I do. I can't handle this."

Her hands were out on the table in front of her. Thea knew that someone with a more tactile approach to consolation would maybe touch one of them. But that wasn't her. She leant backwards, away from Isobel. "We're not asking you to do anything, Isobel. Only tell us what you know."

"I don't know anything. I don't know anything," she sobbed.

15

They had taken even more anti-surveillance precautions on their way to meet Jack's contact. He hadn't wanted to say who it was until they got there. The journey took far longer than it should have done, but by the middle of the afternoon, Adam found himself in a car driving through the Kent countryside, heading towards the coast. Wheat fields surrounded the narrow winding road, towering over the roof of the car on either side. The lack of hedges made it feel more continental than English. It wasn't a part of the world that Adam had been to before, which made it harder to guess who it might be they were going to see.

They passed a small hamlet, almost on the very eastern edge of Canterbury, turning off the main road and following a private track. A large bush marked the outside boundary of the property. A black wooden gate swung open as they approached, letting them drive in. Adam saw that it hid a substantial-looking brick wall, topped with barbed wire that tumbled down the sides like a metallic climbing plant. He knew that nothing would stop someone determined to get into the grounds, but it appeared that whoever lived here was making sure that anyone intent on doing so would have to work for it.

Inside the compound, a gravel drive led up to and around an ornate stone fountain at the centre of immaculately manicured gardens. Adam parked the car up, just to the side of the steps that led to the house's dark brown wooden double doors. "Nice pad," he said as they got out.

"He's not done badly, has he?" Jack replied.

Adam was about to ask who when the door opened. He looked up. Nothing could have prepared him for who he saw.

"Mr Morgan." David Warner was smiling as he said it.

It had been a long time since Adam had last seen David. Almost as long as it had been since he'd seen Jack. Adam had made a point of going to see David whilst he was in the hospital, recovering from the injuries he sustained in what the police had called a tragic road collision, but which the Regulators knew had been a deliberate attempt on David Warner's life. His survival hadn't been guaranteed. It took ten days for him to wake up. Over two weeks before he understood where he was. Three months before he was sent home. Adam had visited him at his home in London, but as work had got in the way and David had begun to get back to something approaching his old self, those visits had dwindled. David was out of the Regulators and he showed very little interest in hearing what was going on. Adam felt as if he was reminding him of his old life and had decided that, as much as he'd miss visiting David, the best thing to do was give him some space.

The smile on David's face as they embraced suggested otherwise. They hugged and Adam felt the frailty in David's body. He had always been thin, but before it had

115

been a wiry, athletic thin. Now he felt delicate. As if made from straw. His grasp around Adam felt light. There was no squeeze. He was still smiling as they stepped apart. "How are you?" he asked.

"I'm good. You?"

"Never better," David smiled, turning and walking into the house, not letting Adam have a moment to point out that he'd seen him far better in the past.

The house opened up into a marble-floored hallway, with an oak-lined staircase leading up along the right-hand side of the room to the first floor. They stayed on the ground floor, passing by a glossily varnished door that remained closed. Their destination was the back of the building. They came out of the hall into a large kitchen-diner, flanked by a glass-ceilinged conservatory which looked onto what could only be described as a quintessential English country garden.

"Now this is some place," Adam said as they reached a white marble kitchen island. He couldn't help but noticed how David teetered against it, grabbing on to steady himself. His smile never slipped. Maybe that was just the norm now.

"I must admit, as places to live out a retirement go, I think I've done rather well."

"You've had help."

The new voice was one Adam had heard before, but not for a long time. It was one he would never have expected to have heard in David's house. Certainly not sounding like it belonged. He turned to see Reuben Arrowsmith smiling at him, perched against the door to the garden, arms crossed, one leg over the other. He looked at David, who must have known the question that was going through Adam's head. Why the hell was he here?

"I've taken in many different people over the years, Adam. From all walks of life. The police, the military, sometimes even criminals. After all, once you start working for me, that's what you become."

"Takes some getting used to. Your big mate over there still hasn't said more than single syllables to me," Reuben nodded in Jack's direction, who just grunted. Jack was clearly also having a hard time seeing a former gangster working for David Warner. That was understandable. The two had gone toe to toe. It had cost Jack his role as Regulator. It had cost Reuben much more. His empire. The life of his girlfriend. The last Adam had heard of him, he was in prison. He had no idea what had happened. He wouldn't have cared if it weren't for the fact he was now working for David.

"Don't worry," David soothed. "The damage to my head was bad, but it wasn't that bad. Reuben was working for me well before that point. And he's been incredibly loyal and efficient."

Jack grunted again.

"Thanks, mate, means a lot coming from you," Reuben said mockingly. He hadn't changed. He was still a cheeky shit.

"I've got a lot more questions now," Adam admitted.

"The backstory can wait. For now, let's get on with the pressing matter at hand."

Adam, David and Jack took a seat each in the conservatory. Reuben left them, busying himself with God knows what. Adam was glad of that. He didn't really see a world where he trusted Reuben. What David had said about them all being criminals now might have been true, but Reuben began as a criminal. He was the sort of person people like Adam spent their lives chasing. They couldn't be on the same team. But that could wait. Now he needed to know why they were all here.

"I wish we'd had the chance to reach out to you sooner, I really do," David said earnestly. "Jack wanted you in from the very beginning, but we decided that it was in your best interests if you were kept out of the loop. After all, we could trust you to work the case from the inside without our input."

"What case? The Nelmes murder?" Adam still didn't have the slightest clue what they were on about. It was still an enigma.

"That's one part of it. Nathan Nelmes was murdered because he uncovered something. What, we don't know yet. All we know is that there is concerted effort by persons unknown to seize control of the government and keep that

118

control. What it looks like, how it will be enacted, we're still not sure."

"Is there anything we do know?"

"It turns out, we made this happen," Jack butted in, taking accountability. Whenever a mistake had been made, he had to be the one owning it.

"We didn't set in motion an attempt to overthrow the government. Like you said to me before, we might have made a vacuum that someone else filled, but we can't take the flack for that. We did the right thing," Adam argued.

"We did," David agreed. "But we also crossed what's known as the Dead Line."

Jack sat back, nodding as if to say 'See?'

"What's the Dead Line?" Adam asked.

"In times gone by, there were lines marked out on the ground in prison yards. These were the Dead Lines. Whilst the guards patrolled on their gantries overhead, the prisoners were free to do as they pleased in the area below. And often they did. Just so long as they didn't cross the Dead Line. Crossing the Dead Line meant that the guards were free to take a shot at you. It turns out that this group, the In Statera, had Dead Lines. Immovable positions that could not be crossed, for fear that they would do so much damage to the stability of the country. The Regulators crossed one of those Dead Lines when they exposed the corruption at the heart of all branches of power in this country. As Jack told you, it left a vacuum. But it's not the people who are filling that vacuum that are the problem, it's the people who are trying to control them. This In Statera want to correct the course as they see it. In their world view, a power controlled is better than a free power. So they're carrying out a plot to ensure that they can wrest back that control. Steer the ship in their direction once again."

"What direction is that?"

"It doesn't matter. It's not theirs to take. So we have to stop them," Jack said bluntly.

"They're probably saying the same about us, you know. I mean, clearly, we've pissed them off here and the biggest problem with that is that they clearly know who you are, who *we* are. We don't give a monkey's about who they are."

"Not as yet, no." David said solemnly. "But that's where we need your help. You still have the access to the Regulators' files in a way that we don't. We're on the outside. I believe the answer lies inside the Kernel."

"What makes you think that the Regulators would have anything on it? I mean, you used to be the top man there. Surely, you'd know?"

David laughed. "I'm flattered you think I can recall everything that came across my desk, Adam, I really am. And I do recall some things. Not as much as I used to," he added sadly, opening his palms out. "But I do recall that Dead Line was brought up to me."

"By whom?"

"Lowri," David said, his eyes cutting away. Lowri Graves had been David's boss, if there was such a thing. She had been a member of the Vehmic Court, which sat above the Regulators and passed judgement on those that the Regulators brought before them. Their number was made up of people in positions within the country where they had access to power and information, but never exerted it. It was the Vehm, as they were known, who gave orders to the Regulators. More than that, although it was never a public thing, there was more than a sneaking suspicion amongst the ranks that Lowri and David's relationship was more than professional. At the very least, they clearly cared for each other deeply. Adam saw the pain in David's eyes as he thought about Lowri. She had been missing longer than Jack had to Adam. Hers hadn't been a disappearance she had enacted. She had been taken from a railway station, never to be seen again.

"Shit," Adam breathed, beginning to understand the magnitude of where they were at. It was impossible to deny that what they had done before was linked to what was happening now. Nelmes's murder. Poole's appearance at the *Daily Inquirer*. A direct link to Lowri Graves. "We're in well above our heads here, aren't we?"

"And we can't call for much more help. Only the people you truly trust," David warned, snapping out of his malaise.

"Your partner would be a good start," Jack added. "She's got her head screwed on, and God knows I can't keep saving your arse. We need that job splitting between the two of us."

Adam wanted to point out that it was Jack's arse that appeared to be in the firing line, but it seemed a little blunt and obvious to be done so facetiously so he just took it and pulled a face at his former partner, who smiled back. "Looks like the band's back together," Jack added.

16

Computers were an ever-increasing part of Thea's world.
Gone were the days when she could claim that she wasn't
technically savvy and pass them off. Even when she was in
the police, the ability to use a computer proficiently was an
advantage. She wasn't some sort of clichéd technophobe
cop who left all the tech stuff to some geek in a basement.
That being said, what she was witnessing now, as the
specialist technician at Five accessed the data from Calum's
computer, was beyond what she had ever seen before.

Josef had only introduced himself with a first name. He
hadn't given his second. He was a tall, red-haired man who
talked a lot whilst he was working. Some of it made sense
to Thea. A lot of it was technobabble. The rest was filler. It
appeared that Josef was no fan of silence.

"It's always great to get some folks down here and
watching," he said as he typed quickly and nimbly. The
program he was using was doing most of the work for him
but as data was being accessed, he was cataloguing it at the
same time. "I always like having a couple of new faces to
talk to. I bet you've had a right busy couple of days,
haven't you folks?"

He'd said the word 'folks' more times since they arrived
than Thea thought she had heard in the rest of her life. It
must have been his go-to androgynous approach to talking
to people. She was surprised he didn't refer to both of them

by name individually. Looking at the way he was breaking down the data he was accessing, he seemed to like everything organised in its own little compartments. Thea didn't know how he could read it all so quickly. She certainly couldn't.

"Don't they normally have AI algorithms for parsing data like this?" she asked.

"They do, but they're slow and, let's be honest, one day they're going to have AI for everything, so I might as well do something before they retire me. It'll probably be the same for you lot upstairs as well. AI that can work out who the bad guys are before they've even done anything. That would be amazing, don't you think?"

Thea did not think. She didn't say it though. She didn't want to be the one who broke the spell that Josef was under as he worked.

"Can we view any of this that you've pulled out already?" Jane asked. She was far more interested in the results than the process.

"Of course you can, folks." Josef flicked a hand quickly out to his right, pointing to another terminal. "Just let me add your login details to this drive and you can view a mirror of it in real time."

There wasn't even time to wonder how long it would take before Josef had told them it was done. They each took a seat at the other computer and looked at what had been sorted so far. There were endless reams of communication between Calum and an unidentified person, calling themselves Umberto. The chats had started on social media, innocuous and friendly enough at first. Calum had confided his unhappiness in his father and how he was glad he had disappeared. "I hope he's dead somewhere," read one particularly angry message. Thea could almost see him writing it through the tears of confusion and anger.

"Wasn't a happy bunny, was he?" Jane remarked as they moved through the logs.

It was an understatement. At first Umberto and Calum had talked about the possibility of a suicide pact. But as their 'friendship' had blossomed, that was cast off. The plan changed from their own deaths to the deaths of people who had wronged them. They had both drawn up lists. Calum's featured people from his college or his old school. Umberto's may well have been just a work of fiction. But they gave reasoning behind each one, as did Calum. *Bullied me at school. Called me a dweeb. Wouldn't look at me, even though I'd been a nice guy to her.* It was all so clichéd, but that just made it abundantly clear how easy it had been for whoever was behind the Umberto persona to manipulate Calum to this point. Then the tone changed. Killing people at college was no good. People did that all the time and what really changed? They needed to go for the people who really made a difference if they wanted to be remembered. If they wanted to be celebrated. And it wouldn't be a suicide mission. Umberto told Calum that they had an 'in' with some other people who were trained. Former soldiers.

125

They would help them to achieve their goals. They just needed a place to start.

"This is chilling," Jane whispered. "How the fuck did they make him make this leap?"

It soon became clear. Umberto got Calum to pinpoint the root cause of his misery. It didn't take much for the finger of blame to go towards Jack. Umberto suggested killing Jack but they dismissed that as impossible. They didn't even know where he was. So they had to come up with a new plan. *What about drawing him out? Killing someone he cared about?* Umberto had planted the seed. Calum had suggested his sister, but Umberto didn't think that was wise. They said they were worried that Calum might one day regret that. Better to find a kill that meant nothing to them. Especially for a first kill. Calum had objected that his sister meant nothing to him, but it didn't take much for Umberto to talk him down off that ledge and admit that, actually, she wasn't all that bad. They needed to kill someone who deserved to die. Someone who had made people's lives a misery, but that Jack Quinn liked.

"They were always going to make him kill Nathan Nelmes," Thea said. It had been what they suspected, but it was good to know that Calum hadn't been the one to come up with it. Maybe that counted for something.

Umberto had researched Calum's dad, or so they said. They had found out what he had done and they were shocked. Or so they said. Being a vigilante was a crime. But if that's what Jack Quinn was, if he took the law into his own hands,

126

why shouldn't Calum? Why shouldn't he punish someone who had caused hurt and in turn draw Jack Quinn out to meet his comeuppance? Nathan Nelmes was selected and the plan was set in motion. Calum had been excited in the lead-up. His mood changed drastically after it had taken place.

"Looks like our boy had regrets." Jane was reading the exchanges that came after. Calum had said how he felt sick. Umberto had said that Calum had been inspirational. They glorified the killing, telling Calum how proud they were. How much of a man he was. There was so much smoke being blown up his arse that, like any teenage boy, he couldn't resist the compliments, and the murder of Nathan Nelmes, instead of being an act he was horrified by, became an act he was proud of. So much so that, when it didn't draw Jack out, it was he who suggested that they go bigger and better.

How about his work? Umberto had said in reply. And then the plans were made. More people were supposedly found, fortunately, by Umberto. *We're building our own little army!* Umberto had decreed.

"There's a lot of 'how' in here," Jane said as they kept reading. "Not a lot of the 'why'. Nothing that links it to any plot on the PM."

She was right. As compelling as the evidence was, this wasn't their case. They were looking for something else and so far, the evidence on the computer was lacking.

127

"Josef, can we run a keyword search on this whilst you're still working?" Thea asked.

"Of course you can, folks!" Josef said breezily. "Just do it as you would normally. It won't slow me down any."

"Thanks, mate," Thea said back, bringing up the search window on the screen and asking Jane: "What are we after then?"

"Start with the PM's name, shall we?" Jane said, leaning over to type the name Agatha Harris as she did so.

The search pane changed, then came back with the results. There wasn't much. Calum had searched her name on more than one occasion, but they were all relatively innocuous. Certainly nothing to suggest that he was involved in the planning of her assassination. There was one solitary result that stood alone. A file of some sort. The name was just gibberish. A string of words and numbers thrown together that meant nothing to either Thea or Jane.

"Josef?" Thea called again. "Any chance you can get this file open or working?"

She expected him to ask which one, or come over to their terminal, but whatever they were doing he could clearly see on his screen, because he answered them without looking up. "It's a partial file. Something that he tried to delete but unfortunately for him, didn't do a very good job of. Let me run a couple of programs on it, see if we can't piece it back together."

In front of them, a new pop-up appeared, showing a progress bar as whatever Josef had set in motion took effect. It didn't take long. Whatever there was, there wasn't a lot of it and the program was able to piece as much together as it could inside a minute.

"Let's have a look, shall we?" Jane said, double-clicking on the file.

A text window opened. Again, it was fragments. Clearly, whatever had been deleted was now lost to the ether. But enough remained for segments to make sense. There was a section on the prime minister that read like a fact file. Family members. Addresses. Routes to and from work. The sort of thing you might want if you were plotting an assassination. Then the data was broken. A huge chunk missing before it returned again. This time with a list of names that sent a chill running down Thea's spine. Nathan Nelmes. Jack Quinn. David Warner. Thea Watts. Adam Morgan. It went on. Some of the names she knew. Some of them she didn't. Some were Regulators. Some were serving police officers. Two of them were the names of journalists killed in the raid on the *Daily Inquirer*.

"You all right?" Jane asked as she read the names.

"I just can't believe they got their hands on Santa's naughty list," Thea did her best to shrug it off. She wasn't scared. Threats were something that came with her job. Her nature was to accept the threat, then face it head on. The problem here was that she didn't know where the threat came from. Right now she was powerless and that was disconcerting.

They scanned the rest of the names, scrolling through more broken text until they reached the very bottom. There lay a link to a document. Jane clicked it. A new pop-up window appeared, followed by an error message that read: *Unable to find U:\DEAD LINE.*

"What the hell is Dead Line?" Thea mused.

"Ah, shit." Jane answered.

"What?"

"I've heard that before."

"Where?"

"You're not going to like it."

There was no going back for Jane and she must have known it. She tapped open a new panel and brought up some videos from the archive.

"Look, let me just say I had no part of anything that happened before, during or after this interview. I didn't know about it till I saw it and by that point my hands were tied. I like it about as much as you're going to like it, but it is what it is."

"What is it?" Thea asked.

Jane showed her. She selected a video and it opened showing what looked like an interrogation room. The walls were a dour green that looked almost like filth. There was a metal table, behind which sat a figure, head slumped forward, their long greasy hair drooping across their face.

The figure mumbled something. Jane turned the volume up.

"Can you say that again," came a voice from someone off screen.

"Dead Line," came the reply. Louder now, but still mumbled. A woman's voice, but broken in some way. Empty.

"Dead Line?" echoed the interrogator.

The figure nodded without looking up.

"I don't know what that is," the interrogator pointed out.

The head in front remained slumped. There was no response.

"Tell me about Dead Line," the interrogator insisted.

The head in front shook, then looked up at the interrogator. Thea swore. She had so many new questions now. Now that she could see the person on the screen.

"I can't," replied Lowri Graves, before slumping her head once more.

17

Jack stepped outside when the moment was right. He did it a lot when he came to David's house. Something about the garden there relaxed him. He didn't know what it was. The softer side of him would have said it was because all he could see in front of him was nature. The green of the bushes and trees that marked the edge of the garden. The rolling fields in the background. All he could hear was the sound of birds. It was idyllic. There was another part of him that knew that he could also relax because of the tall, thick concrete wall hidden in the bushes and trees. The electronic surveillance that meant no one could sneak up on them. Probably it was a little bit of both. There would always be a side of him that longed for freedom and another side that craved security.

He walked whilst the others talked. He had a lot to try and get his head around. He hadn't let his mind linger over Calum's involvement in the attacks. He wanted to wait until the right moment. He thought it would have come at the hospital, but from the moment he set foot inside the place, he knew it had been a mistake. As he'd spotted the vans and the men inside, he'd cursed what he'd called naivety. He had quickly stolen a glance towards his son, at what he hoped was a safe distance. He'd seen Isobel sleeping. The officer guarding the door. And then in the distance, he saw him. Bathed in a light that looked as if it poured down from the heavens, illuminating the son he knew he was going to lose one way or another.

He berated himself in that moment. Why had he been so goddamn foolish to go? To put himself and his family back in the firing line once again. It was selfish. Now he wondered if it had been something else. Love for his son. Something that called him out, regardless of what the danger might be. He'd been surprised that he still had that inside him. It had given him hope. Then he'd reverted back to type. Hurting people. Throwing a guy through a door. That sort of thing. Hope had evaporated quickly. He was who he was and he was never going to change and all of it had led to a place where his son had wound up poked full of wires and tubes, clinging to life under the ethereal lights of the ICU ward.

Jack looked around, wondering if anyone would hear him if he screamed, right there in the garden. Sometimes he wanted to. Just let it all out. Every ounce of anger and hate and regret and pain. He could feel it bubbling and building inside of him on every single day. He was sure people could see it in him. He only had to look at the way they looked at him as he walked down the road sometimes. He had been used to people being intimidated by him in the past. He was a big guy after all and his face bore witness to numerous scrapes and close calls. But recently, intimidation had given way to fear. People looked worried when they saw him coming. They crossed roads. He didn't know what it was inside him, what vibe he was giving off, but people were scared of him. If he'd been asked a couple of years ago, he would have jokingly said he loved the idea. Now that it was his reality, he hated it. He needed to find a way to cut himself free. Otherwise, what was the point?

There was a path that led around the edge of the garden, meandering through neatly kept flowerbeds, full of pretty plants that Jack could never wish to name. He wanted to ask David how he found the time to look after it all. He wondered if Reuben helped. He already did all of David's cooking. Jack even had to admit he was actually quite good at it. Their relationship was still much of a mystery to him. Reuben wasn't the sort of person you expected to fall in line behind anyone, least of all someone like David. But it had happened and Reuben seemed to crave it. Jack could see it in the man. The admiration and respect he held for David. Every time he spoke to him, there was a bond there that Reuben couldn't and didn't want to break. When Jack had first come across him, he'd been the streetwise and conniving head of a London gang. Now he was David Warner's glorified butler with a gun. There was a history that Jack hadn't asked about and probably wouldn't be told if he did. He was learning to believe in it though and that was something. And, more importantly, if someone like Reuben could find redemption, then maybe one day he would find it too.

"I should send you out with a rake."

Jack turned around to see David standing behind him. He had no idea how long he had been there; he'd been so lost in his thoughts.

"What's up?" he asked.

"Thought I'd come and see how you were getting on." David walked slowly and carefully towards Jack, placing a hand on his shoulder out of either sympathy or for balance. Maybe even both. "I can't imagine what you're going through."

A flurry of words formed in Jack's mouth, but none seemed to fit the sentiment in his head. So he said nothing. They walked without talking, the silence extending and giving Jack the chance to find what he wanted to say.

"I've never been here before."

"Where is here?"

"Scared. Truly scared."

"Adam told me you said you were more angry than scared."

"Yeah, well, sometimes we say things we don't actually mean, don't we?"

"We do."

They walked some more in silence.

"It's not to say I'm not angry," Jack finally admitted. He couldn't help but feel that David wanted him to say something. He had a habit of doing that. Saying nothing till you did. It drove Jack mad. He far preferred just saying nothing. But there was something about David's silences. They were always set up in a way that Jack had to fill them.

"I know."

"I'm really fucking angry."

"I can tell."

"Can you?"

David looked at him and shrugged. "Maybe not. Maybe some things are truly out of my scope of understanding."

"I just don't know what I'm supposed to do. With all of this stuff I'm feeling. Where does it go? How do I make it go away?"

"You don't."

"That's fucking shit."

"It is."

"Thanks."

"Don't sound so defeated. Surely in your time in the military, things went FUBAR once in a while."

Jack recognised the acronym. Fucked Up Beyond All Recognition. It felt apt. "More than once."

"Did you surrender?"

"Did we hell." Jack understood what David was trying to say. "We found a new way to get to our objective."

"And if you'd lost men in those situations, completing your objective didn't bring them back, did it?"

"Never once."

"But it made it worthwhile."

"Nothing's worth the life of my son."

"No, sorry," David dipped his head. "That was perhaps a crass analogy. But do you remember when I took you on for this? Where you were at that point?"

"I was at rock bottom. Living my life looking out of a bottle," Jack admitted. His post-army days had been some of the hardest of his life. That loss of purpose had hit him hard.

"We found you a purpose. An explanation for your existence."

"And now that's been taken from me again."

"So take it back."

"I don't think they're likely to have me back."

"Stranger things have happened. I get the feeling that the Regulators and Vehm need you right now."

"I don't think they see it that way. I've still got Grant coming after me."

"Grant is one man and I'd wager quite a lot that his orders don't come with the official stamp on them."

"Regardless, he's still the man in charge right now. Unless you're planning a comeback."

David laughed this time. "No, I don't think that's likely, do you?"

"Shame."

"But my point is this: Jack Quinn works best when he has a purpose. It's always been the case. Right now, finding out who brought your son into this is your purpose. But that moment will pass and it won't heal this hurt you feel right now. Calum may have exacerbated it, but I think if you're honest with yourself, you've been hurting for a long time. And you'll keep on hurting when this is over. Unless you find a reason to live."

"There's always the other alternative."

"No. There's not," David said firmly. "Disappearing was selfish. I should have called you out on it sooner but I didn't. So that's on me. But you can see what it did to your family. When this is done, you need to return to them, in whatever capacity that may be. If that means facing the consequences of what you've done before, from the law or the Regulators or the Vehm, so be it. But you can't keep running and hiding. You can't take enough of yourself with you when you do that."

Jack said nothing. They continued their walk, back towards the house.

Back at the house, Adam was holding a glass of water whilst talking on the phone. When he finished his call, he came over to them.

"Just checking in with the office. Don't worry, I made sure they couldn't track my location."

"Won't that get their backs up a bit?" Jack asked. Adam just shrugged.

"Gentlemen, I have a plan that might get us back on track, which I want to run by you."

They took seats in the conservatory. "Dead Line is clearly the enigma," David began. "We need to know more about it. There are two ways. One is finding someone who knows about it. The only person we know is Lowri Graves and we don't know where she is right now. So that leaves plan B, which I'm afraid to say is going to compromise you greatly, Adam."

Adam remained impassive. "I'm sure I can handle that. What do you need."

"If I'm right, then there will be information on Dead Line locked away inside the Kernel."

"And you want me to get it."

"If you can. Normally with any form of electronic data, we'd find a way to hack it, but as you know, the Kernel is disconnected from the outside world. The only way we can get what's on it is by going there physically and taking it at source."

"Can that even be done?" Jack asked. He knew of the Kernel, the giant supercomputer at the heart of the Regulators' London field office. He'd seen it once. A huge metallic structure that was made up of irregularly shaped towers, formed together in what would have been a cube had they all been the same size. It hung on its axis, attached by two metal poles that ran from the top and bottom, presumably housing the wires and conduits that connected it to its power source and the computer stations in the building.

"There are direct access terminals in the wall of the room where it's housed. You'll need the right passcodes but I can give you those."

"Will they still work? You've been out of there a long time."

"My status hasn't been revoked. I'm currently on sabbatical after all and not considered to be hostile. They should work. If they don't, then we'll come up with a new plan."

"Sounds worth a shot," Adam shrugged.

"You'll need help inside. Someone to watch your back," David said and for a moment Jack assumed he meant him. "Emmie Weston, can you trust her?"

"Completely."

"Then it's time to bring her in."

"I'll talk to her. She'll do it."

"Fine. I'll get the codes and the drive and we'll meet back here when you have the data."

They all agreed and got up. Jack felt a little lost. There was a mission going on and he wasn't part of it. It was only when he left the room that he began to wonder if David had deliberately talked about him needing a purpose and getting back into the Regulators, before implementing a mission where he couldn't support it because he wasn't part of the Regulators.

"Crafty son of a bitch," he muttered to no one in particular.

18

It felt good to be up at this time. Early morning gave solace from the heat that still suffocated the country. Thea had still wound down the windows of the car as they made their way out of London, but it wasn't to stop herself from sweating. It was because the air outside felt good. She knew it wouldn't be long before it changed. Before it attacked anyone unlucky enough to be outside in it. But for now, it felt tame.

"I love driving at this time of day. So little traffic," Jane said, adding another advantage to early mornings. The roads weren't deserted. They never were anymore. But at a little after half four in the morning, they were as clear as you could get.

Their destination was an MOD base out on Foulness Island, on the Essex coastline. It was an artillery firing range, which meant it was somewhere people were loath to tread. But it was also living a double life. Beneath the firing range was a secret. One that if it were ever discovered would cause the sort of shit storm that would reverberate around the world. Secret jails were supposed to be the stuff of thriller films and conspiracy theories after all.

Glasshouse Seven was very real. Thea hadn't heard of it until late last night when Jane had received clearance to let her know just where it was that Lowri Graves was being held. Thea had heard of the term Glasshouse before. It had originated from the glass roof that covered Aldershot Military Prison in the mid-1800s. Over time, the name became synonymous with all military prisons. Thea wasn't sure how many there had been or were now. But if the naming convention was to make any sense, there were or had to have been at least seven.

The journey, although free from traffic, took them over an hour. There were no motorways serving this part of the country. Even the A road only took them as far as Southend. Then it was country lanes to the edge of the MOD site. They were stopped at the gates to the site, well before they even reached the island itself. Their ID was scoured by a miserable-looking security guard before they were ushered through. It was another half an hour before they reached their destination.

The entrance to the prison was unassuming enough. They parked their car next to a small wooden hut and walked in. A single sergeant sat behind a desk. His gun lay on it. He seemed relaxed enough, but Thea was certain that his mood could change in an instant. He had been forewarned they were coming. Unexpected guests would get a very different sort of welcome. They signed three different forms, none of which Thea bothered to read. She knew what the gist would be. The threat of life imprisonment for divulging anything related to this site. As much as the concept of it appalled her on one level, she begrudgingly accepted the need for it.

Once satisfied that their signatures were enough to guarantee their compliance, he led them to the back room of the hut. There they each passed through the same sort of detectors that greeted people at Thames House. They were scanned for everything. Metal, explosives, drugs. Any sort of contraband. They handed their phones over and were issued with visitor passes, before they were finally shown the door to an elevator that would take them God knows how far down, to reach the prison itself.

The elevator was smooth, giving no idea of its speed and so there was no way of knowing the depth they had reached by the time the door opened. They were faced with another reception area. This one was different. The room looked as if it had been bored out of the rock around it. All the colours were earthy and natural. Brown met green on the walls, whilst the floor was a mottled concrete. Above them, metal casing hid the cables, pipes and more that would be needed to keep this place working. In front of them was a desk where two men, presumably guards, sat. They were dressed in grey coveralls. When the first stood up to greet them, Thea could see he had a pistol holstered to his hip. She figured his colleague would be the same, unless of course he had to go out onto the prison floor. There would have to be checks and measures in place for that to stop any inmates ever getting their hands on a weapon.

"Astley and Watts," he remarked, looking down at his screen. "We've been expecting you. I've set aside a room for your visit. I'll take you along; the subject will be delivered shortly. When you go through, you'll need to check all your devices at the security checkpoint. There is a

144

filtered network here. If you need access, you can use these." He slid a card to each of them with credentials that presumably would connect them to the system. Thea took hers, slipping it in her pocket. She had no desire to connect to the Glasshouse system. God knows what sort of monitoring they carried out. As if reading her mind, the guard carried on. "If you do, be warned, your access will be severely limited and monitored. You'll be able to get into your emails and that's about it."

As they waited to be shown through, Thea thought about what the guard had said. 'Subject' was an interesting choice of word. These weren't prisoners. Prisoners had rights. Subjects conjured up the idea of subjugation. Of repression. She hoped it was merely semantics.

It didn't take long for them to be ushered from the waiting room to where Lowri would be brought. It was a room not unlike the one that they had seen in the video. It could easily have been the same one, but Thea was willing to believe that all the interrogation rooms looked similar.

"How many people do they have here?" she whispered once the guard had left.

"I have no idea. Some questions you just don't ask," Jane replied.

"Does it help you sleep at night?"

"It doesn't hurt. Once you realise who you are, you soon get around to accepting it."

Thea went to say something in her defence before she realised Jane was right. She wasn't going to go out and raise the issue with her local MP or sell her story to a tabloid. She was going to interview Lowri and go home. She hoped Jane was also right that once you accepted it, you did sleep more easily at night.

Lowri Graves was brought in between two guards. Neither was armed, Thea saw. They didn't need to be. Lowri had her wrists and ankles shackled, although to look at her, there was no way she would be able to fight her way out of here. Her prison clothes consisted of a brown prison jumpsuit that hung loosely against the contours of her thin frame. Her wrists poked out of the sleeves like white tendrils from dark caves. Her skin looked oily and pallid. Her hair hung low in front of her face, not that it stopped her seeing them. Her head was bowed to the floor as if exhausted. She looked as if she had nothing left to give. The guards shoved her forward into the room. One of them pulled out the chair while the other manoeuvred Lowri in front of it, pushing her hard to sit down. She collapsed into the chair, remaining still as they secured her ankles to the floor and wrists to the table in front of her.

"Any issues, we'll see," the guard warned as he made his way to the door.

Thea couldn't even begin to imagine that he expected any issues. He could have nipped out to the nearest pub, which had to be a good forty-five minutes away, had a round or two, got back and there would have been no issues, even if

Lowri had been left alone. She was utterly emaciated. The proud woman that had once unsettled Thea so much was gone. What had been deposited into the chair in front of her wasn't even her ghost. It was a husk.

"Lowri Graves, I'm Jane Astley, MI5. I believe you know my colleague, Thea Watts?"

Lowri tilted her head upwards slightly. From between the fronds of clumped, greasy hair, Thea could see Lowri's eyes. They stared right at her and, for a moment Thea felt uncomfortable again, as if at least the ghost of Lowri Graves was in the room with them. Then they closed and her head dipped again.

Thea looked at Jane, who shrugged and got back to the script.

"We need your help, Lowri. We're facing a threat to the democracy of this country. Someone has a plan to assassinate the prime minister and I know you. I know what you believe, what you think you were doing. You wouldn't want that to happen."

Lowri slowly turned her head to Jane. For a moment it looked as if she might speak, but nothing came. It did at least seem as if she was listening. As if she was interested.

"We've been investigating whether or not this links to the Regulators. The intel we've been fed tells us it's them behind this threat."

Lowri made a noise that sounded like a leaky radiator hissing. Jane cocked her head and looked at her.

"What?" she asked. When there was no response, she added, "You don't believe that."

Lowri turned away from Jane and looked at Thea. When she spoke, her voice came out as a hollow croak. "You."

"What about me?" Thea asked, keeping her tone mutual.

"You know what we are." Lowri bowed her head again; whether through the effort of speaking or simply because she didn't have more to say, they couldn't tell.

"If you don't think that your people are behind this, then help us prove it," Jane insisted.

Lowri made another hissing sound, but this one sounded angrier.

"Lowri. We know what happened to you. We know that it was us who did that. The British government. And I get why you might not be our biggest fan right now. Fuck it, I wouldn't be. If I were you, I'd be happy to see the fuckers who wronged me burn."

Lowri shook her head. "Too late," she sighed sadly. "Dead Line."

"What do you mean Dead Line? When?" Thea felt they were getting somewhere. Lowri's mind might be clouded and by God knows what. Physical, chemical, mental. She was sure all of it had been done to Lowri Graves during her time here. But she was still standing, still functioning. If only they could find a way to cut through and get one clear answer that could give them the lead they needed.

"Not when. We crossed it. Did what we shouldn't. Now they're fixing what we did."

"Who are?"

Lowri looked up and smiled at them. If you could call it a smile. Her mouth hung limply open and there was saliva pooling in the corners of her mouth, but the corners were upturned. She was enjoying this moment. Probably for the first time in a long time. "You."

"Not us, Lowri." Thea protested as Jane sat backwards, crossing her arms.

Lowri lowered her head shaking it slowly from side to side. "Yes."

* * * *

They left Lowri waiting at the table for the guards to take her back. She offered them very little more. Thea wondered if it was because she couldn't or wouldn't.

"That feels like it added more to the enigma than answered anything," Jane said as they waited for their personal items to be returned.

"What the hell was she on about with this Dead Line stuff?" Thea asked.

"We can get the boffins to run it through whatever algorithms they need," Jane replied. "Hopefully links up to something somewhere. It's clear she still thinks we're the bad guys."

"What if we are? Not necessarily us. But someone on our side."

Jane hummed thoughtfully. "Wouldn't be the first time. And Nick Poole turning up at the shooting when he's played for every team under the sun could mean that there's other people linked to this who should know bloody better."

"Does that affect how we go about things?"

"Does anything affect how you go about things?"

Thea shrugged. "Not really."

"Huh," Jane wasn't looking at Thea now. She had her phone in her hand. "Couple of missed calls from the boss."

"That's ominous."

Jane placed her phone to ear and listened to the message that had been left. "Well, shit," she said once she'd heard it.

"What?"

"Turns out that they've had some intel."

* * * *

"Concrete plans of the Regulators' plot to assassinate the prime minister are being kept at their London field office, the details of which are in the email you should currently be looking at. I've also included a dossier of evidence that proves their intentions beyond a shadow of a doubt."

"And just who are you?" replied the voice on the other end of the phone.

Poole didn't answer. He hung up, before turning to the rest of his team.

"Next stage is a go. Suit up and be ready to move at a moment's notice. We only get one chance at this."

"This'll be a cakewalk, compared to what's next," grumbled Jones. But then, that was what Jones did. He always had to have something to moan about.

He wasn't wrong, though. Whilst their next mission would require precision timing to pull off, what was coming after that was on a completely different level. But it had to be if you wanted to change the world.

19

If he had ever considered a life in crime, Adam had become quickly disavowed of it. He felt the eyes of every single person watching him as he entered the main floor of the field office. Each greeting from a colleague seemed less a genuine hello, more an attempt to get him to divulge just what it was he was doing there that day. Subterfuge felt like the softest word he could come up with. Treachery felt more apt but cut deeper. Even though he knew what he had to do and how to do it, the longer he spent acting as if nothing was wrong, the less likely he would actually go through with it. The Regulators had given him a life after all. They had picked him up when policing had let him down. How could he betray all of that now?

Of course, the only reason he was doing it was because it was David who had brought him into this world and David was the one asking him to go against it. If only just for this one moment. There were questions to be asked later about where his true loyalty lay. Right now, he didn't have time for such in-depth internal dialogue. Right now, he had to find Emmie and recruit her. That was phase one.

"Morning," she said. There was something about the way she did it, omitting the word good, that made Adam feel she was asking something of him. Then he remembered that he hadn't seen her yesterday. Hadn't checked in at all. "You okay?" she added.

"I will be," he replied, sitting down into his seat opposite her, before immediately getting back up. He couldn't sit down. Couldn't run the risk of this turning into a normal working day and everything falling apart. "Drink?" he asked.

"Sure."

"Fancy giving me a hand?"

"Sure."

They made their way towards the kitchen area, but before they got there, Adam veered off course.

"What's up?" Emmie asked, staying in stride beside him.

He had rehearsed this moment over and over in his head the night before as he lay in bed staring at the ceiling and again today on the drive into the office. His mind had been so focused elsewhere, it was a wonder he hadn't caused an accident.

"I need your help."

"Sure." The reply was as breezy and effortless as when he'd asked for help getting the drinks.

"Don't say that till you know what I'm going to ask," Adam warned, checking over his shoulder. There was no one around, so he stopped.

"What is it?" Now Emmie sounded different. Almost impatient.

"I need you to help me get into the Kernel."

"You can just walk… wait." Emmie stopped herself as she realised what he was asking for. "You want to get into the Kernel. Into the actual data?"

"Yeah."

"Why?" There was no warning him off. No trying to talk him down. Just a fair request for further information. That was what trust looked like, Adam figured.

"David Warner asked me to get him some information."

"David's out."

"He is. But he's not stopped working. He thinks we're compromised. That Grant is taking orders from elsewhere."

"I don't disagree."

"So you're in?"

"What information?"

Adam wasn't sure if her avoidance of the question was a good or bad thing. He carried on.

"There's a group behind the murder of Nelmes and the attack on the *Inquirer*. The In Statera. Apparently, they're putting into action some plot because of something called Dead Line. David doesn't know much more about it, other than that Lowri Graves knew what it was. She could be anywhere. The next best guess is that what we're looking for is on the Kernel."

"You know there's fail-safes in place. As soon as you access it, Grant's going to know. He'll come after you."

"So I need you to run interference. To get us out of here."

Emmie pulled a face that suggested she wasn't fully sure this was the best move. "You know, I do kind of like my job here."

"So do I. But we both came into it for the right reasons. To do what's right for this country, no matter what. If David is right, this could remove Grant from the playing field and hopefully we'll come out of this with nothing more than a telling-off."

"And if he's wrong. Or we don't pull it off?"

"Spend our lives in a small concrete room somewhere."

"It's a tough choice."

"Are you in?"

"I've not walked away, have I?"

"Thanks."

"Now, despite the fact you're usually useless at this part, tell me what your plan is."

Adam told her the plan. It wasn't his plan. David had come up with it. He was still not that far removed, and the systems in place were what he had dealt with. He knew their strengths and he knew their flaws. It was the flaws that they were going to have to rely on if they were to be successful here.

Emmie's role required her to go and make a nuisance of herself and distract Grant. Adam had furnished her with evidence of his meeting with Jack. Emmie hadn't been keen on the idea. Selling out Adam? It didn't sit right. But Adam knew it was the best play. They had to give Grant something he was going to want and they had to make sure his full attention was on Emmie. He was certain that Emmie could drag out the preamble, look unsure about whether she wanted to do this or not, then deliver the goods to Grant. The fact that the information was legitimate was another line to her defence that she really didn't know what Adam was up to in the Kernel. If they could keep her in play inside the Regulators after this was all done, then they would be in a really strong position.

He had given her a drive with enough incriminating data on it. Call logs. Locations. Even a transcript of a conversation that he and Jack had staged, that she could "intercept". It was all very thorough. If it bought him ten minutes to find and access the data, then it was worth it.

Emmie had returned to her desk. She was to give him five minutes from their parting before heading into Grant's office. It was at that point that Adam would enter the Kernel. Everything had to be precise.

The lower reaches of the building were far less populated than the upper floors. There were no offices to speak of. Only a few technical stations that were manned periodically. A loan security guard nodded at him as he entered the floor, checking his ID before letting him continue about his business. Why wouldn't he? Adam was senior staff. If he wanted to access the Kernel, he could. He just couldn't take the data off it.

He looked at his watch. Emmie should be leaving her desk. Making her way to Grant's office. Just a few more seconds. He wondered how fast she'd be walking. Would she look as if she was hesitating, or would she be all business? He contemplated giving her a few extra seconds. If she was really getting into character, he'd need to.

He gave her ten. Then he typed his identifier into the keypad that led to the Kernel and slipped inside the room. Immediately all the background noise was gone. Adam had never really noticed the hum of the field office until suddenly it wasn't there. He was left with the soft hiss of the cooling unit that spat air out from vents on the ceiling, keeping the whole room far colder than anywhere else in the building.

There was a small antechamber before he reached the Kernel itself. A little space for someone to prepare themselves for what they were about to do. It had always seemed dramatic to Adam. The Kernel was what it was. A huge chunk of metal that may or may not be packed full of wires and stuff. If that was awe-inspiring to some, it was just convenient to him.

He stepped into the main room, walking around the tilted cube of the Kernel to the far side. There was a pull-up screen which revealed a touch-screen interface. He had to enter David's codes into that to release another panel that would allow him to plug in the hard drive. That was the theory. It was time to put it to the test.

The code was burned into Adam's memory, but all the same he took out his phone and checked it one last time. Then it was entered and he was waiting. It took far longer than it should have. Or maybe time moved differently this close to all this tech. Finally, the screen showed the code was still valid and a small panel slid open to reveal an array of ports. Adam didn't wait. He plugged the cable attached to the drive into the port. Then he was on the screen searching for the words Dead Line.

The Kernel found it in seconds. Fifty-three results all about Dead Line. Adam highlighted them all, then selected 'Copy', sending them to the drive destination. A progress bar appeared, followed by a timer. Estimated time remaining: three minutes.

It would be the longest three minutes of Adam's life.

There wasn't much he could do. If ever there was a way to render even the most capable of men powerless, it was to put them at the mercy of a progress bar. He was pretty certain even the boffins upstairs whose job it was to look after these machines and ensure that they ran at their best, wouldn't be able to do anything to squeeze some extra speed out of whatever bit it was that was working right now.

Two minutes. A minute had passed. Uneventfully. Thankfully. Two more minutes and he could unhook the drive, stash it and make his way to the nearest exit. He knew he'd have to make a call to Laura and invent some pressing job that would have him off the radar for a couple of days. She was used to it. She was brilliant at accepting it. He owed her a lot. More than he assumed he'd ever be able to repay her. Maybe he'd find a way one day.

One minute.

There were sounds outside the door. Adam's heart sank. He knew that it was over even before Grant came storming through the door.

"Morgan, you absolute fucking idiot. What the hell were you even thinking?" he growled.

Two armed security guards flanked Grant, hands on holsters. Adam didn't want to give them any reason to feel that they needed to come out of those holsters. He raised his hands slowly, leaving the drive where it was.

"I left some holiday snaps on the drive. Promised the wife I'd get a copy."

"Apt that, because photos are all she's going to have of you now," Grant sneered.

Grant might as well have hit him with a physical blow. Adam felt the reality of the words sink in. The fear of never seeing his wife or his kids again grew inside.

Before it could boil over, the lights went out.

Adam's first thought was to make a bolt for it. To grab the drive and hope that he could get past the three men in his

159

way in the confusion. But that wouldn't have ended his problem. Everyone in that room knew why the lights were out.

"We're being breached!" Grant snapped. As he did so, the emergency lighting kicked in, bathing them in an eerie green glow.

"I'll pull the plug," Adam shouted back. Pulling the plug was what was called for in this situation. A small EMP device would be let off that would wipe out every single electronic device inside the building. Everything outside would be protected. The framework of the building was made up of a mesh of copper that acted as a block to the pulse. They called it a Faraday cage. That much Adam had taken in during his orientation. Someone had to detonate the device manually. It was perfectly safe to those around it. Just not to anything electronic.

"Are you kidding?" Grant said, but he was already on his way to the door. His duty lay upstairs, not down here. Both he and Adam knew that.

"You don't have another choice." There wasn't going to be a debate. Grant swore and left the room. Then it was Adam's turn to swear. He looked down at the hard drive. The progress bar was complete. He had everything he needed. Now he was about to wipe it clean.

Even as he made his way to the back of the room, ripping the false wall away, behind which lay the lever to activate the EMP, he was hoping that by some kind of miracle the drive would survive. It was powered off. Adam knew that things that were powered off could survive. It all depended on whether or not they were carrying a charge or something. He didn't know if the sort of drive he was carrying would be okay or not. But then, Grant hadn't asked for it. So he had to figure it wouldn't.

He rested his hand on the lever. When he pulled it, the EMP would charge. It would take about thirty seconds. He pulled.

Time went just as slowly as it had when he waited for the progress bar to move. He listened for the sound of footsteps. The next time he heard them, it wouldn't be Grant. It would be whoever was attacking the building. His assumption was that it would be the police. There were precious few organisations out there with the capabilities to challenge the Regulators head on. If someone high up the food chain had decided today was a good day to take out the world's biggest vigilante organisation, then there was nothing they could do. The Regulators had a doctrine of passive compliance when it came to police interactions. They could destroy any evidence before the police asked for it. But once ordered to do something, they were compelled to do so. If someone arrived before Adam pushed the button, he would have no choice but to stand down. It wouldn't have been so bad, but they would probably be taking his drive as well.

Fifteen seconds. Of course, there was the chance that this could be the work of whatever group Poole was working for. Their raid on the *Daily Inquirer* had shown a certain amount of balls. But the Regulators were a huge step up from unarmed journalists. There would be no passive compliance given for Poole and he would know that. Adam hadn't heard anything that sounded like gunfire, even this deep down inside the building. He felt confident he could rule that out.

The clock hit zero. A red circle illuminated a button underneath the lever. Adam sighed. So close to getting what they needed. Now he just had to make sure he found a way out before Grant or anyone else got hold of him. At least the Regulators would be on the same page as he was.

He pushed the button. The lights went out again. This time they wouldn't come back on.

20

It was always the same. The moments before a raid. The building tension. Each officer dealing with it in their own way. Some chatting happily with their colleagues. Banter or banality. It didn't matter. Something light to keep their minds clear. Others were quieter. Focused on the job they were about to undertake. Checking equipment. Putting on helmets or body armour. Checking cameras, magazines. This time was no different, even if each person had their own idiosyncrasies. Thea had seen it all before. She realised now that she didn't miss it. As the officers lined up to the doors of the field office, she thought she would want to be standing shoulder to shoulder with them. It shocked her to find she didn't. She was happy where she was. She was tired. The sort of tiredness that comes from doing something so many times and never seeing any change.

An order crackled through the radio she was holding. She didn't hear the words, but she saw what it was in the actions of the officers as they began their entry. Breaching charges detonated, taking the front door off its hinges. Then the black-clad officers surged in, weapons drawn, shields in hand, ready to take on whatever was inside. All while Thea watched and waited outside.

"I always thought this looked fun," Jane said standing next to her.

She had told Thea very little about her background. The things she had told her were things that she hadn't done. Policing was part of it. Being hands on for the field work stuff was another. Thea could see how it might look cool and exciting. In the past she'd have found it both of those things. But that was then.

More communications came through the radar. The first resistance had been met. It had been light. Everyone knew that was what they were expecting, even if the aggressive nature of their intrusion said otherwise. It had long been known that the Regulators, whilst happy to operate outside the law, didn't like to interfere directly in investigations. That included standing down and surrendering when requested. Thea could see the scene in her head as it was reported through the radio. Vigilantes with their hands on heads, lying on the floor, being restrained one by one.

"Sounds like we're going to have a lot of them in custody." Chief Constable William Hall stood next to them. His cap was on and his uniform looked pristine. Probably hoping for a photo op at the end of this, thought Thea. He smiled at them both, clearly enjoying that it was his officers doing the dirty work. "So far so bloody good."

Then the voices on the radio disappeared.

"What the hell?" Hall grumbled looking at the radio and then around at everyone. "My radio…" he began, before seeing the confused looks from everyone around him. Thea changed the frequency on her radio but there was nothing coming from those inside. Already, more officers were being despatched towards the building to work out what was going on.

"How the hell do you knock out all the radios like that?" Thea asked.

"Jammer maybe?" Jane offered.

"What good would that do?"

"Disrupt comms. Make it harder to coordinate to get people out."

"We've got the whole place surrounded."

"They don't know that."

An officer appeared at the door. "Everything's gone off. Radios, computers, lights, even the bloody torches."

"How the hell did they manage that?" Hall snarled, his dreams of a photoshoot disappearing before his eyes.

"EMP," Jane said gravely.

"How is that even possible?" Thea couldn't wrap her head around it. She had heard of EMPs of course, but from the after-effects of nuclear attacks. Not as a self-contained weapon of their own.

"Beats me. I never claimed to be the brains of this outfit," Jane said as they heard orders being passed around to provide torches and other lights to the teams already inside.

"They've wiped their systems, haven't they?" It seemed to Thea to be the most plausible explanation. She didn't know much about EMPs other than that they were bad for electronics. Stood to reason then that they would be bad for computers and their hard drives.

"Well, this went belly up in a flash, didn't it?" Jane sighed.

"Bloody intel never had anything about them being able to do this," Hall protested, attempting to dissolve his side of the blame. Not that Thea thought it would have mattered. Destroying their data would have been a top priority for the Regulators. Without having someone on the inside to stop that happening, she could see little that they would have done differently. Of course, there would be an inquiry and blame apportioned somewhere. That was just the name of the game. Politicians loved to point fingers. Hall might have come dressed for a photo op but she wondered if he might be needing a headshot for his CV soon.

"Let us know when we're cleared to go in," Jane sounded dejected. Thea could imagine how much she was looking forward to peeking into the collective memory of the Regulators' organisation. Now it was all gone. "We're going to need to identify who is critical to our investigation and talk to them first."

Hall muttered something that Thea didn't quite catch, but it was clear he knew a big part of the brief had been missed. The Regulators wouldn't talk. They didn't have to. Those that ended up with Five, however. They might find it a little different.

* * * *

They were allowed in after five arduous minutes as teams swept every corner of the building. Thea hated waiting. She'd never had to do it as a cop. She'd certainly never had to do it when the scene was so obviously safe as it was now.

Inside the building, makeshift floodlights were being erected wherever they were needed. They dodged past one at the foot of the stairwell that led them into the building and another at the top. As they entered the main office space, there were countless more. Some were on, others were being connected to battery packs. A huddle of prisoners sat on the floor in the middle of the room. All of them had been cuffed, hands behind their backs, either with metal handcuffs or zip ties where the officers had run out. Armed officers guarded them, weapons still on show, in the unlikely event that anyone forgot themselves for a second and decided now was the time to fight back.

"I wish I had a budget like this," Jane cooed as she looked at their surroundings. Thea had to admit, there had been little in the way of scrimping and saving when it came to decking it out. Computers. Monitors. A giant flatscreen that took up almost all of one wall. Everything looked top of the range. Even if most of it was now ruined.

"Let's go pick out our prizes," Thea said.

They made their way to where the Regulators had been gathered. They had made a list of who they believed were the top-ranking targets. It was hard to be absolutely certain. They didn't know the power structure inside the organisation. There had been bits fed in from a couple of anonymous sources over the years and Thea had gleaned some names through Jack, although how out of date they were, she wasn't sure. It had left them with a small list. David Warner, Adam Morgan, Emmie Weston, Eamonn Grant. Jack Quinn. That last one had been more in hope than expectation.

Thea looked at the assorted faces in front of her. None of them looked anything like the pictures she had memorised of their suspects. Jane was talking to one of the officers who seemed to be administering those who had been apprehended. Thea looked over to her, only for Jane to shake her head back. They weren't here.

"Who's in charge?" Thea shouted at the group.

No one rose. Thea thought she was going to have repeat the question, only with more anger and swearing. Then a man stood up. He was tall, slender, athletic-looking. Like a triathlete or something. He nodded. Jane turned to the officer in charge of the prisoners. "He comes with us," she said.

* * * *

"Morgan's still in there." Eammon Grant knew he should feel glad to be out of the office and away from the police raid, but he didn't. It was quite the opposite. His heart was still racing, so maybe that was a part of it, but something deep inside him was telling him he'd made a terrible mistake. One he could never now undo. He'd finally completely turned his back on the Regulators. He'd run when he should have stood. They'd hunt him down over this. Punish him for his betrayal. Maybe he could convince them that he thought it was best to live to fight another day. But he knew what he was supposed to do. He was meant to give himself up and entrust himself to the legal counsel they sent, saying nothing and hoping for the best.

He hadn't done that though. He'd done as he'd been told by his other masters. He'd turned and headed straight for a fire exit in the far corner of the building. One he'd been told had been deliberately left off the plans handed to the authorities. Now he was standing with Nick Poole, the man who had tipped him off, and he couldn't help but wonder if he had gone from frying pan to fire. Poole was a duplicitous son of a bitch and the sooner Eammon could work out a way to get rid of him, the better. After all, Poole was a grunt. Anything of use that he'd once been able to offer was now gone. All his avenues were exhausted. Eammon Grant, on the other hand, had the keys to so much more. If Poole's employers wanted to know about the Regulators, then he was their guy.

"Good to see you, Poole," Eammon said, wanting to keep things light and airy. Best to keep Poole onside for now.

Poole said nothing. He looked just behind Eammon, over his right shoulder and nodded.

It was the last thing that Eammon Grant saw.

21

"What the hell do we do now?" Adam whispered as he looked at Grant's corpse from where he and Emmie were taking shelter behind the door Grant had exited through.

Emmie had found him as they made their way out from the Kernel. She told him about Grant not returning to the office floor, how she'd seen him disappearing into the distance in the direction of the rear car park. So naturally that had to be where they went too. Both of them had been convinced that he'd been in on whatever was happening to the Regulators right now. The fact he had just been shot in the back of the head at point-blank range by a man dressed like an armed police officer, on the orders of Nick Poole, did little to dissuade Adam of that notion.

"We need to get out of here," Emmie replied.

"Well, that much was obvious."

"Don't be a dick."

"Sorry. Okay, new question. How the hell do we get out of here?"

"Well, I'm guessing that Poole and company aren't here to set up camp." Even though she was whispering, Adam could hear the tone in her voice that told him that he should have been able to work that all out for himself. He felt like a scolded school child. "They're not heading this way and towards the bloody police. Unless they hear this conversation."

They paused for a moment. The silence in the car park lingered. Thankfully it was echoed from the corridors behind them. When he was satisfied, Adam moved from where he was crouched and eased the door open, looking around the corner. The car park was clear. Only Eammon Grant's body remained to tell the tale that anything had happened.

"How come there's no police down here?" Emmie asked as they edged nervously into the space.

"I'm guessing because the person who leaked the details of our location neglected to mention the entrance to the car park."

"You think Poole was in on it?"

"I'm certain," Adam said. "It wasn't coincidence that he was hanging around. They wanted us out of the picture. They got it as well."

"Then fair to say we must have been onto something."

Emmie wasn't wrong. That would be playing on Adam's mind until he had it sussed. Just what was going on? Why did the Regulators have to be taken out of play? He knew it all led back to this Dead Line, whatever it was. He also knew that he'd let their only lead slip through his hands, following an order from a guy who was now dead.

"Let's get out of here," he said. "I'm fed up with surprises today. I don't need another one."

Getting out of the building and then the surrounding area proved to be a far easier process than Adam could have ever hoped. There were no police in the area. If it was Poole who had set this area up as some kind of avenue to aid his escape, he'd done a very thorough job. Both of them had shed their phones. They were likely useless anyway, thanks to the EMP, but there was no sense in keeping them just in case. They'd have to get new ones and soon.

They took a cab out of the area, which dropped them at London Bridge station where they were able to catch a train out east into Kent. They paid for their tickets in cash. One less way that they could be tracked if someone was looking for them. There was always the risk that their faces would show up on a camera somewhere, but they did their best to keep their heads down and as obscured as possible.

By the time they arrived in Canterbury, a little over two hours had passed since the raid on the office. Adam wondered if word had reached David by now as he picked up a burner phone from a shop just outside the station. He walked with it to a nearby pub where he found Emmie had already ordered a round of drinks and was waiting for him in a booth that was wedged up against a wall at the far end of the pub, furthest from the door.

"Socket?" he asked, sitting at the table and opening the box containing the phone.

"Under your side. Even got the Wi-Fi password."

"Great job," Adam said, taking the charger from where it was stowed in the box, inserting one end into the phone and then after some scrabbling around, the plug into the socket. He took a sip of his drink once he was done. "Give it five minutes, then I'll give David a call. Not that he's going to be happy."

"You didn't have a choice," Emmie said. "You had to set off the EMP. David would have done the same."

"Yeah," Adam blew out a long breath. Emmie was right. Of course David would have done the same. It was who he was. He'd do his duty and then he'd find another way. At least, that's what he kept telling himself. "But what if this time he wouldn't? What if this time what we were doing was bigger than the integrity of the Regulators? I mean, he had us working against them."

"Drink your drink and stop over-thinking things. It never does you any good." Emmie raised her glass and nodded at him to do the same.

"Cheers," he said, taking a larger swig this time. He felt a little of the tension releasing as he did so. It was amazing what a good pint could do sometimes.

Five minutes passed quickly, which Adam took to be a good sign. He called David, told him their location and David agreed to send someone to pick them up. Adam assumed it would be Reuben, but he was surprised when the car they got into was being driven by Meg, another of the old Regulators team. Meg had been David's eyes and ears. She may have been sitting at the reception desk, but Meg Tanner wasn't just a secretary. Her PhD in Psychology let her be the one who knew more about what was happening inside the heads of the Regulators than they probably knew themselves. Adam knew that she collected the gossip on the office floor and used it, with her own intuition and education, to put together a picture of how the teams were functioning, which she could feed back to David. She'd taken a leave of absence when Eammon Grant had come in. At the time, Adam guessed her loyalty was to David first and foremost. Although now that he sat in the back of the car hearing her talk about what they'd been up to in the interim, he wondered if Meg had been far more loyal to what they stood for than he had.

"We always feared something like this would happen," she said as Emmie explained the story of the raid.

She had sat in the front whilst Adam had tried to check out in the back. Try as he might, he couldn't. Every word they spoke in the front had his mind racing. Nothing that was happening was random. It had to have a point. It had to have a conclusion. Given the scale of what they'd already seen, that concerned him.

"You thought someone might take out the Regulators?" he asked, trying not to sound incredulous. It had never crossed his mind after all.

"Why not?" Meg replied, glancing quickly over her shoulder at him. "It's not like we can go to the police and

175

put in a complaint. We're on our own. You step on the wrong toes once and that's it."

"Yeah, pretty much sums up where we are now," Adam crossed his arms and shrugged. He could see Meg still looking at him in the rear-view mirror.

"In all honesty, it probably makes our job much easier going forward. At least you don't have to try and be clandestine anymore. You can concentrate on the task in hand."

Adam hadn't thought about it like that. He wasn't sure he saw it as the positive Meg did.

"We still lost a huge tactical resource," Emmie pointed out. "I'm sure David and the rest of you have your own set-up, but we went to the Regulators to try and get information and came back empty-handed. That information is gone now."

"In one guise."

"The other being talking to Lowri Graves, who, forgive me if I'm wrong, is languishing in a prison that no one knows the location of."

"Not necessarily no one."

Meg didn't expand on the point, even though Adam and Emmie asked her too. Apparently, it was better coming from the horse's mouth. When they arrived back at the house, Adam had expected that the proverbial horse would be David. He was wrong. It was Jack.

"We've spent the last eighteen months, each of us in our own little ways, on the back foot," he began. He was standing in the orangery. Adam, Emmie, David and Meg had taken seats. Reuben hovered behind them all, leaning against the kitchen island, still well in earshot, but just that little bit apart from the rest. Adam wasn't used to seeing Jack pontificate. It didn't seem as if he was enjoying it. The words sounded forced for him. Rehearsed. Adam wondered how many times he'd said them out loud before this moment. "We've all been playing catch-up on this thing, but we've been doing it from the shadows. But whoever we're chasing has fucked up. They thought we were hiding because of them. But the thing is, our biggest threat was always the Regulators. The Vehm. We were hiding from them. I was hiding because I knew they wanted me out of the way. Dead. Locked up. Didn't matter. David, they locked you out. Thought you were broken. Meg, you chose David over them. Adam, Emmie; you had Eammon Grant lording it over you. Reuben. Fuck it. No idea."

"You're all good, bruv," Reuben called back.

"My point is, we're not looking over our shoulders anymore. We knew who the threat was before. Now we know shit. In my experience, the best way to deal with knowing shit is to find a way to punch it in the face."

"You punch shit?" Adam couldn't help himself. He knew Jack was struggling to find a way to explain his ideas, but that was too good a chance to pass up.

"I'll punch you," Jack warned, smiling as he did so. "But yeah, I mean take it on. Have a go at it. Shit or no shit. We need to take the game to them, to use an old footballing cliché. Right now, they think they've got us sidelined. We're a handful of people who don't know who they are or what they're planning to do. We've got one last real shot at changing that. We need to get Lowri Graves back. And to do that, we do something that, I have to admit, doesn't come naturally to me."

Jack left a little dramatic pause and Adam realised he was waiting for someone in the audience to set him up. Given their previous exchange, he supposed he owed it to him. "What is it?"

"We ask nicely."

"Ask nicely?" Emmie paced the words out to make sure they'd all heard him right.

"Yeah."

"Ask who?"

"Lowri was picked up by Nick Poole and other known MI5 agents. I don't think asking Poole will get us anywhere. Asking Five might."

"You want to ask Thea Watts?" Adam already knew what Jack was thinking. It was ridiculous. It was risky. It was unfortunately probably the only viable option they had left.

"She owes me a couple of favours," Jack said it like he was talking about borrowing a garden strimmer.

"The kind of favour that releases a high-value prisoner?" Emmie was using a tone he'd heard her use on him when he'd had 'bright ideas' in the past.

"Or just tells us where she is."

"Your boy here wants to bust into a prison. I'm down!" Reuben whooped from behind them.

"You are joking, right?" Emmie was looking straight at Jack now.

He shrugged. "It could work."

"We could all die. Or get locked up in the same hellhole as Lowri Graves."

"Isn't that always the risk?" David hadn't spoken, but now he stepped in. "When we signed up for this life, we knew that was what we were facing, if things went pear-shaped."

"That doesn't take away from the fact that, on so many levels, this is a terrible plan. I mean we risk exposing ourselves to a group of people who would love to lock us all up. We ask them to give over someone who must be one of their highest-valued prisoners. All the while hoping that they don't betray us."

"I didn't say it was a good plan," Jack agreed. "I just said it was a plan and in the absence of any other plans it is, at this point, terrible or not, the best plan in the world for dealing with our current situation."

"The best plan in the world?"

"For dealing with our current situation," Jack repeated.

"I think we all need to take time to think about this," David interjected. He was still very much everyone's boss. Adam knew that if he said they were doing this, then that's what would happen. He was also pretty sure that in all likelihood David, had made his mind up long ago. He would have known what it was that Jack wanted to say. He wouldn't have let him get up there if he didn't agree with it being the best option on the table.

There was a quiet murmur of assent. Emmie still looked perturbed by the whole idea. Adam decided he'd talk to her. Listen to her worries properly. Jack was blunt. He was also a terrible talker. Adam knew how he thought. Maybe he could explain away some of those worries. Not all of them though. It was a terrible plan after all.

* * * *

"Quite the day you're having."

Poole looked at the man who'd greeted him out of the van. He wasn't wrong. Five hours ago, he had left his team in London having completed their mission to ensure the Regulators were crippled and that Eammon Grant, who knew far too much to end up in custody, was dead. Now he was a little under 300 miles away. In a place he didn't need to be. The people here had the job in hand. But he wanted

180

to be here. There was nowhere else on earth he would rather be in this moment. It was the final domino to fall before it was all done.

22

Agatha Harris shivered. Looking around, she wasn't quite sure why. The sun was high in the sky and when she'd glanced at the thermometer in the car, it had read twenty-seven. That was hot down south, never mind up here. But still she was shivering. A sharp bite of cold wind came in from the North Sea, whipping around her shoulders.

"You okay, ma'am?" The voice of Booth, her close protection officer came from just behind her.

"How on earth can one get cold in the middle of the hottest summer on record?" she asked, turning to smile at his concern.

"The North East will do that to you, ma'am.

She nodded and smiled again, before turning back to the job in hand. There were people to meet and greet. The cameras were ready now. Journalists had their questions. Hopefully, they would be banal. Things had been pretty quiet of late after all. Agatha Harris sometimes felt as if she hadn't achieved much of note in her short time as prime minister, but then after recent years, that seemed to be the charm. Her approval rating was high. Her analysts thought she was as close to guaranteed to win the next election as they would ever say. It was just a matter of when she was going to call it. She wouldn't keep them guessing much longer. The announcement was being prepped even now. A team had been assembled, quietly, in London. It wasn't the done thing to have an election in October. But how could she turn the opportunity down? Other prime ministers had fallen at the first hurdle by not striking at the right moment. And this was her moment.

"Show time," she said to herself, stepping towards a beaming local councillor.

* * * *

An hour later and it was all over. Agatha Harris was back in the car, her secretary Debbie Lamont to the side of her. Booth sat up front with the driver.

"Can we get the air con on back here?" Agatha said, feeling the heat in the car. The tinted windows might have done some work in keeping the sun out, but it had still felt like an oven when they got back in.

"Warm now, are we?" Booth joked from the front.

"Must be the menopause."

"Don't say that. Sure-fire vote loser," Debbie warned. She did that a lot. Warning Agatha about what to say, despite it being patently obvious that Agatha would never say such a thing in public. Agatha used to chastise her for it, but over the years she'd grown to appreciate it. It was always useful to have a little voice in the back of your head making you double-check every thought before it came out of your mouth. Agatha's little voice sounded very much like Debbie.

"Air con is on, ma'am. Should cool down," Booth reported.

"You're not going to let me open a window, are you?"

"No, ma'am."

Booth was thorough. He always had been. The last month or so, he had taken that to another level. There was chatter about a threat to her life. Agatha wasn't foolish enough to dismiss it entirely, but she knew that it went with the territory. The last thing she should do was to look as if it bothered her. So extra precautions had to be taken around her, but she had to keep doing the job she was doing. It had meant extra police at the event today. She could see them now. Outriders on their bikes, flanking her car as it moved along the quiet seafront road that would take them back into the centre of Sunderland and then the station where a train waited. Roads on her route would be blocked. Cars would be made to wait until they'd passed. On certain sections, such as the bridge across the River Wear, only her car and the police outriders would be allowed. She knew all this, because Booth had made a point of telling her all the lengths they were going to. It was some sort of alpha male tendency he had to not only protect her but let her know he was protecting her. It was a little bit cringeworthy, she had to admit. Agatha Harris hadn't needed anyone to protect her. Certainly not more than any other prime minister.

She looked out of the window. A small row of shops overlooked the beach. Here it was hard to tell that they were in a city in the North East of England. This part looked like a quaint seaside village. She looked out towards the sea and saw the seawall arcing around towards the lighthouse, the sea glistening behind it. It was almost idyllic. It made her want to come back and spend a little bit of time around here.

The car turned and started heading up a hill, back towards the city centre. "We have a direct service down to London King's Cross," Debbie started talking. "I've arranged a conference call with the Whips ahead of the dissolution of Parliament."

"Great. I want them briefed before anything happens. Not that I expect there will be any issue."

"No, none. My understanding from speaking to them is that they're all raring to go."

Agatha thought about what was coming next. The whole idea of fighting an election seemed daunting. She'd done it before, of course. As an MP. But that was completely different. The first election campaign she'd run, she'd been expected to lose. It was simply a practice run, to get her name out there. That she'd ended up running the incumbent far closer than had been expected had been a bonus. She'd hoped that would mean they'd put her into a tighter swing seat, but the party had had other ideas. They wanted to preserve her. To ensure her seat was safe, no matter what outside factors came into play. So, every election she'd faced ever since had been a formality. Her anointing as leader of the party hadn't been much in the way of a fight. There had been debates, but her real rivals had quickly stepped aside for the good of party unity and her election had been more of a coronation.

Even now, people were telling her this was a cake walk. That she should easily do what was required to guarantee five more years. It felt different, however. This one mattered more. It wasn't just about her or the party. This was about the country. It might look easy on paper, but it wouldn't feel that way to her.

"This is the right thing, isn't it?"

"Of course. Your lead has been stable now for a number of months and—"

"I don't mean for me," Agatha cut Debbie off. "I mean for the country. After all it's been through with my predecessor." She didn't like saying his name. After everything had come out, about his involvement in what had happened to those children, he didn't deserve to be thought of as a leader of this country.

"The country is resilient and you've helped with that. You've given them someone to look up to again. Someone to lead them."

"Have I?"

"You're bloody right you have," Booth chimed in. "I hear it all the time, ma'am. You're not like the bastards who came before."

Agatha smiled. She certainly wasn't.

The car carried on to a three-laned road that ran behind the university, then swept onto the Wearmouth Bridge. To their left, modern apartments and the university lined the river, leading to the sea. It still looked incredible.

"I really should come back," she said. She didn't get to expand on the thought.

The road in front of them erupted upwards. A volley of concrete shot into the air, cascading as if from a line of fountains placed in the road. Then their car jerked, the back end kicking upwards. There was a huge bang followed almost immediately by a crescendo of smaller impacts hitting the bottom of the vehicle, ripping into the armour plating. Debbie screamed, Agatha ducked, her head going between her legs. She braced for the impact of the car crashing down onto the tarmac. It didn't come.

Agatha felt her stomach lurching up inside her. Her seatbelt tried desperately to keep her in her seat as gravity ripped in the opposite direction. They were falling. Why were they falling? They couldn't be.

"Hold on!" Booth shouted from the front.

How did they have time to hold on? Agatha looked out of the front window. She saw the river rising up to meet them as the car fell nose first toward it, surrounded by falling masonry from the broken bridge. They slammed into the water and she blacked out.

23

The Regulators had been taken to various police stations over London. It hadn't been an easy task to separate them. There were so many after all. But the Met Police had done as well as they could. Thea liked to think that by her and Astley taking custody of Raf Hoban, they'd done their bit to help any congestion in the cells. Whether Raf Hoban was as happy with the situation, she wasn't so sure. He hadn't said a single word since they got there. Not even to ask for a lawyer. He'd just sat impassively. Thea couldn't even say if he'd been listening to what they'd said. For three hours they talked and he ignored them. Nothing they put to him roused a reaction. If he ever played poker, Thea could see how he would easily clean up.

"This is fun, it really is." Jane wasn't hiding her sarcasm. This wasn't the first time that the two of them had interviewed a person of interest together. It was certainly the first time Thea had seen Jane on the verge of losing her cool. But the threat was immediate. And it was high. The pressure Thea was under would be nothing compared to the pressure that Jane would be facing from those above them. She never mentioned it to Thea. She didn't have to. Thea had heard the terse tones from Jane's side of phone calls and video meetings. The "Yes, sirs" and, "No, ma'ams" that seemed to come incessantly from her office in those conversations. People were putting a lot of trust in Jane and, by extension, in Thea to stop whatever was meant to happen from happening. Thea really didn't know how she felt about that. It was probably better that she didn't think about it.

Raf Hoban, on the other hand, seemed like a man with no cares at all. If he was feeling any pressure from being locked away inside a small room in a warehouse at Luton Airport, he wasn't showing it.

"Thea? Can you check this guy's notes again? I don't remember them saying he was a fucking mute." Jane sounded all out of ideas. She was just trying to take out her frustrations on Raf now. Insult him. Laugh at him. Something to make her feel a little bit better. Thea had seen it happen to other investigators before. When they knew that they were going to get nowhere. Silence was always a suspect's best friend. Leave the other side to prove the case against you. Don't make it easy for them. In normal circumstances, it was a winning strategy. But these weren't normal circumstances. Raf Hoban was going away. It didn't matter what he said or didn't. Freedom wasn't a thing he was going to experience again for a very long time. If ever.

"Raf. We all know what happens when we step out of this room. You're gone. I've looked at your file. I know you've no family or anything, but I can't believe you're happy for your life to be all over bar the shouting. If you can help us stop this, it can make a difference. Not just for you, but the whole bloody country. I know you lot think you're doing the right thing with all this vigilante shit, but we're giving you the chance to do the actual right thing. The real deal.

Just tell us what you know. I mean, it was my understanding that you were supposed to help us if you could."

Raf turned his head this time. For a moment she hoped he might speak. But then the moment dragged on and she realised he wasn't going to.

Sighing, she leaned back in the chair, wondering what else she or Jane could do. She knew, when she looked back, she would have to admit she'd known that defeat was coming very early on. Asking wasn't getting them anywhere. She wondered what would happen when Raf was in the hands of the sort of people who wouldn't ask as nicely as they had.

A rap at the door punctuated the moment. A face peered in. A young man dressed in a shirt and tie. "Ms Astley. Call," he said as Thea tried to remember if she'd been introduced to him when they arrived. It had all seemed very surreal. Driving into an airport in mini-vans with blacked-out windows, bypassing security, felt like the sort of thing people did in movies. The idea that a secret corner of such a complex could be sealed off whilst some threat to national security spent their last moments on British soil was almost unbelievable. But it was happening now. And it had happened countless times before. All of it felt like fiction. Not the sort of thing that a real democratic society would do. Yet now here she was. A part of it.

Maybe surreal wasn't a strong enough word to describe it.

She took another look at Raf. He hadn't moved. He'd showed no interest in the knock at the door or Jane leaving. Maybe he had been waiting for this moment.

"You know that I, of all people, know how you lot work. I don't for one moment believe that you're in on this." Thea knew that this was as good a moment as any to play the good cop. "Don't make me a part of disappearing you, Raf. I don't want that. I want to stop whoever's doing this. Jane thinks it's you. Five thinks it's you. I don't. So help me. Otherwise, bollocks. You deserve everything they're going to throw at you."

Raf was looking at her now. The corner of his mouth twitched. She'd said something that had landed. If she could just push him a little bit more…

The door swung open. At first Thea didn't turn her head, but then the sound of it slamming into the wall and Raf turning his head towards the door made her look. Jane was already at the desk.

"You fucking piece of shit."

She launched herself straight into Raf, knocking him from his chair and falling on top of him, her fists raining down over and over in quick succession on the side of his head as he tried to cover himself up.

"What the fuck?" Thea lurched from her seat, rounding the table, grabbing an arm under Jane's and struggling to pull her off Raf. "We need help in here!" she called out to the corridor.

Then another hand was helping her wrest Jane from off Raf. Blood splattered on the floor where she'd opened cuts on his face and head. The man in the shirt and tie had come to her aid and between the two of them they were able to stand Jane up. She didn't resist, but Thea could feel the tension in her body anyway. Everything felt contracted. Hard. Coiled. Could they hold her back if she wanted to go again?

"You're fucked. You hear me. I hope they pick you apart, you fucking cunt," Jane spat.

"What the hell's going on?" Thea stepped in front of Jane, pushing her hand into her chest. Jane shot an angry glance at Thea. It might have made other people think twice. Not Thea. "Don't even fucking try. Talk to me."

She saw the tears in Jane's eyes. Saw them running down her cheek. Not sweat. Tears. Everything fell into place.

"They did it. They fucking killed her."

24

Everyone sat in stunned silence staring at the screen. The yellow ticker bar at the bottom wound its way across the screen delivering the news. Prime Minister Agatha Harris was dead. Killed after an explosion on the Wearmouth Bridge following a visit to the North East.

Adam sombrely voiced what they were all thinking. "They're going to think it was us."

* * * *

Jack managed to tear himself away from the screen first. Once the first rotation of the news was over, he knew he wasn't going to learn anything else. Whoever had killed Nelmes, attacked the *Inquirer*, involved his son, had now set up the Regulators and assassinated the PM. That wasn't going to be talked about, no matter how in-depth the rolling news coverage got. They were going to get a far more digestible story of a desperate vigilante group in its final act. What a win that would be for whoever wanted to claim it. The suspects were already in custody. They'd probably eke out a few more bodies to account for whoever was supposed to have pulled the trigger on the bridge. Wrap it all up very neatly. It was absolute bullshit of course. But the public would swallow it, because why wouldn't they? Right now, there were going to be a lot of scared people wondering what was going to come next. They were going to need answers. They were going to need reassuring that it was all going to be okay. And maybe it would even feel as if it was. Time would tell on that.

He didn't even think about taking his phone from his pocket until he found himself staring at the contact card for Thea Watts. He hadn't called her in years. He wondered if she even still had this number. He'd be able to find it eventually. David would have some back door into the directories that would dig it out. But given what had just happened, David could easily stress caution and push back against reaching out to an MI5 agent. Jack wasn't happy to sit and wait.

"What are you doing?" Emmie was standing behind him, arms folded. He looked at her, the phone in his hand, wondering what lie he could come up with. Nothing came quickly enough. "You're going through with it, aren't you? Calling Watts?" she said.

"We need to get out ahead of this." Jack was fully prepared to argue the toss on this one.

He didn't have to. "Fine."

"You're cool with it?" He knew that sounding surprised would probably be unfair, so he did his best to make it sound as if he was just seeking approval.

Emmie shook her head. "Is anyone cool with anything at the moment? This whole thing is a mess. It's rank. I don't know if calling Watts is a smart move or a dumb move or what. All I know is it feels like we're in the shit whatever way you look at it, so why not try something."

"Thanks," Jack said. "You reckon you can make sure no one else walks out here?"

"Do I look like a bouncer?"

"I reckon you'd scare any teenager with a fake ID into thinking twice about trying it on, yeah."

"I think you've forgotten what it's like to be around teenagers."

That one hurt and Jack looked down.

"Sorry," Emmie apologised. "Shit. That was insensitive. I didn't mean it."

"It's okay. You're right."

"No. I wasn't. Not my place."

"The only person not in their place was me, when I should have been with my family."

"You can't beat yourself up over it either. Self-flagellation didn't work in the dark ages. Certainly doesn't work now. Own what you did. Use it to push forward."

Jack swallowed. "My kid's lying in a hospital bed with machines doing his breathing for him. I don't know how to own that."

"That's because you want to go back and make it all okay. You're thinking like a soldier. You've suffered a defeat. You want to avenge it by hurting the enemy more. But that won't change anything for Calum. Or your wife or daughter. You can't help them by being angry. You help them by being there in the future. To support Calum in his recovery. In his reckoning. Because he is going to have one. He is his own man and he is going to face consequences for this. He needs his father standing beside him. Telling him that he's sorry. That he knows he made this happen at least in part. That he will be there for him through the hardships to come and will wait for him when he has a chance to start again."

Jack looked at her, trying to wrap his head around what she'd just said. There was a lot of truth in it. All he had in mind was revenge. He just hadn't thought of that as being the wrong thing to do. That there might be other things. More constructive things. "I…" he stuttered.

"For now, deal with what you do best. We still have a job to do. If we get through this, find a way to be a dad then."

"Thanks," he said, meaning it earnestly. He didn't really know Emmie. Certainly not enough to ever want to turn to her for advice, but he had the feeling that what she'd just dished out was probably some of the best he'd ever received.

"Good luck." Emmie turned and walked back into the house. Jack looked at the phone. Time to make the call.

* * * *

"Hello?" Jack felt relief at hearing Thea's voice at the end of the line. That was one worry scrubbed out. She sounded tired. She also didn't sound as if she knew who was calling.

"Thea. It's Jack Quinn."

Silence. Jack could imagine Thea composing herself. Or maybe she was signalling to someone nearby that the call needed tracking. It wouldn't help. Jack's phone had been on a scrambled signal since he got hold of it. Part and parcel of life on the run.

"Shit me," she finally said.

"I need your help."

"You need more than that."

"Someone is setting me up. The Regulators. All of us."

"So they weren't behind it?" Even though she didn't expand, Jack knew what she meant by *it*.

"Course we fucking weren't."

"So who was?"

"The In Statera."

"Who?"

"The same shady bastards as the ones behind the paedo ring you took down."

"We took down. And I thought we got everyone."

"Not the top dogs apparently. It appears we created a vacuum at the top that they're working to fill with their own people. Taking out the Regulators and making them look complicit gives everyone a bogeyman and an easy win."

"There's no win here. The PM is fucking dead."

"Preaching to the converted."

"What help do you need?"

"I need Lowri Graves."

"Lowri Graves?" There was something in the way she repeated the name that caught Jack's attention. A lack of surprise.

"You know where she is." He didn't ask. He didn't need to.

Another pause. "Why do you need her?"

"There's something called Dead Line. We lost all our records with the raid. She knows about it."

Another pause. "She can help you?"

"I think so."

"Let me see what I can do."

"Thanks."

"Jack?"

"What?"

"Take care out there."

"You too. Good to hear from you."

The call ended. Jack looked back up at the house. They were committed now. No going back. Through to the end.

25

"I can't work out if this is good fortune, or we're fucked seven ways to Sunday."

Jane and Thea were sitting in a coffee shop on the other side of the river. Thea had insisted that she had something to tell Jane but it had to happen off site. Surprisingly to Thea, Jane had agreed. Her reaction when she had heard the news hadn't given away much.

"I think we have to see it through," Thea said. In truth, her mind was made up. It didn't matter what Jane said now. Thea was meeting with Jack. It would be nice to have Jane onside, but it wasn't a deal-breaker.

"I take it you've considered all the possible ways this stitches you up? And then me up?" Jane asked.

"He could be in on this all along," Thea began her list.

"He could be in on this all along," Jane agreed. "He could be looking to give you false information. Or simply to find out what we know. Could be setting you up for a sting operation using our own side, even. Or maybe just waiting to lure you to your death."

"You should be so lucky."

"Are you sure you want to do this?"

"It's not about wanting to do anything. It's about doing the job."

"Pardon my French, but that sounds like a load of bullshit." An elderly woman on the table behind shot them an annoyed glance, whilst Jane took a loud slurp from her mug. Clearly that sort of industrial language wasn't commonplace in here. Perhaps they should have gone to the pub.

"I thought you said you'd read my psyche-evaluation prior to bringing me on your team?"

"Touché. Okay, so given that I can't talk you out of it, let me ask you this. Are you planning on giving him what he wants?"

"Giving him Lowri Graves? How the hell am I going to do that?"

"Not thought this all the way through then, have you?"

"Lowri Graves is locked up in a prison that, earlier this week, I didn't even know existed. I wouldn't even know who to ask and I certainly couldn't tell them why I wanted her even if I did. Jack isn't going to want his name sharing around. He'll be seething that I told you."

Jane took another swig from her drink, then smiled. "He won't be when he hears my idea."

* * * *

Thea had set the location. A small, wooded area just south of Bexley station. She travelled by train, paying for the ticket at the barrier using her own card. Telling everyone where she was going seemed to be the best way to broadcast to anyone who might be watching her that it wasn't worth the effort. Not that she thought anyone was.

She walked the short distance from the station to the woods. The skin on her face, neck and arms seemed to prickle in the heat and she was glad when she made it to the trees where the canopy offered at least some shelter from the sun. There were several wide paths that wound their way through the wood, giving a long, unobstructed view of everything in front and behind. Someone could of course take refuge in the treeline if they wanted to spy on them, but it didn't seem likely. Thea had selected a location on What Three Words that she had sent to Jack. Right at the heart of the woods. If he was half as confident as she was that this was a secure place to meet, he'd be there.

Thea arrived at the spot. Jack was nowhere to be seen. She waited. A couple of dog walkers and a lone jogger, who looked to be regretting his choice, came and went. But there was no Jack. Thea checked the time. One minute till the meeting time.

She looked both ways. There was no sign of him heading in either direction. She turned slowly on the spot, hoping to catch sight of him in the trees. There was no sign of movement. No one lurking in the shadows. Where was he?

She pulled out her phone. As she did, the screen lit up and it vibrated in her hand. An incoming call from a scrambled number.

"Watts." She kept the conversation neutral. The last thing she needed to do was announce Jack's name down the line to God knows who.

"Follow the path south-east, all the way out." Jack's voice was firm. Thea couldn't tell if he was irritated or not.

"Where are you?"

There wasn't an answer. Jack hung up.

"Shit me." Thea sighed and began walking.

The path finally led between two gardens, exiting in a small alley between two blocks of smart, decidedly suburban semi-detached houses. A car was parked right in front of the exit. The engine was running. The passenger door ajar.

Thea climbed in and sat down.

"Good to see you," Jack said in the same tone as he had on the phone, which made it sound anything but good to see her.

"You too," Thea said, reaching for her seatbelt as the car accelerated away. They took a quick loop through the housing estate and then out onto the main road towards the A20.

"How have you been?" she asked, realising that she was going to have to make any form of conversation.

"It's been quite the year or so."

"Where have you been?"

There was a pause, Jack probably working through the risks of telling her. "I have a bolt-hole out in Wales." Apparently enough to give her the country he was living in. Which was a start.

"How's that been?"

"Quiet," he said abruptly, before adding, "Nice."

"Didn't have you down as the quiet life sort of guy."

"Recent events suggest you'd be right."

"I don't suppose you have any idea what the hell is going on here?"

Jack laughed. "Are you kidding?"

"It was worth a shot."

"I was hoping you'd know more."

"I know the Regulators are a thing of the past."

"Not quite."

"Who's left? You? Morgan?"

"A couple, of others. Forgive me for not mentioning names. Better for everyone and all that."

"Fair enough."

"So shall we get down to business?"

"Lowri Graves?"

Jack gave a little sideways nod. Thea realised that his eyes only ever stayed on the road or the rear-view mirror. He wanted to make sure they weren't being followed.

"It's going to be complicated."

"I didn't expect a cakewalk. But I need to speak to her. Do you know where she is?"

"I do." Thea wondered how best to explain to Jack. She suddenly felt extremely guilty for what had happened to Lowri. The two of them had butted heads in the past. They certainly weren't friends. But admitting where Lowri was made her complicit in the existence of Glasshouse Seven and that sickened her.

"What is it? Is she dead?" Jack asked and Thea realised she'd taken far too long to answer his question.

"No. She's being held in a prison."

"Which one?"

"Not one on any map."

"That figures. They were never going to put her anywhere official." If Jack was shocked by that news, he didn't show it. "So can you get her out?"

"No. That's way outside of my powers. You know that, Jack. That's top brass only sort of thing and, let's be honest, you're far more likely to have someone on your side with that access than I am."

"Not anymore. You're our one and only shot." Thea's last hope of a simpler solution faded away. She had hoped that Jack would be satisfied knowing that Lowri was alive and inside the system. That he would be able to take that away with him and use whatever contacts he had left to get access. Fat chance.

"There is another way."

"Which is?"

"I can get you to the location."

"Inside a secret prison facility? How?"

"You're a wanted man, Jack Quinn. We can get you inside. You just have to get out."

Thea looked at Jack waiting for him to tell her that her plan was crazy. That there wasn't a chance in hell he was going to allow himself to be taken into a secure facility as a prisoner. He didn't say anything. He just smiled.

26

It took a day for Jack to source everything that he thought he would need. There had been the usual complaints from everyone else. No one thought it was a good plan. 'Suicidal' had been the politest description. Tellingly, no one had tried to dissuade him. Not properly. All their attempts had been borne out of friendship. Duty however meant that none of them had tried that hard. Everyone knew what they had got themselves into. And with the situation as it was, this was their one and only chance to get some answers and finally get ahead of the curve.

Adam walked into the small room where Jack was assembling the kit. He had insisted that he check each team member's loadout personally. It was his life on the line ultimately.

"How are you getting along?"

"All right," Jack said, closing up one of the backpacks. This one would belong to Reuben. Jack had tried to give him as little as possible to do. Of all the people out there, Jack wanted his life in the hands of Reuben the least.

"Still think this is a good idea?"

"It's a fucking horrible idea. It's on a par with the remake of *Porridge*."

"That is bad. I'm not going to even try talking you out of it, mind."

"Good. Truth to be told, I might even enjoy myself."

"Well, here's hoping. I'll buy you a pint if you make it out."

"I reckon this is worth a couple."

"You would."

Adam clapped a hand on Jack's shoulder. "Good luck, mate."

"Thanks, mate. You lot too."

"I'm hoping it doesn't come down to luck. I'm banking on my incredible talent to be enough."

"You're fucked then," Jack said, deadpan.

An hour later, for all his bravado, it was Jack who felt a little fucked as he waited at the spot he'd agreed with Thea. Adam and the other Regulators had their orders. He trusted them to do their bit. But now, everything that had to happen to give him the best possible chance of getting out of this was in other people's hands. It wasn't a situation he was accustomed to being in.

His phone rang. It was Thea.

"I'm running late," she said.

"You don't want to do that. I won't wait," Jack replied firmly.

"You will. You need this."

"Not as much as you do. Get here."

He hung up and looked around. The foyer of the hotel was busy with people moving through, to their rooms, to the car park, or on into Gatwick Airport itself. A myriad of different routes. Perfect if you wanted to try and make an escape. And Jack would want to try and make an escape. He'd already done his bit of scouting out the routes. To the front was the car park. If he wanted to escape by car, that was the best way. The road deposited him almost immediately onto the M23. There were enough junctions nearby that he could slip off the grid and away from any cameras. It would just be a case of losing anyone chasing him. Jack fancied his chances there. The police trained well, but so did he. The difference was that they operated with rules. He didn't. If little scrotes in souped-up hatchbacks could do enough to have a chase called off, he was certain he could too.

If that option didn't present itself, he'd make it out on foot. There were many exits to the hotel, including a bridge that led to the airport and its train station. Multiple car parks offered what amounted to a labyrinth of concrete and steel. Depending on how many people came after him, Jack again backed himself to be able to make good his escape. It just all depended on how much time he had between seeing the trap and it being sprung.

The phone on the reception desk rang. He watched as the smartly dressed concierge picked up the phone, greeting the unseen caller with a smile that came with years of practice. The caller clearly had a query of some sort. The smile gave way to a look of mild confusion as the concierge listened and began to put together an answer. Jack stood.

He looked at the people in the room. All oblivious. No one was looking at him. No one seemed to care that he was there. Everything was as it should be. All he could do was wait. He rolled his neck, then his shoulders, then yawned. The concierge finished their conversation and stepped away from the desk, heading out back. Clearly the phone call had required further action. Jack looked at the front door. Surely the wait wouldn't last much longer.

A double staircase led away from the reception area and towards what the hotel hopefully proclaimed to be an executive lounge. Something for travellers with more money than sense to splurge on whilst they waited to go away. Jack would have been happy with finding some fast food and a pub. Anything else was just excessive. He looked towards the stairwell. No one was going up or down. Business must be quiet at the moment in the executive lounge. He spun around once more, taking everything in.

Most people wouldn't have noticed the change in the atmosphere in the room. But it didn't evade Jack. Something shifted on some level. People stiffened. Nerves accelerated. Maybe certain pheromones were released as fear or surprise took root in the onlookers. Whatever it was, Jack felt it. It was happening.

The shout came from behind him. An unseen opponent closing in, making the most of their assumed invisibility. "Get on the ground, now!"

Jack didn't look back. He let the shout come again, seeing the other team of armed officers coming through the front door. A moment of recognition as he contemplated his situation. He took a step towards the door, feigning that he hadn't seen the second team. Then he stopped. He spun around looking at the first team, making sure that his arms were out at his sides. No point in giving anyone an excuse to take a shot. Six armed officers closed in on him, their weapons trained on his sizable centre mass, their faces obscured behind helmets and face masks. More shouts came as Jack slowly raised his arms. He swore and shook his head as he began to kneel, then he lay on his front, fingers interlaced behind his head, and waited for them to swarm him. It took seconds for the cuffs to be fitted and Jack to be dragged to his feet. He made it easy for them. No point fighting. No point running. The game was up. They'd found him. Surrounded him. Secured him. Textbook.

A minute later he was being bundled into the back of a black armour-plated Land Rover, which took off quickly from the car park, heading for the M23 and then north, towards Essex and the place where Jack Quinn would spend the rest of his life.

27

"They got him." Jane smiled as she leaned back in her chair, the phone at her ear.

"Any problems?" Thea knew there wouldn't have been, but all the same she felt she needed to hear it.

"Went quietly, they caught him on the hop. Seems he really thought you were going to meet him. Turned up on his own with just a side arm." Jane pulled the phone from her ear and started scrolling through her contacts.

"He always was a cocky bastard."

"See how cocky he is when he gets to Glasshouse Seven."

"Do you reckon we'll be able to get in and see him?"

"I'll put the request in, but I can imagine there's going to be a queue of people desperate to see him." The phone went back to her ear.

"We bagged him. That's got to count for something."

"I'll be sure to mention it." Then the call she was making connected and Jane's attention turned to the person on the other end.

Thea half listened as Jane made the case for them to see Jack Quinn as soon as possible. She knew no answer would be immediately forthcoming. Even if a decision was made, the usual bureaucratic procedures had to be followed. The right people in the right places had to believe that they were calling the shots. That was just the way it was. It was all a load of bollocks of course. But it was the game Thea was finding herself playing more and more frequently. At least policing had kept her in some way insulated from it all. Being in Five, it felt as if all there was between her and these people was Jane. And one day there wouldn't even be Jane. It would be Thea making these calls. Listening to people make themselves and others out to be important or more deserving. All of it for show of course. Thea wondered how long it would take before that became unbearable.

In the meantime, it would be the waiting that would become unbearable. Waiting to hear that Jack had been securely moved to the facility. Waiting to hear when she could go and begin the interview process. Waiting for everything that was about to happen.

Setting up Jack had been simple enough. He'd called her using a scrambled phone, but fortunately for MI5, it had been scrambled using a frequency they'd decoded before. That meant that as soon as that first call was complete, the tech teams downstairs had been able to begin the job of triangulating his position. From there they'd monitored him as he'd left his bolt-hole in Hertfordshire and made the journey around the M25, south towards Gatwick. Algorithms had been used to determine exactly which car was his. From that point on they'd had eyes on him all the way until he had taken his seat in the lobby of the hotel. Thea had called, placating him to ensure he didn't leave early. Then the police teams that had taken up his trail once he'd crossed the Thames at Dartford moved in. They'd been able to avoid detection by hanging a couple of miles back on the road. Well out of sight of Jack. No way to arouse his suspicions. The whole operation had been flawless. The Met Police were pleased. MI5 were pleased. A whole host of politicians and civil servants were basking in the collective glory of the apprehension of Jack Quinn. Thea wondered who else would be happy once the news reached their ears. If Jack's worries about this In Statera group were true, someone would know soon enough.

She couldn't help but feel a degree of guilt. Subterfuge wasn't her style. She was honest to a fault, so her superiors had often said. She preferred to deal with things up front. To look the person in the eye whose day she was about to ruin. Something about all of this felt a little bit wrong. It made the itch to get to the prison, to see Jack eye to eye, all the greater. She knew Jane was working her magic and she trusted that she'd come through, but the question was, when? It couldn't be too much longer. She couldn't let Jack just wallow in some secret facility for too long. Especially if word did get out to those who wouldn't be happy with him just being locked up.

She looked at her watch. It had barely been fifteen minutes since the arrest. It felt a lot longer. Jack's escort would be on the M25 by now, heading east back up towards the Dartford Crossing. They wouldn't have to wait in the traffic like everyone else. They would sail through, escorts lining the route. Trying to make it all safe in the same way they had for the prime minister. Best laid plans, Thea thought.

Jane was still talking on the phone. It sounded like perfunctory bullshit. The sort of small talk middle managers have to make when they're going to ask for a favour. Thea decided it was best if she was out of the room. She found her way to the canteen, ordered a cup of coffee and took a seat. She had to say one thing for Thames House, they made great coffee. Obviously spooks were considered important enough to get the good stuff.

She spent as long as she could nursing her drink, doing everything in her power not to keep glancing at her phone. Then, when it was done, she ordered two more to go and made her way back to the office.

"Fantastic, just what I need," Jane said as she saw Thea entering with the drinks.

"How did it go?" Thea asked, trying not to sound too eager.

"We're in."

"Brilliant. When?"

"They want to get him in and processed. That could take a few hours. I imagine they're going to be pretty thorough. But seeing as we're the ones who got the collar, we're being allowed the first interview."

"Amazing." Thea smiled.

"I thought you'd be happy with that. Tell you what, let's get the reports written up for the call. Make sure all the paperwork looks how it should do, then head over. We've got time to do this right, so let's make sure we do."

* * * *

They were in the car a couple of hours later. The drive was arduous as ever. London was not an easy place to get out of at the best of times and the ongoing heat seemed to have made everyone on the roads a little bit edgier. Thea missed the days of patrol cars and blue lights. Traffic seemed less of an issue when you could command it to get the hell out of your way. That was the problem with being invisible.

They arrived at the facility a little before dusk. Clouds were forming up over the North Sea ahead of them. Behind them, the sun was setting and where it met the clouds, the sky burned red and orange as purple blotches sought to creep across the sky. The air felt heavy and threatening.

"Reckon we might finally get some rain tonight," Jane said as they approached the entrance to Glasshouse Seven. "Long overdue."

They followed the same procedure on arrival as before. Passing through the scanners. A thorough pat down. Phones and tablets were passed over to a guard who assured them that they would be returned. Then they were seen down to the same reception area as they had been in whilst waiting to talk to Lowri. Even in here there was an electricity in the air. Something was different about the room. The people in it. The guards spoke bluntly to Thea and Jane. Their orders were to the point. Their tones clipped. Perhaps the arrival of a new prisoner was the sort of thing that put everyone on alert. Thea couldn't imagine it happened all that often. This wasn't the sort of prison the local magistrate was going to be sending people to after all.

After what felt like an age, a guard arrived to show them down to the same interrogation room where they had found Lowri. Thea recounted the route in her head. Remembering the distances between corners. Remembering where doors were. Remembering where she expected people might come from.

The guard opened the door to the interview room and they stepped in. Jack was cuffed to the desk, waiting for them. They'd taken his clothes and given him a grey-green overall and paper slippers. He looked up and nodded but said nothing.

"Mr Quinn. A pleasure," Jane began as she sat down. "I believe you know my colleague here, Thea Watts."

"Jack," Thea said.

"Thea," Jack replied. He turned to Jane. "I can't tell you how much I'm looking forward to this."

All the lights went out.

28

A light flickered somewhere over the North Sea. Adam saw it, wondering for a second what it was. A second flash rippled across the horizon. Lightning. A storm brewing somewhere out east. He didn't expect it to head this way. Whether there was anything coming up from down south was another question. The last forecast he'd seen before they arrived on location showed a possibility of storm cells bubbling up just about anywhere. Apparently they weren't the easiest thing to predict. Adam wasn't sure if a storm landing on them would be a good thing or a bad thing.

"You okay?" Emmie must have sensed his nervousness.

"Fine. I just hate waiting. How about you?"

"Days like this are what I signed up for."

"Ain't that the truth," Adam said, wondering if Emmie meant it as little as he did. He turned to look over his shoulder to Reuben and the men he'd gathered for their team. They'd had brief introductions, surnames only. Dean, Moore and Hadland. They all looked capable. Reuben vouched for them, which didn't mean much. But David vouched for Reuben and therefore, by extension, they passed first inspection.

"Itching to get started, big man," Reuben grinned.

"So long as it isn't those trigger fingers that are itchy," Adam warned. They had agreed that minimising casualties was a must. It was the only way all the parts of the puzzle had come together.

"I still can't believe we've gotta play nice with these mugs in here. You know what they do, right? Lock people up. No trial. No chance of freedom. Just stick them in a hole."

Adam said nothing. He didn't know if Reuben was making a point about the Regulators or not. He didn't want to find out. Some comparisons hit a little too close to home.

He looked once more at the entrance to the building. There was no sign of movement. No sign that anything was happening inside. He wondered how he'd know when it was time. That was the part of the plan that they hadn't got a real handle on. There weren't many details about Glasshouse. Satellite imagery that David had managed to obtain suggested that at the very least there was enough shielding between the surface and the building to mask both its heat and electromagnetic signature. As well as hiding the facility, it also stopped signals getting in or out. It meant their way of knowing if things had kicked off was tenuous at best.

"How long have they been in there?" Adam asked. There was at least one way of estimating how things might be going. They'd tracked Thea and Jane until they arrived at the facility.

"A little over forty-five minutes," Emmie replied. Things had to be happening soon. If they weren't already. "How's the signal?"

The signal was crucial. It was their way of knowing what was happening. At least to the point of knowing whether or not Thea's phone was still on. They'd used the manufacturer's own location service. Right now, the phone was on. There was no location data. That was probably being scrambled by the Glasshouse Network which Thea had connected her phone to on arrival. But it hadn't seen any point in stopping the phone from communicating that it was at least on. Why would it? What use would that be to anyone?

As Adam watched, the signal went out. The phone was off.

"It's time," he said.

* * * *

A guard entered the room. Just as Jack knew he would. He had a fluorescent tube attached to his jacket, which cast an eerie green glow over him, the shadows of the features of his face hiding one of his eyes and making him look almost grotesque.

"We've had a power failure. I need to get you both out of here," he said to Thea and Jane.

"What about me?" Jack asked. The guard didn't answer. Either he didn't know or didn't care.

"Come on," Jane said. "Let's get this bottomed out and come back."

"Do we have to leave?" Thea asked.

"Protocol, ma'am," the guard replied, making it clear there was no room for discussion.

"Fuck's sake," she sighed as she stood. "Barely even got the chance to get going."

"There'll be plenty of time. He's not going anywhere," Jane said, eyeballing Jack firmly, which made him want to laugh. He hoped the guard hadn't seen the start of a smile forming on his face, but if he had, he hadn't said anything.

"Any chance of a light for me?" Jack asked as they moved to the door. The guard ignored him again and then they were gone.

The room was pitch black. He couldn't see a thing. He counted to five, then got to work. He took the thin lock pick that had been curled inside his hand since Thea had secreted it there and set to work on the handcuffs. He'd done this countless times before. Most of the time for practice, but once or twice for real. The practice had been worth it. He could do this blindfolded. Which in the pitch black was definitely a bonus. Picking a lock was all about finding the pressure, the moments of give. He could visualise the lock in his mind as he worked at it, seeing the mechanism as it heeded to him, releasing his wrists, one by one, within a minute. He stood, remembering the number of steps he'd taken from the door to the chair, then moving off to the side of it. Now he had a decision to make. Wait for someone to come for him or take the fight to them.

He chose the latter. It could have taken them God knows how long to come and get him. If they ever did. But that wasn't his main motivation. Ultimately, Jack just wanted to get on with it. He eased the handle to the door down, then pushed it slowly open with his shoulder. He'd half expected it to be locked. That was interesting. He wondered whether it was a result of the power going down. When they'd entered the room, an electronic lock had been used to allow access. Maybe it reset to 'unlocked' in the event of a power failure to ensure no one became trapped. The cells of course would be different. Or maybe the guard had been given an order to leave it unlocked to allow someone else in to see Jack.

There was very little light in the corridor. Strips of some kind of reflective material ran along the edges of the floor and ceiling, giving the space a dull grey glow. Jack assumed there would be an emergency power system somewhere, but for whatever reason it hadn't yet kicked into gear. He looked back the way he'd come. That led back to the holding section. He didn't want to find his way back there. He assumed that more esteemed guests such as Thea and Jane would have come from the opposite direction. He headed that way, moving slowly and carefully so that he could listen for the sound of footsteps.

He didn't have to wait long to hear them. He had only just made the first corner when they came. Retreating back around the corner, he pressed himself against the wall, then waited. One set of footsteps. Heavy boots. Heading this way. A guard. Or someone similar. The footsteps came closer. Jack held his breath until they were right on top of him.

The figure turned the corner, walking casually, completely relaxed. A critical error. Jack stepped forward just as the figure moved into the same bit of space. There wasn't room for both of them and Jack's elbow drove up at where he expected his opponent's jaw to be. He caught it sweetly, his arm extending and crunching into the bone. The figure staggered, tumbling into the wall. His head crashed into the concrete that made up the far wall and he slumped down on his side, his head at an angle. Unconscious or dead, Jack wasn't bothered. He'd seen the gun in the man's right hand. Someone had decided that Jack didn't need to leave. He bent down, took the weapon. There was a round holstered in the chamber and a flashlight attachment underneath the barrel. Both useful. As was the set of keys clipped to the man's belt like an old-school gaoler. He didn't hold out much hope that the man's electronic pass card might work. Definitely less useful were the man's shoes. Easily two sizes too small for Jack. But then, most shoe shops didn't stock his size. Still, didn't hurt to check. Finally, he checked the man's pulse. He was still alive. Jack stood and delivered a hard kick to the guard's unprotected chest. He had been coming to kill him after all.

Jack found a comfortable grip with the gun and headed the way his would-be killer had come from. He wondered how many others would be in his wake. It stood to reason that there would be at least one more person on site who knew that the order was to terminate Jack Quinn. Could be that everyone had been given the same briefing. Could be that it wasn't even personal. In a situation like this, where the shit was hitting the fan, it was probably better to clear house. It meant Jack had to work fast. He picked up the pace, moving to a jog, keeping his feet light. Which, he had to admit, was easier without shoes.

He rounded another corner. Double doors blocked his way. Jack reached them and eased against them, opening them slowly as he had done with the door to the interrogation room. They opened up into a small vestibule area flanked by what looked like a checkpoint. A thick window showed where a guard would check visitors in and out, relieving them of their possessions. Which was exactly what he was after.

The security inside the checkpoint was less complex. There were just two sets of possessions held in there, both contained within clear plastic Ziplock bags. As low-tech as it got. There was a seal on each to show that it hadn't been tampered with when it was returned to the rightful owner. This time, there would be tampering.

Jack ripped both bags open in turn, taking just one thing from each. The phones. He didn't know exactly which was the one he was after. He didn't care. It had to look as if it was something else. As if he was taking both. There was nothing else of note in the bags. No cash in the wallets and purses. Nothing he could use. As it was meant to be. The only things that would matter to him were the phones. It would make sense to take them and to leave the rest.

He stepped back out into the corridor, recalling the route he had to take to the muster point. Adam and his team would be in the building by now. They had a couple of floors to make their way down. Jack would try and intersect them en route. Part of him hoped he might run into some resistance on the way. He could help the others get in easily. But the building was deserted. He saw no one ahead and he heard no one behind. By the time he found Adam and the team hurrying down the steps, he wondered if any of the guards had remained at all or whether their emergency plan called for a complete evacuation.

"All good?" Adam asked, taking off his backpack so that Jack could get kitted up.

"Not sure," Jack replied. "The place is quiet. Too quiet. I think we've missed something."

"Like what?"

Jack pulled a night-vision headset over his face. "I've no doubt we'll find out soon enough."

29

Adam had been to numerous prisons in his previous life as a police officer. Whilst each one had been different, they had all, in some ways, been the same. The smell. The sounds. The overwhelming sense of oppression. Despite it's unconventional nature, even Glasshouse Seven was the same. Take away people's freedom and some things didn't change. In the eerie iridescence of the night vision, he could see things that told him instinctively where he was. Security checkpoints. Barred gates. Heavy locks. Hidden from view or not, this prison was built with the same purpose as all the others. To keep people inside. Which was where they were now.

Jack had got himself kitted up quickly and was explaining what he'd seen to the rest of the team.

"It's a small operation. Minimal staff, which suggests minimal number of prisoners. All good for us."

"Any sign of our helpers?" Emmie asked after Thea and Jane. Their role had been crucial. Smuggling in a small EMP device that had just enough kick to fry the prison's electronics. It had been hidden inside one of their phones.

Jack shook his head. "They were ferreted away within seconds of the lights going out. I got the phones. Hopefully they're still okay."

"We need to keep that in mind when we're engaging," Adam pointed out. "Not everyone in here is a hostile. Non-lethal force."

"Tickling sticks only, boys," Reuben laughed. Adam was pretty certain that his bravado was down to his discomfort with the order.

"Try not to shit yourself before we've even got started." Adam hated being dismissive of someone during an op, but the snicker of laughter it brought from everyone, Reuben included, told him he'd made the right choice.

"Come on. Jobs to do." Jack had quickly assumed charge of the operation.

They didn't need any more orders. They'd planned to split into two teams. Jack would lead one with Emmie and Moore. Adam would lead the other with Reuben, Dean and Hadland. They would sweep through the complex to find Lowri, rendezvousing back within ten minutes. They figured that would be the maximum amount of time before someone from the nearby barracks was sent to find out what was happening. The prison would be monitored off site and someone, somewhere, would be wondering what was going on over here now that everything had gone dark. Hopefully ten minutes would be more than ample and they would be long gone by then.

The two teams split. Adam led the way down the darkened corridors, coming out into what looked like a reception area where a large desk looked as if it would offer perfect cover for anyone preparing a defensive position. Adam sent Reuben and Hadland to circle round one side whilst he and Dean closed on the other. They crept slowly and carefully towards the desk. Guns raised. Adam knowing that he didn't want to have to pull the trigger. Hoping that the other three would show the same restraint. They reached the desk. The final moment for someone to spring out. There was no one there.

"The fuck have they all gone?" Reuben asked. No one offered an answer.

There were two more doors out of the reception area other than the one they'd come through. One was on the opposite wall. They went for the other one. Another small security checkpoint. Once more unmanned. Then a short corridor that led to two sturdier-looking doors. The sort of sturdy someone might use at the entrance to a high-security prison.

Adam raised his hand as they reached them. The other three fell in behind him, kneeling as he placed his hand on the door and pushed. It was far heavier than the doors that had preceded it. Slowly it swung open revealing a cavernous circular expanse that dropped down below where Adam could see. A metal gantry came out across the hole, criss-crossing in the middle, running back out to where it circled the room. Thick metal doors with small portholes that looked as if they should have been on a submarine were spaced equally apart. The cell doors. They'd found what they were after. Adam let his gaze scan the space. All the doors were closed. The prisoners were still in their cells.

All his plans of moving into the room were shattered when the thunderous boom from a shotgun rang out, followed by a cascade of smaller impacts as the shot hit the door. And him. Small fragments bit into his arm, his shoulder. His face burned and his helmet hammered against his skull as he toppled over. He heard a shout from behind him, then someone was dragging him backwards as gunfire seemed to ring out from everywhere.

"You good? You okay?" Adam heard the voice but he couldn't see anything. He panicked for a moment, forgetting the pain, worried he'd gone blind. Then someone was pulling something off his head and he remembered his night-vision goggles. He saw the flash of fire from the muzzles of guns around him.

"You're a fucking lucky bastard." Reuben had finished his once-over. "Cosmetics, mate. Come on."

It didn't feel like cosmetics. Anything but. Adam's arm felt as if it was burning from the inside out. He shuffled into a sitting position and looked as Hadland stepped out into the space he'd just been in. There was no delay this time. He opened fire with his automatic weapon. Bursts of hot lead and death in the direction of whoever had just shot at Adam. He wanted to protest. To remind them to try and use non-lethal force, but he knew it was ridiculous. What were they going to do? Appeal to the guard's better nature? The first shot hadn't been a warning shot. Once that happened, all bets were off.

Hadland fired off three volleys of shots before sparks erupted at his feet. He went down grabbing at his boot, howling in pain.

"Fucking hell!" Reuben grimaced as he grabbed hold of Hadland and dragged him back into the safety.

"Someone below," Hadland shouted, the pain he was in apparent. "Shot my fucking foot and my arse."

"Couldn't miss could they?" Reuben quipped. "You good?"

"No. But I'll live," Hadland replied indignantly.

"What's the bellyaching for then?" Reuben said before turning his attention back to Adam. "You need a plaster or something or you getting on with it?"

Adam didn't know if he could get himself to his feet. He didn't want to say so, but Reuben must have guessed, holding out a hand for Adam to grab onto. He hauled him up roughly. "Thanks," Adam winced, the pain only marginally starting to subside.

"Don't fancy being a permanent resident. Fight through it."

Dean was shooting down from the doorway to where whoever had shot Hadland had stood. "Got two of them holed up down there," he reported.

Adam couldn't see much of anything anymore. He turned to Hadland. "You out?"

"Let me just get patched up," Hadland replied through gritted teeth.

"Goggles?"

Hadland didn't say anything else, just removed the night vision from round his head and passed them to Adam. He put them on. The room came back into view. The criss-cross of the gangway. The circular void. The stairwell down was on the far side. Someone was going to have get across or round the room. The only problem was that they were going to present a much more viable target to whoever was below them. Simple angles and all that.

"Reuben, Dean. You two need to circle to the left. I'll go right. Hadland, you okay to cover us from here?"

"I can't see shit."

"Just cover us. Doesn't matter if you hit anything. Call that a bonus."

"I can do that."

"Stairs on the other side," Reuben said aloud, explaining the plan to himself.

"Let's move." Adam felt a burst of adrenaline. He wasn't sure if that was a good or bad thing. The pain had subsided. Should it have done? He wasn't used to getting shot. He hoped he wasn't bleeding out from somewhere unseen. Losing feeling. His legs didn't feel wobbly as he took off though and that felt like a good thing. There was no time to dawdle or hobble. He broke to the left, gun raised, aiming to where the men below were hiding. The moment he saw one, he had to shoot. He couldn't hesitate. The people he was shooting at wouldn't.

A head popped out. Looking upwards. Not at him. Towards where they had been. He fired. Someone else fired from the other side. The noise echoed around the room. The man fell. There was no sign of his partner. Adam didn't know if it was his bullets that had hit. He didn't know why it mattered. Joint enterprise and all that. He kept going. Kept looking. Kept waiting. Finger on the trigger. He reached the stairs before Reuben and Dean, not stopping, not taking his eyes off the space where the other man had to be.

The lower level looked the same. Same layout. Another set of stairs on the opposite side now. Where the men had been hiding. Had the second man gone down? He slowed, easing away from the foot of the stairs to leave room for the others. There was no sign of movement ahead of him. Surely he'd be able to see the man now? The recess that they'd been hiding in was dark and empty. It seemed to stretch on. A corridor perhaps. If he had bugged out, he could be anywhere. Adam looked to see Reuben and Dean fanning out to the opposite side of the gantry, circling like they had before. Adam pointed at the recess and got two nods in response. They all moved together, reaching the it in unison, training their guns on the darkness. A door was set back about ten foot from the opening of the recess. Adam knelt, ready to place his hand on the neck of the fallen man. Stopping when he saw the hole in his neck. No point. He stood and looked again at the others. No need for a nod. Everyone knew what they had to do. They advanced on the door.

Adam got there first. The door wouldn't move when he pulled. Someone had locked it.

"Gonna need to blow that," Dean said from behind.

Adam held up his head. "Give me a second." He stepped against the door, shouting to whoever was inside. "Look. In thirty seconds, this door is going to be gone and we're coming in shooting. You want to live, you open this door now, you throw down your weapons and I swear, nothing will happen to you."

There was silence from inside.

"They ain't buying that for shit," Reuben hissed.

Adam tried again. "If you don't believe we'll let you go, fine. I get that. But ask yourself this. What chance do you think we have if we come in shooting?"

They waited. Then the door moved. Slowly. The butt of a pistol appeared from the crack. "My weapon," a voice called out.

Adam grabbed the butt of the gun as the door swung open. The guard dropped to his knees, placing his hand on his head. "Thank you," Adam said.

The guard didn't reply. No plea for them to uphold their word. Just the silent fear that comes from placing your imminent fate in the hands of someone else. Someone you've just been shooting at.

Adam stepped into the room. He saw blank TV screens. Computers that would never work again. This was clearly the control room for the cells. At least for this block of the prison. He had no idea if there were more.

"We need to get into the cells," Adam explained to the guard.

"You can't."

"We can and we will."

"They're electromagnetically sealed. When the power went off, deadlocks kicked in. All the doors are firmly shut."

"You're telling us there ain't some sort of master key you can use?" Reuben asked, searching to see if they were getting the whole truth.

There was a pause before the guard answered, which Adam knew meant they weren't. "I don't know."

"Where is it?" In Adam's experience, it saved time and effort to get straight to the point. No use telling the person you know they're lying and have them deny it. It had caught many a suspect off guard in interviews in the past. It did the same with the guard, whose face dropped as his gaze danced through the three of them, fearing violent retribution for his lack of candour.

"You can't. It opens everything."

"Everything?" Adam could guess what that meant and it wasn't good, but just in case he was wrong...

"All the cells. They'll all be out. And these people, they're not right. They can't be let out."

"How many people are down here?"

"Forty-six."

"That's a problem."

30

"All of them?" Jack replied through the comms. Adam had just explained the situation with the master lock system. "Well, that's going to bring up some crowd control issues. Might work to our advantage though."

"How so?" Adam's voice came through in his ear. He could see Emmie and Moore looking at him as he talked. They were hearing all the same things too. Their faces said they had the same question in mind.

"If we are going to get company from outside, then let's give them more to deal with."

"And the guards. And anyone else in here."

Jack knew what Adam really meant: what about Thea and Jane? He wouldn't say it out loud, so as to not alert the guard to their involvement.

"They'll have to make their own luck." He felt callous as he said it, but there wasn't really another option. The whole mission was about getting into the cells. If that meant all of them had to be opened, then they all had to be opened. They would just have to deal with everything else. "How does it work?"

"Each cell block has a master key in the control room. Three cell blocks. Three keys."

Jack sighed. Two teams. Three cell blocks. Adam was clearly in one. They were in another. They'd met light resistance and, with Adam's directions, found the control room. If Lowri was in one of these two blocks, they were in good shape. If not, things got even more complicated.

"What's this key look like?" he asked.

"There should be a big metal wheel on one of the walls. You see it?"

"I see it," Jack said. "Suppose we best get this show on the road. Don't suppose your friend had any idea where Lowri was, did he?"

"We asked. Names don't tend to mean much down here though. Said there are female prisoners in each cell block. The description of a middle-aged woman, grey hair, looking gaunt didn't help much."

"Figures. Okay. Here goes."

He moved to the wheel, turning to Emmie and Moore as he did. "This is about to get fun then." They didn't respond.

He began to turn the wheel. The sound of some unseen but large mechanism could be heard rumbling inside the walls. Jack felt the vibrations in the wheel as it turned. Larger clunks and clangs felt as if someone was hammering at it from the inside out. It didn't feel like a well-oiled machine. If it had ever been used before, Jack would have been surprised. Checking the maintenance on it had probably been low priority. After all, who was going to complain if the prisoners were stuck inside the cell of a secret military prison?

He kept turning. Moore went out into the corridor to watch, tossing a fluorescent glow stick down into the middle of the cavern, the green glow at least giving some definition to the space. "It's working," he called back. Jack grunted and worked the wheel until it came to a sudden but inescapable stop. He sighed. That had been hard work.

"You want to get out here?" Moore shouted from the entrance.

When Emmie and Jack were with him they saw the open doors. Already one or two prisoners had begun to emerge from their cells on all three of the floors. One above. One below. The one they were on. They moved warily. Scanning around in the darkness trying to pick out what they could. Wondering if this really was freedom.

"I don't see her," Emmie said. Jack didn't either.

"Let's check the cells. Quick as we can."

They stayed on the same floor together. It would have been quicker to split up, but the newly released inmates meant that safety in numbers felt like a preference. None of them knew what these individuals were in for. What they were capable of. Most looked emaciated. One or two still had enough about them to show that they could at least be problematic if they chose to be. But the sight of three well-armed people moving through the darkness was enough to make them think twice. At least for now. Sooner or later, they would begin to decide this was the time to escape.

Then they'd want every advantage they could get their hands on.

The first clutch of prisoners that had emerged from their cells didn't contain Lowri. There was only one female amongst them and she was much younger and sporting a cropped hairdo that left no chance for error when looking at her facial features. That meant that if she was in this block, she was still in her cell. They worked their way from the lower level upwards, checking each cell quickly but thoroughly. She was nowhere to be seen. She wasn't in this block.

"All clear. No sign," Jack radioed through.

There was a brief delay before Adam replied. "Same. She must be in the final block.Do we know how we get there?"

"We're working on finding out," Jack replied. He hoped that whoever was going to provide that information did so quickly. For everyone's sake.

31

Jack's team had reconvened with Adam's. The guard they had captured had been more than eager to give up the information on where the third set of cells could be found. It hadn't taken much more than a look to convince the guard to give them directions to the cell block. Jack had considered threatening him if the directions were wrong, but the look on the guy's face said that he didn't have the capacity to bluff or bullshit at the moment.

They shut him into the control room, letting him lock the door from the inside. With a bit of luck, he'd be able to hold out till someone came to rescue him. His directions had been concise. The third cell block was accessible via a small corridor that ran from the lower level of this block. It was where they held the higher-security prisoners. It was also overseen by the control room that they'd just been in, which meant that the doors had already been opened.

Hadland had managed to stem the bleeding from his foot and buttocks and was able to hobble along with them. Jack had taken the lead as they made their way through the narrow passage that would take them to the cells. A forty-metre-long, two-metre-wide rat run down which he was certain escapees were going to come. It made for an interesting tactical situation. Jack didn't necessarily relish the idea of killing unarmed people. That crossed a line even he wasn't comfortable with. But these weren't just normal people. They were clearly seen as a threat by the British government. Big enough threats that they had been disappeared. The fact that he might easily find himself in such a predicament wasn't lost on him. So, there was some sympathy. But he didn't have time to check people's backstories as they hurried towards him. And he didn't have room to get far enough away from any improvised weapon. And desperation did strange things to people. But one of them could easily be Lowri. Target identification wasn't going to be easy. Especially if there were people lurking behind those at the front. Shooting on sight was out of question. None of it was ideal. He was going to have to control the situation as best he could and hope that whoever came listened.

He didn't have to wait long to find out. As they reached halfway he saw a figure shuffling down the corridor towards them, arms drooping, shoulders slumped, head down. They looked like something out of a zombie flick. Long hair dangling over their eyes. The paper jumpsuit hanging loosely around their thin frame. It would have been easy to dismiss any threat from them, but Jack couldn't. Just because they were broken didn't mean they weren't capable of making things go sideways quickly. It probably made it more likely. What did they have to lose? They wouldn't want to go back. Might as well die trying.

"Get on the ground," Jack shouted, lighting the corridor up with the torch on his gun and lifting his night-vision goggles. He wanted the person to see him coming. To know that he was there and that he was in charge.

The figure did nothing.

"Get the fuck on the ground or I will shoot."

Still nothing. Jack raised the barrel of the gun high and fired into the roof just ahead of him. Well away from the figure. He didn't want a ricochet heading down the corridor into who knows who. The explosion of noise echoed down the corridor and the figure's hands instinctively reached up to their ears. They paused, unsure for a moment. Then slowly they lowered themselves down to the ground. Jack edged forward, reaching the figure as they finally lay down. He was able to see them a little better now as they looked up at him. It was a man. Asian. His eyes were sunken and his face thin. Jack couldn't even begin to guess the guy's age.

"When we're gone, you move. You don't come back," Jack's voice did its best to convey the urgency, without sounding threatening. He needed the prisoners to at least believe they were on the same side.

Leaving the prone man behind, they covered the last fifteen or so metres quickly, coming out in a room not too dissimilar to the cell block they'd been in before. The only difference was this one was just a single storey. There was no gantry, just a stone floor separating the cells.

"Check the cells," Jack ordered as they fanned out.

He headed left, to the cells at the far quarter of the circle. The doors were all open. No prisoners had been milling in the space. He wondered how many had been occupied.

How many still contained occupants unable to leave, either physically or mentally.

The first cell was empty. The second wasn't. A man sat in the corner on the floor, his knees up to his chest. A thin grey mattress hung from the wall and something that looked like a toilet protruded from the opposite side. There was no sink. No desk. No chair. Just somewhere to sleep and somewhere to relieve yourself. A life distilled to two bodily functions. Not a life at all.

Jack moved on. The third cell. The layout was the same. The only difference was that this one wasn't empty. Jack saw the body on the floor immediately. He saw the long light-coloured hair drooping down into the pool of blood. The slender fingers sprawled out on the ground.

"Oh shit."

He raced to the body on the floor, turning it over, knowing it had to be Lowri. That someone had got to her before they did. Then he saw the face and it wasn't.

"She came for me," a voice croaked from behind him.

He turned. "Lowri! Thank God." He left the woman on the floor, turning his attention to Lowri. She was sitting next to the mattress, leaning against the wall. Her eyes were wide, staring at the woman on the floor. She was sweating and her hair was tussled. "What happened?"

"She came for me," she repeated.

"We need to get out of here. Can you walk?"

Lowri finally looked away from the body and to him. She nodded.

Jack put his arm underneath hers, lifting her up. She felt light. Too light. He worried whether or not she'd be able to stand. He should have known better. Lowri didn't want to be carried. She pushed his hand away, wobbled, but held herself upright.

The sound of distant automatic gunfire echoed through the room.

"Shit," Jack muttered.

"Adam. Was that you?" Emmie was already on the radio checking with everyone else.

"Not us. Sounded like it came from where we went in," Adam's voice sounded Jack's ears.

"Dammit. We're out of time." Jack grunted.

"What's wrong?" Lowri asked. There was no emotion in her voice. No fear. She was assessing the situation. Just like Lowri of old. Even if she sounded frailer.

"Someone came to find out why the lights went out. Came in through our way out."

"Is there another way?" she asked.

"Not technically. But we have something in mind," Jack replied.

"Plan B," Emmie groaned over the radio.

"Plan B," Jack nodded.

"What's Plan B?" Lowri asked.

"It's shit."

32

"Rescue team on site," one of the guards reported as they heard gunfire coming from somewhere above them.

"You hope," another guard replied. "Could be more of whoever's attacking."

"Why would they be firing up there then? They're already in," the first guard replied. He'd been the one in charge since they had all come together. Thea hadn't seen him before, but the way the others had deferred everything to him said all she needed to know. She hadn't liked him much. He had revelled in the moment and this moment was decidedly a defeat for them. Clearly all that had mattered to him was keeping his own arse safe.

"You heard the cells open," the second guard retorted. "Prisoners probably made it up there by now."

"Fuck 'em. Who gives a shit?" the first guard shrugged, completely on brand.

The room they had sheltered in was cramped and hot. Unsurprisingly, given that there were thirteen people crammed into a space a little more than nine by nine. If anyone did find a way to breach the doors, it wouldn't take much more than a quick spray of bullets to finish everyone off. There was nothing to find cover behind. Just shelves against the wall full of cardboard boxes that on inspection contained first-aid kits, spare jumpsuits, cardboard dinner trays. Nothing that seemed to be of any use right then.

"You know these fucking berks could easily get us killed," Jane whispered to Thea as they sat on the floor against the back wall of the room.

"We'd at least get the amusement of watching them die first," Thea pointed out. "I think if they'd had to stay in here for another hour they might have done the job themselves."

The mood hadn't turned sour yet, but there were hints of it in the way the guards were talking to each other. They were all scared and they were all looking for a way out. The fact that one wasn't presenting itself was causing them concern. Concern would eventually give way to panic. Panic would force action. The sound of the gunfire had raised more questions between the guards than it had answered. It would probably remain the case till someone came through the door.

"If they wanted us dead, they would have killed us by now, right?" one of the guards said. Thea couldn't see which one it was in the dark. His voice sounded as if he needed someone to say something to convince him that was the case.

"Hang fucking tight," came the growled reply from the leader. His patience was wearing thin with those around him. Probably something that was an asset when dealing with dangerous prisoners. Not so when you were in a situation like this.

"I think you're right," Jane commented quietly to Thea.

"Someone have a look, see if they can see anything," another voice from inside the room suggested.

"Well volunteered," came a snarky reply.

There was a pause as the first voice tried to come up with a compelling reason why it shouldn't be him. "I'm all the way over here," was the best he could manage.

"You've got legs." There was laughter this time. Not necessarily good-humoured. The sort of snickering you heard from a group of playground bullies picking on the weak kid.

The first voice sighed. Thea saw his shadow as he stood and picked his way uneasily through the room. He bumped into at least two people as he went, apologising as he did so, although Thea was sure he didn't mean a word of it and that his actions were deliberate. He reached the door, then hovered. Slowly, he eased it open and looked one way then the next.

"All quiet," he called back.

"Not so fucking loud," the leader shushed.

The man apologised again. It sounded more sincere this time. He shut the door and eased back into the room, returning to the spot he had been in before. "Done my bit now," he pointed out.

"Fucking hero," the same voice who had replied before came back at him.

"Piss off, Jones."

"Twenty-two minutes," Jane noted. They had both worn analogue watches to keep abreast of the time after the miniature EMP had gone off. They'd assumed that it would take the response unit less than twenty minutes to arrive on scene and begin taking back control of the facility. Whether the guards' safety was deemed a priority or not would determine how long it would take for them to be rescued. Neither of them expected it would be top of the list. There was no way anyone could be allowed to leave. If word of a secret prison facility got out, there would be all sorts of hell to pay.

"You think anyone escaped?" Thea asked, careful to keep the true meaning of what she was asking hidden. She didn't care about the prisoners after all.

"I guess we'll find out soon enough."

"You think we'll be told?"

Jane took a moment to ponder. "I think it'd be hard to keep some of those names from us."

"That's assuming we'll still be employed."

"Or alive."

"Cheerful."

They waited. There was nothing else they could do. The men in the room said very little. When they did, it was born from fear and often met with derision from their colleagues or snapped at by the leader. It was clear he didn't want to hear about how they felt. Again, probably another good personality trait to have when dealing with dangerous prisoners who, for all intents and purposes, don't exist.

Finally, there was the sound of footsteps heading towards them.

"What's that?" a voice asked, which Thea was pretty sure belonged to Jones.

"Someone coming?" another voice asked.

"Who?"

Everyone stopped and listened. Thea knew instantly. The footsteps were heavy and fast. Confident and numerous. The door opened. Lights shone on them.

"Bravo Unit. We have the guards," someone reported into a radio.

"Thank fuck," the leader stood and walked towards them only to be met by a raised hand, halting him.

"Is this everyone?" the soldier asked.

"No. We're missing three."

"We'll find them," the soldier nodded. "In the meantime, we're going to escort you to the surface. Transport is waiting to take you to be debriefed."

"What about the prisoners?" the leader protested. "We need to get them back in."

"You have your orders. Let's go." The soldier either couldn't or wouldn't answer the question. Thea knew the answer. The prisoners were dead or would be. This facility, as it was, was finished. The guards would be debriefed. Reassigned if they gave the right answers. Who knew what if they gave the wrong ones. The prison would eventually return with new staff. New prisoners. But for now, it would be purged.

There wasn't much in the way of dissent from the guards. All of them saw this as an upturn in their situation. At least for the short term. The soldiers escorted them through the prison, their flashlights illuminating the way. They only passed the body of one prisoner. Whoever it was lay on their front, a pool of blood spreading out below them. It wasn't anyone Thea recognised. Their head was shaved, their body still relatively strong-looking. Clearly not a long-term resident.

When they emerged from the prison it was raining hard. Thunder and lightning rumbled in the distance. It was hard to tell if it was heading their way or not. Four black Land Rovers were parked in a line outside the door.

"Transport will be on its way," their escort shouted as they fanned out. "In the meantime, stay here where we can see you. Don't wander off. We don't want anyone mistaking you for a target."

"That's a polite way of saying you're under arrest," Jane said, quietly enough so as to not reach their escort.

"You think we're fucked?" Thea asked.

Before Jane could reply, a flashlight was turned on their faces. "Astley and Watts?" a voice called from behind the light.

"That's us," Thea replied.

"This way."

The light turned and a soldier began walking towards one of the Land Rovers.

"I definitely think we're fucked now," Jane said as they walked.

33

"Say it." Jack said.

"Say what?" Adam protested.

"Say it."

"I don't know what you mean."

"Just get on with it."

Adam smiled. "This is a shit idea."

It really was. But it was their only option. Other than trying – and ultimately failing – to fight their way out.

"Hope you got your jabs done recently, Hadland," Reuben slapped the wounded man on his shoulder.

"This was the best you could come up with?" Lowri asked.

"We were working on a short lead time," Adam explained. "And we didn't have much in the way of information on the site. We managed to get a couple of passes with the satellite. Obviously couldn't see much; this place is too deep down. But we did see a structure just off from it. Looked kind of like a septic tank."

"A septic tank?"

"People gotta poo and that poo needs emptying."

"You'd have thought they'd just pumped it straight into the sea," Moore said as he began strapping Hadland's suit around his wounds with thick black gaffer tape.

"The whole premise of this site is that there's no easy way in or out, for anything. A sewage pipe, no matter how small, would still allow access. A septic tank is a lot harder to get in and out of."

"How are we going to do it?" Lowri asked.

"It was Jack's plan," Adam looked to his partner.

"So, brute force," Lowri filled in the blank.

"It seemed the simplest option," Jack shrugged before turning to Adam. "You want to strap your wounds up too."

Adam sighed. "Yeah, I reckon your plan might have needed a bit more oversight. I never thought about this."

"They can give you a thorough clean-up inside and out when we get back," Jack replied

"I'm going to be puking my ring up for weeks, aren't I?" Hadland moaned.

"I think we all are," Jack said grimly.

Adam knew that Jack had planned operations like this before. Coordinating different aspects of a military operation to coincide perfectly was second nature to Jack. It wasn't to him, however, and it meant that as they prepared he couldn't help but be nervous. What if something went wrong? What if there was a delay? It wasn't going to take much longer for the rescue team to arrive at their location. Jack and Dean had begun placing breaching charges around the corridor they used to reach this cell block in an effort to slow down their would-be pursuers. But again, what if that

255

went wrong? What if they didn't detonate? What if someone got through? He knew part of his nerves were because he felt he wasn't doing anything constructive. The sleeve of his tactical jacket was completely shredded. It meant he needed to tape his whole arm. Other than him and Hadland, everyone else had simply taped the gaps between clothing. Cuffs and collars. Rebreathers had been fitted. But he had more to do and it was slowing him down. Stopping him from being a useful member of the team. That made him feel nervous.

"Charges are set." Jack was back in the main room. "Thirty seconds."

Adam quickly pulled on his rebreather, the mask covering his face. He tightened the straps. There wasn't time for anything else. Jack's plan couldn't wait. He looked at his own watch. Less than twenty seconds to go.

"Everyone in the middle of the room," Jack barked. "It's gonna get loud."

Adam crouched, covered his ears and opened his mouth. He had no idea how big the explosions that were about to come were going to be. All he knew was that they were going to be like nothing he had ever felt before.

Jack began his count down. "Five... Four... Three... Two... One..."

The two charges around them went off instantaneously. The sound echoed through the chamber, dust and debris flying out of the cell where the first set had been placed and from the corridor. Before the noise subsided and the debris had landed, there was another explosion. This one shook everything. Silently at first. Then a split second later the sound wave hit. A deafening boom as the whole room seemed to rise up around them. Adam wondered for a second if they'd taken a direct hit. But then he realised a direct hit from a drone-launched bunker buster bomb would have evaporated them. Instead, masonry fell and someone shouted something he didn't quite catch.

Then came the roar. A ferocious sound that bellowed from all around them, screeching and screaming as waves of fire rushed out from the walls of every cell. The septic tank and, to a lesser extent, the sewers that fed it, were full of methane. The bunker buster had ignited it. The fire leapt and licked all around them as if belched out from a horde of dragons imprisoned in here with the internees. Adam felt the heat on his face, even behind the rebreather. The air shimmered around the holes in the walls that had once served as toilets. The shaking stopped and the flames abated.

"Move!" Jack was the first to his feet, ushering everyone else forward. They all knew the plan. They all knew there was no time to waste. Adam led the way. As he was supposed to. Jack would bring up the rear. He wouldn't have had it any other way.

The hole in the wall was big enough for someone to crouch and jump down through. Adam went first. It was a ten-foot drop and he bounced as he landed, trying to ensure he didn't fall. There was no way he wanted to tear his clothes, or the taping. He staggered to his knees, crouching below the low ceiling. The sewer was at best five foot tall. Not perfect, but it could have been a lot worse.

He turned, helping the others down as they came. Catching them, supporting their landings. Emmie first, then Hadland, Lowri, then the rest until finally Jack was in and they were heading east towards the remains of the tank.

Small fires burned around them. Flames licked from the walls as God knows what smouldered where it had landed. Ahead of them there was an orange glow where the sewer emptied into the septic tank. Huddled over, they moved as quickly as the space allowed. Around their feet, water flowed back towards the septic tank, debris riding the current with it. There wasn't time to think about what was around them. They had to get out quickly. Otherwise they'd be trapped there.

Adam was the first out. The down draft from the helicopter hit him as it hovered above the hole, keeping him crouched low. The crater was impressive. The walls of the septic tank had been blown outwards. Earth had fallen into the gaps, creating haphazard banks and hollows. At the heart of the hole, the contents of the tank that hadn't been ejected by the explosion were alight, the flames dancing as they were buffeted by the rushing air from the blades of the helicopter. A searchlight found him and the others as they emerged. He shielded his eyes, looking for the ladders. The chopper they'd commandeered was big enough for everyone and the doors on either side were open. The ladders dangled from each. The pilot was doing the best he could to keep it in place around the hole, despite the currents coming up from the uneven ground and the heat of the fires surely causing him more trouble than he would have liked.

"Let's go!" Adam shouted over the sound of the blades. He didn't know if anyone heard him. He didn't know if they had to.

Somewhere in the distance there was another explosion. The drone was patrolling the skies above them. Jack had been very clear with his orders to David. There was no way that the drone was to target any encroaching soldiers. It could slow them down. Fire in their paths. Make them think twice. But it wasn't to engage them personally until the very last minute. Jack didn't want dead soldiers on his conscience. Ex-forces looked after their own, even if Adam was certain that the soldiers approaching them wouldn't show similar restraint.

Lowri was the first one ushered onto the waiting ladder. She was the reason they were there. Once she was onboard, the pilot had strict orders not to wait and perform heroics for anyone else. If things got hot, the chopper left and everyone else was on their own. Hadland followed on the other side. Wounded men always went first. Another rule Jack insisted on. A rule Adam would ignore. Then Dean and Moore were following. Reuben and Emmie next. More explosions came from above them. Louder this time. Which meant nearer.

"Let's get out of here." Jack had his hand on Adam's shoulder, shouting at him. Adam hadn't even seen him exit the tunnel. He'd been so focused on the job in hand.

Together they each grabbed onto a ladder. The pilot must have been given a signal because within seconds the aircraft was rising. Adam clung on tightly. He didn't want to fall off at the last minute. Then he was climbing again. Steadily and safely as the chopper nosed itself low towards the North Sea. Adam made his way up, rung by rung until finally he was being yanked into the cabin, the door slamming shut behind him.

"Holy shit! We did it!" Reuben whooped.

Adam laughed. It was all he could do.

34

The Land Rover had taken them back to London. Back to Thames House. There had been no one waiting in the car other than a driver, who said nothing more than a polite "Ma'ams" when they got in, then nothing again until he repeated the words as he brought the vehicle to a halt in the car park. The storm from the night before had passed and the last traces of thin clouds were being chased away as the sun reasserted its dominance.

There they'd been met by a junior analyst who introduced himself as Richard Hadley. He asked if they needed a drink or something to eat, before showing them to a small but comfortable-looking room. A small grey fabric sofa sat along one wall. Four more chairs were arranged around a glass coffee table. There were cupboards that neither of them opened.

"Well, that was a night, wasn't it?" Jane said, more than a little theatrically. Clearly she thought they were being listened to. The thought had crossed Thea's mind. Everything seemed a little too disarming. If anyone at Five had suspicions that Thea and Jane were in on it, letting them think they got away with it might have been one way to get their guards down. Thea was almost a little insulted if that was the case.

"It was something all right."

"Do you think anyone got out?" A completely innocuous-sounding question. But one that they both must have been pondering. It was the whole point of being there after all.

"I wouldn't like to guess."

"No. Nor me. Fuck. What a mess." Jane sighed herself into silence then sat. Neither of them said anything else.

Hadley returned with drinks and food and a chirpy message that they wouldn't be waiting much longer. Thea wondered whether, if she looked close enough, she'd be able to still see the green behind his ears. But she only thanked him, then drank the coffee and ate the breakfast rolls he'd brought.

Ten minutes later there was a knock at the door. It opened without them replying and two suited men walked in. They were older and far more experienced than Hadley. They'd also spent time in the field. Thea could see it in the way they walked. Confident and precise. Every movement considered. There were only two sorts of people who walked that way. Covert field operatives and actors.

Someone had a suspicion then.

"Ms Astley. Ms Watts. My name is Kris Pegg, this is Phil Cartwright. We'll be handling your debrief today," the first one said. He had dark hair whilst his partner was fairer. The two of them were similar in height – not too tall, not too short – and similar in build – not too skinny, not too fat or muscly. Short back and sides for each. Completely nondescript. Forgettable.

Thea and Jane had sat around the table when the food came, so Cartwright and Pegg took the sofa. One at either end. Cartwright, the fairer-haired one, leaned forward and began.

"Let's start from the beginning shall we? The apprehension of Jack Quinn. A masterstroke."

"Or luck," Pegg added. He had an arm up on the back of the sofa, and one leg crossed over the other. Thea realised that this would be how they liked to play it. Cartwright laying out the facts as they'd been told by Thea and Jane, Pegg butting in where there were question marks. They would be hoping that Jane and Thea would jump in to defend themselves. To say something that could be picked apart. Thea had no intention of doing that. She hoped Jane knew interrogations well enough to do the same.

"Or luck," Cartwright repeated. "Although we were due a bit of that. You can't hide forever, as Mr Quinn found out. So, tell me, how did he come onto your radar?"

"He called me." Thea answered the question in as closed a manner as possible.

"When?"

"The call logs will give the exact time, but four days ago. In the morning. About 10:30. I need to double-check that to be certain."

"I get that. Long night and everything. Have you slept?" Cartwright asked. Jane and Thea said they hadn't. Thea knew that wasn't going to work in their favour. Tiredness led to mistakes. She'd tried in the car. She saw Jane had too. But there was still too much happening for her to switch off. The thought of sleep now reminded her of how tired she actually was. That wasn't a good thing. She wondered if that had been deliberate.

"What did he want?" Cartwright pressed on.

"He's convinced that there're people out there who want to bring down the government. Replace it with their own people."

"Assassinating a prime minister would fall under that category, wouldn't it?" Pegg butted in.

"It would fit the profile," Thea looked at him as she spoke.

"You're not convinced?" Cartwright asked.

Thea turned back to him. "I didn't have a chance to be convinced. We went to interrogate him. The lights went out."

"Timing," Pegg tutted.

This time Thea said nothing. The bait was too obvious. It was insulting to think she'd take it.

"Look, you know why we have to ask this. You bring him in, then there's an incident at the prison. You've got a past history with him. It's not that we want to make things personal, Mrs Quinn. Sorry, Ms Watts."

Thea sighed. "For God's sake. Is this really your script? Thea and Jack sitting in a tree? I didn't realise they let the work-experience kids do debriefs these days." She knew she shouldn't have reacted, but the clumsy nature of Cartwright's insinuation needed pulling up. Next to her, Jane frowned.

"No, sorry, honestly, a slip of the tongue," Cartwright apologised and for a split second he sounded as if he meant it. Only Pegg's slight smile behind him suggested otherwise. "But let's face facts. You have a history with Jack Quinn. One of bending the rules. You had a chance to apprehend him three years ago. You didn't. In fact, a year later, you then brought him into a police matter without even seeking approval. Now it's you who finally brings him in from the cold, only for there to be a security breach at a secure facility."

"That neither of you have asked about," Pegg pointed out. Thea realised then, that had been a mistake. They had been so set on staying silent that they hadn't considered that if they had been innocent, they would have wanted to know what had happened at the facility. Had Jack escaped? Who had been behind it all? They'd asked nothing. It made it look as if they knew.

"We haven't had the chance," Jane said indignantly.

"Okay," Pegg's tone was dismissive.

"And to the point, Glasshouse Seven is, as you said, a secure facility. What happens there is far above my level of security clearance, let alone Ms Watts'. Do you think we suddenly forgot the rules? Do you think that people of our calibre suddenly believe that, because we're personally involved in a situation, we should get a free pass? All four of us in this room know that when you work here, you don't know everything. You don't need to know. You don't ask to know. What you're told is what you're told. Poking your noses into business that doesn't concern you is the sort of thing that ends careers by putting you in a cell. Or worse. Frankly, I'm of the same mind as Thea. You two are an absolute shambles. I don't know who has sent you in here, but I suggest that you toddle off now and send in the grown-ups. And maybe polish up those CVs because by the time I'm finished, you'll be lucky if you're cleaning the floors in here."

As Jane tore into them, Cartwright seemed to shrink backwards. Pegg never moved. The slight half smile remained in place.

"I tell you what," he said. "I think this would be better if we reconvened when everyone has had the chance to catch up on their sleep. Shall we schedule something for later in the week?"

"Let's," Jane snarled.

"Wonderful. We'll be in touch."

Cartwright and Pegg stood and, without saying anything else, left the room.

"That was fun," Jane said once they were gone.

"They think we're involved, don't they?" Thea made it sound as if she was surprised. You never knew who was listening.

"They think they're hot shit on a scalding shovel," Jane shrugged. "I can eat them for breakfast."

35

Lowri had leapt from the car when she saw David. For that moment, the effects of her imprisonment had been forgotten. The two of them had met in the middle of the courtyard outside his house, embracing each other, their broken bodies both suddenly full of energy as the relief of seeing each other dissolved anything else that might afflict them. Adam stepped out of the car but stayed where he was, watching the moment as it unfolded. There was no rush from either of them to end the moment. It felt to Adam as if it went on for minutes. To them, he was sure it felt like an eternity.

They pulled apart slightly, a murmur of words exchanged only between them, though their smiles said everything to those watching on. Adam felt a squeeze on his shoulder and he turned to see Jack. They nodded at each other, then left David and Lowri alone.

Jack had disappeared on his own as well. He needed to go and check in with the hospital. Calum was never far from his mind. The pilot had been updated with his condition before setting off, but they hadn't wanted to make a call whilst in the air, for fear of giving anyone a chance to pair their location with that of the helicopter.

Adam found himself back in the orangery staring out at the garden.

"Penny for them?" Emmie asked.

"Not a lot going on I'm afraid," Adam replied. "Just drinking it all in."

"It makes you realise how close we skate to oblivion when you see places like that, doesn't it?"

"Sure does."

There was a moment's pause. When Emmie finally spoke, Adam realised that it was probably because she was working out if what she was about to say was the right thing.

"You know, no one is going to think any differently of you when you walk."

Adam didn't know how Emmie knew that had been playing on his mind. He didn't even know that he'd realised it. Not properly. She was right though. There was no way that he wanted to end up in somewhere like that. No way he wanted to be separated from his family. The thought of it scared him more than death. It had always been an abstract thought, but now it wasn't. The stakes had been laid out. He didn't care if he had a winning hand. They felt too high.

"I'm going nowhere," he said firmly, almost believing it himself.

Emmie didn't say anything else. He looked at her and she smiled. It was the sort of smile you gave to someone who said they were doing all right after the death of a loved one or a divorce or something. The sort that said: *I know you're not okay, and I'm here.* He smiled back. His way of saying: *I know. Thank you.*

Jack returned five minutes later. His eyes were red and for a moment Adam feared the worst. Then Jack said, "All good," through a cracking voice and Adam realised that the tears had been relief.

They made food and drinks before finding spaces to settle and catch up on some sleep. It was early afternoon before they were all back downstairs ready to begin thinking about what came next. Adam had showered, feeling as invigorated as he was likely to in the heat as they all waited for Lowri to tell them what she knew.

"Dead Line is the end game," Lowri began. She looked remarkably better already. She'd cleaned herself up and been given clothes to wear that weren't made from paper. It looked to Adam as if she might have even tried to cut her own hair. It all made her look more like Lowri and less like the husk they'd found less than twenty-four hours before. "It's the final act of a desperate organisation in an effort to cling on to what they have."

"Which is what?" Jack asked.

"Power," Lowri said matter-of-factly. "What is it ever about? There's no ideology to these people. Just greed. They've run everything for generations. A small group of people who have nudged and cajoled but have never really had to do much more. They were already so rich that their input went unnoticed. Or if it was noticed, no one who noticed cared. What could they do? What did it matter? To our fault, that was the mindset many in the Vehm had. It didn't matter to us because what they were doing usually was maintaining the status quo. We didn't go looking for them and they left us alone."

"Kind of seems against the whole game you lot say you been playing," Reuben gestured towards her with a half-drunk mug of coffee.

"Consider this the reckoning for our apathy." Lowri wasn't one to make excuses.

"Where did it all go wrong then?" Emmie was the next to send in a question.

"That was what I couldn't understand. When I was first picked up, I assumed we had upset someone by bringing down Briar. I expected my rendition to be a short but bloody affair. Revenge for what I had allowed to happen. But then came the questions. They wanted to know everything. Not just about Briar and the operation there. Everything about the Regulators. The Vehm. They wanted to pick us apart. I realised I had a chance to survive if I could prove useful, yet not so useful that they would exhaust me."

"You gave up information?" David sounded shocked.

Lowri bowed her head as she replied. "No. Not at first. But after time, you have to realise, you are no longer the person who went in. You don't operate in the same way. You don't have the same resolve. You forget what it was you were

271

holding on to. They call time the great healer because it makes you forget the pain. But it also makes you forget your duty. Forget who you were, who you are. I could feel myself losing sight of what it was I was fighting for. I needed to refocus so that I wouldn't give up on everything. So I made a deal with myself. One I knew that I would be able to keep because I would never stop wanting to make it happen. I decided I was going to do whatever it took to keep myself alive so that I could get out of there. I knew you would come for me. I knew I had to keep going until that point. So I told them things that I knew they wanted to hear. Sometimes, yes, they were true. But I made sure they knew I was holding stuff back. They thought they were breaking me. I was just making them think that I was useful. Because if I wasn't useful, if they decided that they were never going to get anything out of me, I was far too big a risk to keep around."

"You gave them the location, didn't you?" Adam knew she had to have done. For a long time, he'd blamed Grant. Now he was wondering if he'd been unfair to do so.

"I did. And that they would find the Kernel there and that it contained everything that the Regulators had ever worked on. I didn't tell them that the protocol would be to purge the Kernel the moment they set foot in that building and that there was nothing they could do about it. I knew that if I did that, I would accelerate your desperation and I hoped that would lead you to finding me. I was right."

"I'm totting up all the times you've given me an absolute bollocking for doing something reckless in the past, and I reckon, for once, I might be in credit after that." Adam counted on his fingers up one by one. It made Lowri laugh, which in turn made a couple of other people in the room smile. That was no bad thing.

"I don't imagine it'll take you much longer to level the playing field. It might even be necessary."

"I still don't understand what their plan is," Jack pointed out. "Just to get rid of the Regulators?"

"No. They want to clear the whole deck. Put their people in place, either short term or long term. They've removed the Regulators. Then the PM. My guess is that next will be to install someone in their pay to Number 10. By which point I don't know what we can do."

"The In Statera. Who exactly is behind them?"

"I don't know the names. I do know where we can find them, however. There is a secure backup, hidden away where very few people know of it."

"A backup?" David asked. Clearly "very few people" meant that even the Director of the London office was excluded from that list.

"Everything that was on the Kernel. There is a hard line that runs to an exchange underneath the building. If the Met find it whilst pulling the office apart, they'll find nothing that will tell them the location of the backup. The exchange runs through a million different physical locations around the world."

"I thought the whole point of the Kernel was that it was isolated. It didn't go anywhere."

"The whole point of telling people that was to ensure that that's what they believed. But every system needs a redundancy. To not have one would be foolhardy."

"Then we get this data and we can take the fight to them?" Jack looked up eagerly. Adam almost believed he could see the energy in his eyes.

"That would be my plan," Lowri said.

"Best plan I've heard in a long time. Let's get moving."

36

Sleeping in the back of the car hadn't seemed likely as Thea climbed in, but within minutes of leaving Thames House, she had sprawled across the back seat of the roomy saloon and nodded off. She only woke when the car pulled up outside her house.

Groggily, she sat back up and took a little moment to compose herself quietly, taking in her surroundings and working out where she was. She looked at the driver through the rear-view mirror and he acknowledged her with a courteous nod.

"Here we are, ma'am," he said, unbuckling his seat before getting out of the car and walking around to Thea's door to open it. Being chauffeur driven wasn't something Thea was accustomed to, so she muttered her thanks and hoped to hell that none of her neighbours had seen her. She'd enjoyed the relatively low-key life she was living here. That would change if people thought she was some sort of big deal. People always asked questions. The walk to her front door seemed longer than normal and she felt an unaccustomed sense of relief as she finally managed to shut the door to the world outside her.

It felt like a lifetime since she had been back home. Thea didn't know what she should be doing with herself. Her orders had been to get some rest, but the sleep in the car had left her feeling more rested than she probably was. It would catch up with her, but not just yet. Far better to do something first, to try and turn her brain off once more. She settled on having a shower. She felt sticky and dirty having slept in her clothes in the car. A good cleanse of the body might help kick-start the process of cleansing her soul. It would at least help get her in the right frame of mind to perhaps catch a little more sleep.

Her bathroom was situated behind her bedroom; a narrow room, just enough space for a bath and toilet to stand next to each other, the sink protruding out between the toilet and the door, creating a small but not insurmountable obstacle, although Thea couldn't recount how many times in the dead of night she had clipped against the hard porcelain bowl when she couldn't be bothered to turn the light on. A window ran along most of the length of the bath, at head height but less than a foot tall and made of frosted glass. It could be pulled inwards to let any condensation out of the bathroom. Thea liked to do that when she showered, letting the noise of her small back garden filter in, almost allowing her to daydream that she was showering outdoors. After all that time spent underground it was reassuring to hear something of the outside world. What must it be like for those that worked there, or worse still, those interred there, who most probably would never see the surface again?

No. She couldn't go down that rabbit hole. She needed to switch off. The people in there were in there for a reason. She couldn't allow herself to feel sympathy for them. Crimes had consequences and all the people holed up in that facility were criminals who deserved to have justice served on them. Thea tried to let that idea settle but every time she did, she felt another side of her psyche asking whether that wasn't what she was supposed to be fighting against? Thea hadn't seen a criminal case brought against Lowri Graves, or any of the inmates in that facility. What worried Thea most was that, in truth, she didn't really disagree with that.

Frustrated with herself, she turned the shower off. That hadn't worked at all. She was more worked up now than before she had stepped in. She wrapped herself in a towel, leaving the water to drip onto the floor as she stared at herself in the mirror that stood above the sink. Why couldn't she leave this world well alone? There weren't easy answers. It wasn't as black and white as she'd believed before she got mixed up in all of this. Before she'd met Jack Quinn, Adam Morgan, Lowri Graves and the rest of the Regulators. Before then, she'd fought crime and put the bad guys in jail. It had been so simple. Now there were grey areas everywhere. Never had she ever imagined that there were people who could break the law and find ways to get away with it. Some brazenly, others less so. Yet it was happening everywhere. The more she looked, the more she found people scheming to get around the system. More blind eyes being turned. More people on the take. It was a nest of corruption and piss-takers.

She sighed, standing up straight. There was only one thing she could do. See this through and try and make the world a better place. Almost immediately, her head dropped again. What the hell was she thinking? This wasn't for her to change. She was a cog in the machine, but she wasn't turning anyone else; they were turning her. No matter how much resistance she seemed to apply, she always got spun the same way, round and round, always in one direction, never to her end.

Dejected, she walked into the bedroom, losing the towel and finding a sweater top and some shorts. She wrapped her hair in another towel, then pulled out a wicker box under her dressing table, looking for a hairdryer. It wasn't there. Where the hell had she put that?

She let out a huff of indignation as she tried to take her mind back to before she had left the house for the last time. Nothing rang any bells. Then she remembered. She had done her hair in the kitchen because she had been trying to make breakfast at the same time. Another rushed morning.

The kitchen was at the front of the house, a small room that merged into the living room allowing both to benefit from the bay window that looked out onto the street. Thea was in there in seconds. Then she froze.

Half in, half out of her window, one foot on the worktop, was a man dressed all in black. Their eyes locked on each other. If there was a doubt about what he was here for, it quickly vanished as he hauled the rest of his body quickly into the room, clambering over the worktop to get down and towards her.

Thea couldn't see a weapon yet. No gun or knife in his hand. He was a big guy, however, clearing six foot easily, broad shoulders. There was something familiar about him. A face she knew. The sort of face that could tell a hundred tales of fights through its myriad of scars, pockmarks and dents. He wasn't going to go down easily, but then again, neither was Thea.

She lunged towards him, a move that must have shocked him, because his eyes widened as he scrambled down from the worktop. In his head he must have seen her turning and running to get away, something most people would have done without a second thought. A head start, knowledge of the house, a chance to find a weapon. Thea knew there was no escape by going backwards, and she already had a weapon.

As she made her move, she was already unwrapping the towel from her head, flexing the fingers of her right hand through the material, grabbing it tightly and flailing it down on the man. It wasn't a knockout blow, but it was enough to make him stagger and sway, unbalanced already by the act of getting off the worktop, his hands coming up to protect himself.

The two of them were together now, seconds after their first sighting of each other. Thea knew what she wanted to do. She needed to get behind him; the problem was he was still backed against the worktop. She needed to spin him around or find a way to move him off the counter, just enough to still be able to reach him but not enough that she couldn't get enough purchase.

The man tried to grab at the towel, his fingers snatching at it, getting a loose grip, but not enough. Thea pulled it away, kicking him in the back of the knee, dropping him down on it. He tried to turn away from her, looking to regroup. She had a towel, nothing more; he would be able to overpower her if he could disentangle himself from her.

A fatal error.

Thea grabbed the towel with both hands now, wrapping it around his neck, her left hand circling over his head, then both hands pulling backwards as she let her body drop behind him, pulling him down.

The impact of the ground and then the man on top of her hurt like hell. Her head rattled on the tiled floor, but she knew she couldn't let go. She wrapped her legs up and around his torso, then pulled the towel tighter, choking him, hearing him gurgle and splutter as the hastily prepared noose bit into his neck. She let the pain wash away, channelling her mind to the job in hand. Tightening her grip. Locking in her muscles. Her arms pulling back further and further as the man squirmed and clawed at the cord around his neck, fighting for his life. She felt his efforts to fight back, felt his fingers pulling at the towel, doing everything he could to free himself, but it wasn't working. Then she felt his right hand move away. She didn't know where it had gone, she just knew it wasn't pulling at the towel anymore.

She pulled tighter, trying to crush his neck, then she looked. His right hand was fiddling in a pouch on his hip, looking for something. A weapon. She loosened the grip on her legs so she might try and pin his arm down, but as she did, he wriggled his body, trying to snake away from her grip, so she tightened it again, her eyes going back to the pouch.

His hand came out and she saw what he had been after. A syringe. He clumsily tried to get the cap off with his fingers, but he was running out of air now; his movements weren't as refined as they should be as his brain started to switch off the functions it didn't need in an effort to stay alive. She watched as he battled, at first in vain, then with success. The black plastic cap on the needle popped off. He went to raise his arm and bring the syringe down into her leg. Thea had no idea what was in there, she just knew she couldn't be injected with it.

His arm came down in an arcing motion. Thea made a judgement call and let go of the towel, swivelling her hips and lifting herself up and off him. The needle scraped her leg, scratching her skin but not breaking it. The man gasped, finally able to breathe again, the air rushing into his body in a moment of triumph. It was to be short-lived. The deep breath made him hesitate. Thea didn't. She didn't have that luxury. She spun around again, facing the man now, her legs behind her. She grabbed his right hand and forced the syringe down into the top of his chest, just below his neck, pushing the top of the plunger.

She looked at his face. His eyes were wide as he looked down at the syringe, then up at her. "Bitch," he gasped, before letting out a deep, guttural groan.

Thea backed away as the man clutched at his chest, his fingers curling up on both hands, his body locking into a foetal position as whatever was in the syringe worked through his body. The groan grew more and more pitiful until it was finally a whimper. Then his body twitched one last time before it was over and there was silence.

Thea sat down next to him, breathing hard. She looked at the man. Trying to place where she knew him from. Then it clicked. The video call Jane had been on with the man who had collected the DNA from Emmie Weston's home. That man was now lying dead on her kitchen floor.

37

If ever there was an unlikely place to store a backup of some of the most confidential data assembled in the world, underneath a spoil tip would take some beating. That it was also placed in the centre of a nondescript Midlands market town also added to the sheer implausible nature of the location. As Jack looked at Mount Judd, he couldn't help but admire the audacity of it as a hiding place.

"I mean, I'd have never guessed, would you?" he asked Adam.

"What? That Nuneaton is currently the home of the largest store of covert intelligence gathered by a private entity in the history of man, or that this thing is also called the Nuneaton Nipple?"

Jack laughed. "Really?"

"Really. Won an award for the UK's best landmark as well."

"Get out."

"That's what happens when you let people vote for things on the internet."

Jack hummed. "I'd vote for it."

"You like nipples?"

"Who doesn't?"

"You are a nipple."

Mount Judd was a little over 500 feet high, although on one side, where it ran down into the quarry below, the slopes ran on for 700 feet. It rose steeply on three sides, with a fourth more gentle slope up which Jack assumed lorries and excavators would have travelled to deposit whatever it was that made up the hill. Jack and Adam were viewing it from the north-west, on the far edge of the quarry. They could see a small scattering of outbuildings around the base of the north slope of the hill. That was where Lowri had said their access point would be. They expected it to be quiet. To be secure. But all the same, there was nothing wrong with being certain.

"Happy?" Adam asked as they looked.

"As I ever will be," Jack replied. He didn't want to say that he wasn't. But there was something that was making him uncomfortable. He hadn't quite been able to put his finger on it yet. But it was there in the back of his brain. The survival instinct that had kept his ancestors alive for generation after generation. It was the reason he'd packed an extra weapon and a couple of extra clips. As he looked down at the entrance to the backup, he knew there was something amiss. He wasn't sure what.

They made their way around the edge of the quarry on a single-file track that wound around the perimeter. A chain-link fence kept anyone safe from the dangers of the quarry. Jack could imagine it being a magnet to teenagers. It would have been to him. The risk-and-reward balance was so great. He could picture himself as a kid climbing the sides of the hill. Not the gentle one that trucks could work their way up. The steeper ones. The ones that had formed as material had rolled off the top. He doubted they would be an easy climb for an amateur. Definitely not for a teenager. He would have loved it. How many local kids had tried the same? He hoped they'd all made it, although in his experience, quarries usually had tragic tales to tell.

Eventually they came to a locked gate. A combination lock. It was a token gesture, of course. Anyone who wanted to get past a chain-link fence would do. But Lowri had been able to give them the passcode and they through the gate itself. Jack wondered if there were likely to be any security guards on duty. Again, they would have to keep up appearances. Especially if they didn't want dead teenagers on their hands. It was an easy route to having your top-secret data hub shut down if you didn't stop kids from getting themselves in trouble. Lowri had been able to issue them with digital IDs that they each had on their phones, which she said would straighten out any issues they might encounter. Jack was still less than convinced. Security guards in places like this didn't know what they were guarding. They wouldn't be as high on protocols as those Lowri was used to dealing with. Things got forgotten. Egos got trampled. It could easily become problematic. Thankfully, they saw no one and they were able to reach the buildings they'd seen unimpeded.

There were three buildings in total. Two smaller ones, not much larger than mid-sized garden sheds. Storage space for whatever might be needed. Jack guessed at first-aid kits, or buoyancy devices in case someone fell in the water that had pooled at the bottom of the quarry. The final building was larger. A temporary hut. The sort of thing that Jack could remember being used as a classroom at schools when he was a kid. Temporary, in that it shouldn't have been there as long as it had been.

This was where the illusion of normality began to shatter. There was a keypad on the door to allow entry. Jack and Adam didn't need that. They needed what was underneath. Pulling the fascia forward from the keypad revealed a hand scanner. Adam had to use it. His details were still on the system. Jack was long since expunged. The scanner not only opened the door, but everything else that they'd need to get into the backup.

They walked into the hut. There was a long plastic table on wall on which sat an urn and an arrangement of mugs. Not that anyone would have been wanting to warm up with a hot drink recently. There was a water butt next to it. A tatty-looking grey sofa sat near another lower table. Probably where security sat and ate lunch or dinner or whatever meal their shift covered. On the other side of the room were metal lockers. Five of them in total. Two hung open, completely empty. The others were closed. None of it was of interest to Adam and Jack. What they wanted was just in front.

Accessing the building via the scanner had also released a hatch in the floor. It was currently rising from the floor. A four-by-four slab, driven up by telescopic metal poles. Underneath was a metal cage. When the floor panelling reached the ceiling, the whole thing came to a stop. A lift that would ferry them to the backup.

"Fancy," admired Adam.

"They spared no expense," Jack agreed.

The two of them squeezed into the lift and Jack regretted his comment. Clearly they could have spent a little more to make it slightly larger. They pulled the door of the cage shut. There was only one control. Two buttons. One with an arrow pointing upwards, the other pointing down. Adam pressed the down button and, with a jolt, they were moving, the roof closing above them as the lift retreated underground.

The lift shaft was lit and Jack was able to estimate by the spacing of the lights that they had gone down twenty feet or so by the time they stopped. He opened the cage door of the lift and they stepped out into a corridor that stretched out ahead of them.

"Not likely to get lost in here," he said. The survival instinct in his brain tingled again, telling him he wasn't likely to get lost, but he could easily get trapped. "Let's get this done quickly," he said.

The corridor was unlike the ones they'd come across in the prison, even if they were back underground again. Metal

287

grates ran underneath and above as power cables led down to the backup. More than one. Redundancy systems. The walls were made of polished metal. He could hear fans pumping air around. A draught circulated, the cold air catching his cheeks and seeping into his fingers. Again, the instinct in his brain spoke up, wishing he'd brought gloves. Something to keep his hands warm. Just in case. He saw his breath condensing in front of him.

"Got to keep your supercomputer nice and cool, I guess," Adam said. Jack saw the goosebumps forming on his arms.

"Bit of a shock to the system."

"You know it. Going to feel hotter than the sun when we do go back topside."

The corridor stretched on for what Jack guessed was nearly a hundred claustrophobic yards. He wondered if this was how submariners felt. Trapped in a tin can, well below the surface. It couldn't be a nice way to live. In all the different operations Jack had done, be it for the military or private contractors, he'd never had reason to find himself on a submarine. Now he felt glad not to have.

The corridor came to an end with a nautical-looking door next to another scanner. This time it was a retinal scan. Adam looked into the camera. A light passed up and down his eye once, then a second pass. There was a momentary pause before a sound of locks being released and the door moved slightly. Jack heaved it open. It was as heavy as it looked. Behind it lay the backup. A carbon copy of the Kernel. Even the layout of the room looked the same.

"I guess they got a discount for keeping the same style," Adam remarked.

"Buy one get one free?" Jack asked.

"Probably not that good."

They had brought two drives with them. Always worth having a redundancy in case something happened to the first drive. Adam inserted the first into the ports next to the computer terminal, then began to work his way through the menus until he found the information he was looking for.

"Right, this thing reckons it's going to take about five minutes to copy across," he announced.

"You'd think they'd have something in here to help pass the time," Jack said, shivering. He thought back to the urn upstairs. "Fancy a brew?"

"Sounds like a plan." Adam smiled. "You want me to get it?"

"Nah, just don't shut the doors and I should be able to get back in."

"What about the lift?"

"I'll leave the door open. Probably got some sort of failsafe in place to ensure it doesn't chew up the mechanism."

"Fair enough. If you don't come back, I'll just meet you topside when I'm done."

Jack left Adam and headed back down the corridor. He was glad when he was back in the lift. The tactical situation down there was less than ideal and whilst there was no reason for them to be interrupted, that side of his brain that had served him so well in the past was still nagging at him to be vigilant. Maybe it was events over the past couple of days. Maybe it was simply being back doing this line of work. It had been a long time, after all.

The lift reached the top and he swung the gate open, leaving it out of place, hoping that would stop the system from retracting. He wandered over to the urn, lifting the lid. There was more than enough water in it to make a couple of drinks, but not so much that it would take too long to boil. He bent down, finding the plug socket and flicking the switch. He heard the urn come to life and the soft but growing sound of the water being heated by the element inside. He picked up two cups and began to look for teabags.

Before he could find them, a car approached.

38

Jack's mind worked quickly. He could have gone back to the lift. He could have pressed the button, ridden it down to the bottom floor and found cover with Adam. But he knew that the car was there for a reason and that whoever was in it knew about the backup. There was no question. Coincidences weren't a thing as far as Jack was concerned. It made for an uncomfortable truth. But Jack would deal with that in time. Right now, he had other problems to deal with. The number of which depended on how many people got out of the car.

Jack looked around the room, working out his best plan of action. The lift was an issue. Ideally he would send it back down. Just in case whoever was about to come in didn't have a way to access it. But that would only be a temporary measure. Adam would have to come up and if he did, he would be the one coming up into a bottleneck. That deep underground, Jack wouldn't be able to send him a message. At least if someone went down in the lift, Adam might have the wherewithal to pay attention and see who it was in time to take cover.

The car was getting closer with every second, but it was on the opposite side of the building to the door. Jack ducked and moved quickly, rushing outside, hoping he wasn't spotted by the occupants of the approaching vehicle.

Around the building there were small thickets of trees and banks of dirt. Perfect cover. Jack was sliding down the far side of one of the banks before the car even stopped. He had time to turn around and watch the men as they got out. Four of them. One for every door. He'd guessed as much.

They fanned out from the car. All of them already had weapons drawn. No chances being taken. They weren't rank amateurs then. Which was a shame. They performed a quick visual check of the location. Jack stayed perfectly still. Ducking would have created movement. Movement attracted the eye. It also meant he wouldn't be able to tell if they'd seen him or not. He'd bet on his reactions being quicker than theirs in that scenario.

They didn't spot him. The bushes provided enough cover. One of them edged back to the car. His shoulders relaxed a little as he did so. He could die last. The other three headed towards the building. They allowed themselves to focus on the door. Banking on the fourth guy to have their backs, even though he was already thinking about getting a tan whilst he waited. Their first real mistakes.

The next mistake was their impatience. Coupled with their confidence. They bunched at the door. One at the scanner. The other two on either side. Concentrating on what was ahead of them. The man working on the scanner knelt as he did so. He would clear out of the way once it was unlocked. The two on either side of the door would burst in, almost instantaneously. One taking one side of the room, his compatriot the other. Only they'd never make it that far.

Right now, they were three unguarded, unaware targets, all nicely bunched together.

Jack eased his pistol into position. He lined up the first shot. Went through the procedure in his head. Take out the guy on the right first, then the kneeling man in the middle, then onto the man on the left. Double tap on each. Less than two seconds. He would arc left, to the car, find the final guy who would be scrambling out of his relaxed position, looking for a target he couldn't see. He'd put two into him last. Over in seconds. Too easy.

Only, the next moment, it wasn't easy.

Jack didn't think he'd made a noise. Didn't think anything had glinted off the metal of his gun. But something had made the man by the car look his way. Perhaps he shared that same animal instinct that Jack had inside him. Perhaps he could almost smell the danger. Pheromones in the air, or something. Jack didn't know. What he did know was that the man had seen him. Or seen enough of something where Jack was. He hollered at his colleagues.

The sound of the shout made Jack want to instinctively turn to face it. He fought the urge. If he turned, he lost the shots he had mapped out. He would be starting from scratch and chances were that when he did, there were going to be bullets flying in his direction. If he wanted to bring the numbers down, he had to stick to the plan for as long as he could.

He fired. The guy on the right. As was the plan. He didn't even have the chance to fully appreciate what it was his partner was shouting about. He was falling to the ground as Jack was already moving onto the second target. The kneeling man. He wasn't kneeling anymore. He was diving for cover. Towards the man who had just fallen, which struck Jack as odd. Perhaps he'd committed to the move before his colleague had been shot. Perhaps he was just nuts. Most people tended to move away from where the bullets were flying.

In this case, however, it saved the kneeling man's life. For now, anyway. Jack found himself aiming at the door. He kept moving. Looking for the next target. Not reversing. Not slowing down. The man who had been on the left-hand side of the door was also scrambling now. Looking for cover. Heading back toward the car and the fourth guy. The one with the instincts. Jack fired. As he did, he heard the sound of gunfire exploding from behind the car. Someone shooting back.

He ducked down behind the cover, hoping he'd re-emerge. Bullets cracked through the treeline. Jack heard a shout of pain. Presumably from the scrambling guy. He'd find out shortly. First, though, he had to move. His angles to the fourth guy were all wrong now. And in Jack's experience, the people who stayed in one place in a gunfight were the ones inviting trouble. Especially when they were outnumbered.

He clambered on his hands and knees through the undergrowth. Four more shots cracked into the treeline behind him. Then a further volley came from a different direction. Almost square on, it sounded like. Presumably from the kneeling guy. Nothing from the guy who'd made a break for it. At least, so it seemed. Maybe he'd pulled himself back to the car. Maybe he was getting strapped up. Stopping the bleeding. Ready to go again.

Another burst of gunfire. The bullets ripped leaves from branches where he had been. He risked a look. The kneeling man was back kneeling. One knee. Gun trained on Jack's old position. The scrambling man was writhing slowly on the floor. He didn't look as if he was getting up. Jack couldn't see enough of the car to spot the fourth man. Nor did he want to wait. Whilst the kneeling man had his eyes elsewhere, he was easy pickings. Jack snapped his gun up into position and fired. Two shots. Then two more. Then he was ducking. He didn't need to wait to see. He knew he'd hit his target. A burst of gunfire came from the direction of the car. Leaves fell on his head. But nothing came from where the kneeling man had been.

One on one. An even fight. Almost.

Jack was still tactically disadvantaged. He was stuck in a rut. Literally. The bank provided cover but it kept him fenced into one area. He couldn't replenish his ammo. He was halfway through already. Who knew how much more the fourth man had access to? Best to assume it was more. Jack had to put something else between them. The building itself seemed as good an idea as any. To get there, though, he'd have to break cover. He hoped that he could move quickly enough to catch his opponent out, but the fourth guy had already shown he had an uncanny instinct and Jack was a big target. It was a risk. But a risk that he had to take. He took a deep breath.

Gun in hand, he leapt over the bank, crashing through the thickets that had hidden him. He didn't stop to look. He kept his head up, looking at where he needed to be. Behind the cabin. Tunnel vision. He didn't want to lose focus. Didn't want to slip or stumble. Waiting for the gunfire to come. Because it had to come. Because the fourth man had to try and take the chance Jack was giving him.

Then it came. When it did, it made Jack realise the mistake he'd made. Of course they'd brought other ammunition with them. He'd thought of that. That's why he was running. But he didn't think about other weapons. Didn't think about semi-automatics until one was firing at him and he was diving for cover. Bullets bit into the wall of the cabin. They scattered dust from the sides of the hill behind them.

"Shit!" Jack gasped, quickly getting back to his feet, continuing to run, not just round that first corner, but the second as well. Now he had a problem. He had a heavily armed opponent on the opposite side of the building. The side of the building with the door down to the backup. If that guy could find a way in, then Jack wouldn't be able to stop him and neither would Adam.

Jack risked a look through the glass. He couldn't see the fourth guy. Either taking cover or making his move. There was no more time to wait. Jack had an obstacle in his way. It was time to get round it.

He jogged backwards five or so yards, holstered his pistol, then ran, leaping as he reached the building, pushing his left foot into the wall, as he did, straightening his left leg to propel him higher. His hands sought out the edge of the roof. He knew the noise would have alerted the fourth man to his intentions, but Jack was now pulling himself onto the roof. His opponent couldn't stop him. Now they were fighting in three dimensions and Jack had the higher ground.

He flattened himself against the roof and waited for a response.

Nothing.

The fourth man wasn't going to be drawn into a rash reaction. He probably figured, as Jack had, that despite its appearance, this building would be reinforced. Bullets weren't going through it. Not the calibre that they had. It meant that they both knew the same thing. The first person to make a mistake dies.

Jack moved slowly, slithering on his belly. He couldn't risk crawling or crouching. He didn't want to be seen. Didn't want to make a noise. He just needed to get into position and be ready for his chance. He turned his body around, facing almost back to where he'd come from. It was a gamble, but he hoped he was going to make it irresistible to the other guy.

Lying on his belly, he reached his right leg out, driving the toe of his boot into the ground. He dragged it slowly, the sound of the roof and boot grating together barely perceptible. But it was there. Then he stopped. Suddenly. He waited. Reached his leg out a little further. Another slight drag. Then he stopped. He repeated the motion three more times. Each time he moved his foot a little further away. As if someone was creeping slowly over the roof towards where his opponent had last been. Taking up a position.

Which was what he knew his opponent would be doing. Only he wouldn't be waiting. Why would he be? Jack knew that this guy was good. He probably thought a little bit like himself. He'd be searching for the same advantage.

The higher ground.

The problem he had was that Jack already had it. He was about to come in second and in this contest, silver medal was awarded six foot under.

To his credit, he must have been wary of Jack's plan. As he stepped into view he had his eyes firmly fixed on the roof of the building. He didn't let his guard down for a single second. But Jack didn't need a single second. The fourth man's head came into sight well before his weapon was high enough to find Jack's. Jack fired. The man fired back.

Dust kicked up around him as bullets bit into the sides of the building. Jack ducked. The angles were on his side, but there was no point being bold. The salvo was short-lived. Jack waited a second then looked. The man was lying crumpled on the floor. Even from here Jack could see the blood pouring from his head.

The kneeling man was also dead, as was the first guy Jack had shot. Scrambling guy was still clinging on. He lay on his back staring at the sky, barely breathing. If you could call it that. It sounded more like gargling as the blood seeped into his lungs. Jack moved slowly towards him. His hands were empty. If they hadn't been, Jack would have shot him again. Put him out of his misery. Better than choking to death on your own blood. He might do it anyway, but first he had to ask him a question.

"Who sent you?" he asked as he stood over the man.

"Fuck you," he spluttered defiantly as blood bubbled around his lips.

Jack stepped around the man, picking up his weapon. "One last time, or I leave you to die slowly."

"Fuck. You."

Jack shook his head. "Your choice."

Jack walked back into the building and finished making the tea. The lift was still there, so he took the two cups down to Adam. He was just packing the two drives away when he reached him.

"You took your time," he said before seeing something in Jack's expression and adding, "What?"

"I think we have a massive problem."

39

His body wasn't what it once was. Hadn't been for a long time. He'd started to get used to that. Even so, as he ended the call, his legs felt even weaker. His arms were trembling. His mouth was dry even if he could taste bile. The hammering of his heart in his chest felt irregular. Misplaced. Like his loyalty. Like his love.

David took a second before he tried to stand. His head spun for a second when he finally did. Lights dancing in his eyes as the blood drained temporarily away then rushed back. His body didn't know where to send it. Didn't know what to do. Neither did his brain. Nothing was making any sense.

He opened the door to his office, making his way down the panelled corridors of the first floor, back to the room where he knew he'd find her. As he walked he told himself he had to be strong. He had to be to the point. He had to know the truth. When he reached the door, he knocked softly and waited for permission to enter.

"David? What's wrong?" Lowri looked up at him from where she was sitting on the bed. Her head was in her hands, her expression blank, the colour that had been coming back had drained away. The croakiness in her voice told him that she knew exactly what was wrong.

"Why?" he said, the question sounding like a soft wail.

She placed her head in her hands again and cried. That was his signal to move to her. He wrapped an arm around her and consoled her. They could work this out. They could find a way to undo what she'd done. He just needed to know what exactly she'd done. She pushed her head into his chest. She was scared. Lowri didn't do scared.

"What happened?" he asked.

She sobbed and pulled away from him. "I couldn't say no anymore. I couldn't do it."

"Do what?"

"I was in there, that place. And I couldn't be any more. I wanted it over."

"You made a deal to be released?"

She shook her head.

"What then?"

"I… that place. It's impossible to survive it. I knew I was dying in there. I made my peace with it. I embraced it. I tried to end it. But I couldn't. There's no way to kill yourself. They lock you to the wall. They force you to eat. They keep you alive. Any way they can. Doesn't matter if they're forcing things into you. They're not going to let you take the easy way out. And in the end I just couldn't go on. I begged them to kill me. I pleaded." She looked up at him mournfully. "And they agreed."

"But we saved you," he said firmly. "We got there in time. They didn't kill you. No one blames you for talking. What you went through, it was inhuman. Anyone would have talked."

"No," she shook her head. "You didn't save me. You did what they wanted. They made sure people knew where I was. People who would tell you. They knew you'd come for me. I gave them what they wanted."

"What did they want?"

"The backup. If they couldn't get the Kernel, they wanted that and to get it they needed access. They didn't want to use one of the prisoners they picked up from the raid. Someone decides to be a hero, enter the wrong code, the whole thing goes to hell. They wanted someone who had a reason to be there and they wanted to intercept them."

"It's okay," David felt his spirits rise. "Jack and Adam, they survived. Took out the team sent to get them."

Lowri laughed and looked away and David smiled and hugged her. It was going to be okay.

"Then we die for nothing," she sighed.

* * * *

The force of the blast had thrown Reuben backwards. He couldn't tell how far. The last thing he remembered was making his way up the steps towards the front door. Now, there was no front door. There was no building at all. Just rubble, fire and smoke.

He tasted blood in his mouth. He spat. There wasn't a lot. He hoped that meant he wasn't bleeding out from the inside. Not in his lungs at least. He went to rise, but pain shot from his leg in protest. Looking down, he saw why. A shard of the door had impaled itself through his thigh. In through the front, out through the back. The point at the front higher than at the rear.

"Fuck!" he hollered at the sky, his head dropping down, his fists slamming the floor in frustration.

He couldn't wallow. He had to get up. He was alive. Others might be. Somehow. He needed to help them.

The wound around his thigh didn't look to be pissing blood out, but all the same, he took his belt, tightening it around the top of his leg as a makeshift tourniquet. He pulled it as tight as he felt he could bear, then forced himself to go even tighter.

Satisfied he'd done the best he could to stem the wound, he dragged himself to his feet. In front of him, the remnants of the house were laid out like a jumbled pile of Lego. One chimney stack remained where it had been part of the east wall. It looked to Reuben as if it was swaying but he couldn't be certain that wasn't just him. He grunted and hobbled up the steps he'd been climbing just as the explosion hit.

When he reached the top he saw the crater. A large depression in the middle of the debris field. The centre was almost free of rubble, ejected away by the blast, save where some parts had tumbled back down the slope. Water was already pooling, rising up from a broken pipe somewhere amidst the wreckage. The smell of gas hit him first. Had a main burst? He heard the hiss of something escaping to his left. Saw flame licking from a pipe. He moved right. The further he walked, the more the smell of gas subsided. He could taste metal. There was an acrid burning smell that he couldn't describe and didn't recognise.

"Anyone there?" he called.

The pipe hissed its reply. Everything else remained silent.

"Hello?" he called again, swearing to himself when no one responded.

He moved off again over the rubble, watching each footstep, looking for some sign of life; anything. The bricks below him cracked and chattered as they moved against each other. The pain in his leg grew and grew. It was impossible to keep his balance and he slipped, landing on the rubble, which moved as he came down on it.

He was about to stand when he heard another noise. A new noise. At first he thought it was someone pounding on something. A door. But there were no doors still standing. He looked skywards. He couldn't see it, but he could hear it. A helicopter. All the pieces came together as his mind cleared. This wasn't an accident. How could it have been?

Someone had attacked them. Now they were coming to clean up the survivors.

"Oi!" he hollered. "We got to get the fuck out of here."

He listened. The thumping grew nearer. Somewhere stones slipped and moved. It took a second for him to register the noise as something he should be listening out for. He went to spring to his feet, excitement wiping out the pain momentarily, only for it to come back with a bite as weight went onto his leg. He couldn't sit down again. Not if someone was alive.

"Hello? Someone there?" he shouted.

Another noise. More stones moving. Maybe a voice or a groan. He thought he knew roughly where it was coming from. He scrambled on hands and knees, his right leg half trailing, half crawling behind him. A token gesture, but not completely useless. He saw her hand first. Poking out of the rubble, fingers spread and pointing as she waved.

"You okay?" he called, grabbing the hand, not knowing whose it was. Emmie? Meg? Lowri?

"Help me," a voice called out. Whoever it was sounded barely with it and sapped of energy as if the effort of waving had taken more out of them than it should have done.

"Hold on," he called, pulling desperately at the material around it. It didn't take long to make a hole big enough that he could see Emmie's face. She was grey, caked in dust and plaster from the collapsing building. Her eyes were open and she focused on him.

"Are you stuck?" he asked.

"No. Some sort of pocket." She'd got lucky, but they could talk about her fortune later. Reuben didn't say anything else, just heaved as much as he could as quickly as he could, widening the hole. He never stopped to think about what might happen if he pulled the wrong piece out. The sound of the helicopter was getting louder.

The hole was large enough now for Emmie to pull herself out. He gave her his hand and between the two of them they got her out onto the rubble. Physically she looked remarkably unhurt, but he could see her eyes drifting in and out of focus. Just concussion, hopefully. But if something heavy had hit her on the head or the pressure wave of the blast had found a sweet spot, who knew.

"You're going to need to help me here, my leg's seen better days," Reuben tried to keep it light. He couldn't tell if Emmie had heard the chopper. He didn't want to add another thing for her to think about. He could see she was struggling with that, even as she nodded her agreement.

Together, they clambered back across the debris, away from the front of the house, towards the rear garden and the woods behind. There was an outhouse there. It had a weapons cabinet secured inside. If they were going to have to make a fighting escape, or even a last stand, Reuben wanted to be prepared.

It was easier going once they were off the ruins of the house. As they made their way across the garden, the helicopter came directly over their heads at about fifty feet.

"In the trees," Reuben leaned into Emmie, steering her to their left and the trees that ran along the wall of the garden. They disappeared into the foliage as the helicopter spun over the house, landing gear extending. Reuben couldn't tell if they'd been seen, but he didn't want to hang around. Whoever it was wasn't on a rescue mission.

There was a gate that took them out of the compound into the woods. It had a keypad lock that Reuben hoped would slow down anyone following them. Closing the gate, he heard the whine of the helicopter as it landed and the pilot powered the engines down. Had they really not seen them? The helicopter had come in low, fast and right on top of them. They could have been in the blind spot.

"We need to keep moving," he said, as much to himself as Emmie. There was no time for hoping or complacency.

They found the outhouse a few minutes later. Reuben hopped to the cabinet where the guns were kept whilst Emmie sat down on a table and watched. Reuben got them both a couple of pistols and turned to her. When she looked at him he could see the absence in her eyes.

"There's a gamekeeper's lodge about a half mile from here. He keeps a car there for us, for situations like this. Won't take us long, but you are going to have to help me get there."

Emmie blinked and looked at him. "What happened?"

"I don't know."

She nodded and looked down.

"Hey, come on," he placed his hand under her chin and lifted it up so she looked at him. "We need to stay alive. We need to get to that car. Can you drive it if we do?"

"I…" she shrugged. At least she was being honest.

He offered her his hand, pulling her to her feet. She nodded back at him as if she was trying to get that focus back, which he hoped counted for something.

"Well, let's deal with that when we get there. Jesus, we're a fucking pair."

40

Police statements were an arduous thing when you were taking them. Thea had just finished giving hers and was of the opinion now that the latter was far worse. At least the officer doing the questioning didn't already know the story. Thea had replayed the attack on her over and over again in her head whilst she'd waited for the police to arrive. Now, as the body of her attacker was being bagged up by the undertaker, her story had been committed to paper. The officer at the scene had told her he was sure that someone would be in touch to talk to her in more detail. Thea had said she "couldn't wait". The officer had shrugged as if to say, "What do you want me to do?" then left her alone in the room.

Not that she was alone for long. Within seconds, Jane Astley, who she knew had been loitering in the house waiting for her moment, was with her.

"Wondering if you should expect a visitor of you own?" Thea asked as Jane idly looked around her kitchen, hands in her pockets.

"Sleep with one eye open and all that?"

"Don't expect to be doing much sleeping till this is done now. We're proper fucked, aren't we?"

Jane sighed. "Not necessarily."

Thea shook her head. She couldn't believe that Jane was already trying to spin this to make it into some kind of advantage. "With all due respect, Jane, someone just tried to kill me. Someone who works for us, supposedly. And I don't know who sent them."

"I hope I'm not reading between the lines there. Because, correct me if I'm wrong, *we* don't know who sent them."

"I only ever saw this guy once. That was when you were tasking him to break into Emmie Weston's house."

"We called him Morris. I don't know his real name," Jane sighed. "He's our go-to for jobs that require a certain level of stealth and a certain level of coldness, should the need arise."

"An assassin. I figured that bit out already."

"My point is, he's not just my bad bastard. A lot of people use him and, I'll be honest, if you want to carry this conversation on, one of is going to end up saying something they really regret, and believe me, it's not going to be me."

Thea shook her head. "There are certain levels in life you can find yourself at and the level we're at least hovering dangerously close to is 'proper fucked'. I mean, I almost got injected to death with God knows what."

"Yeah, but you didn't though." There was some inflection in Jane's tone that made the comment sound blasé. Disarming. There was only one reason for that.

"What *did* you do?"

"I had a theory. And I was right. Two in fact. The second being that you'd be okay. And that was less of a theory, more of a fact, if you like, because here we are."

"You fucked me over?" There may have been numerous police officers in the building, but Thea knew already that if she wanted to get to Jane and inflict some real damage, she could do. It was tempting. For now, though, she left the menace in her voice. Jane didn't seem to notice the danger she was in.

"Clearly not," she shrugged. "I fed some information out. Pointed it in the right direction. Waited to see who took the bait."

"What information?"

"Well, believe it or not, it turns out your clandestine meeting with Jack Quinn was less clandestine than you might have hoped. People knew that you were in cahoots with him. You were there with Cartwright and Pegg. You know that they know. I had to do something that first and foremost covered my arse and secondly drew out anyone who might be playing the other side. So, I said that you'd been handed a drive with information on it. They love things like that."

"You didn't think it was worth warning me?"

"No." Jane said bluntly. "For a couple of reasons. Mainly because I didn't know who was watching me. It had to be convincing if they were going to go for the bait. And, like I said, I believed you'd be able to deal with whatever they threw at you. Admittedly, I didn't think they'd go for something like this. Although I do admire it. I imagine toxicology is going to show nothing amiss in his blood work. If it wasn't for the fact you stuck him with his own needle, I assume his death will look natural. As would yours. Fascinating."

"Well, that's reassuring to know that I would have been murdered and no one would have been any the wiser."

"I would have been wiser. I would have known and you wouldn't have died in vain. Anyway, let's stop talking about hypotheticals. It didn't happen. It's not worth getting bent out of shape over."

"Bent out of shape?"

"Whatever you want to call it. This was the best course of action so I took it and it worked like a dream. When your response is one that's less emotional and more about the bigger picture, you're going to see it for what it was."

"A masterstroke?" Thea asked indignantly.

"It's on that level, yes. Whoever opened the file I created regarding your meeting with Quinn set off a trojan that revealed the device they were using. It was then a case of cross-referencing whose system had accessed it. Guess who came up?"

"Cartwright and Pegg."

"Both of them."

"So now what do we do?"

"We need to reconvene with you know who."

"The Regulators?" Thea said in a hushed voice in case anyone was watching or listening. Jane gave a half nod.

"Although there might be a bit of a problem with that," Jane added.

"What do you mean?"

"David Warner and Lowri Graves are dead."

"What? How?"

"They're calling it a gas explosion on the news. The fact that it's on the news means they're bragging about it. They want everyone to know what they've done."

Thea sighed. "What about Jack? Adam? Has anyone heard from them?"

"Nothing yet. Five bodies have been recovered so far, but only two have been named."

Thea felt her heart sink. If the others had been killed then it was over. There was nothing they could do. Whatever was happening would happen and they wouldn't even know where to look until it was too late.

"I need to try and call him," she said taking out her phone.

"You can't," Jane put her hand on Thea's, stopping her from dialling the number. "If they came for you and failed, you can be sure they're listening to you as well."

Thea went to pull away. "Bollocks to them, they can listen all they want."

"And where will it get any of us?" Jane held her arm even tighter. "Jail? Dead? Stuck in a hole in the ground? Forgive me for passing on all of those."

"So what do we do?"

"The only thing we can do now. If Jack's still alive, we let him do his own thing. In the meantime, we go after the ones who paid your sparring partner out there. Then we take them down."

Thea looked at Jane who returned the stare. She knew her boss was right. There was little point arguing. If any of the Regulators were left, they were best left to their own devices now. Jack had a plan. Those who remained, if any, would be enacting it. She had to trust the process. Even if it was hard to push back the need to know if anyone had made it. If the death toll stayed at five, someone had to have done.

41

"Stay safe." Adam hung up.

Reuben had sounded beat up. Shaken up as well. Adam had done his best to help the two of them. There were certain safe houses dotted around the country where they would be able to go, get looked after, get a sympathetic doctor to pay a visit. It wouldn't be ideal. Probably wouldn't be the sort of treatment it sounded as if the two of them needed. Reuben was dealing with a chunk of wood embedded in his leg. God knows what damage that would do by the time he got some place safe. Removing it would be fraught with danger. Then there was the risk of infection. If Reuben still had both his legs by this time next week, Adam would call that a minor win. As for Emmie, it was harder to say. Head injuries always were. He hoped it was nothing. He didn't want to think about anything else.

He looked at Jack and shrugged. They had parked the car in a small car park next to a nature reserve one town over from where they'd retrieved the data from the backup. For a moment they sat in silence, staring straight ahead at the woods. Adam couldn't help but feel it was somehow apt.

"Best get cracking then," he said.

The plan had been to take the data back to Kent, but they had a second option. There always had to be a second option.

In the boot of the car Adam found a laptop. He took it into the passenger side where he'd been seated and turned it on. It didn't take long to load. The computer was relatively new and the programs installed on it were only the essentials required for the role. Nothing on there that would slow it down.

"Let's see what we get." Adam plugged the drive in. There was a whirring from the device as it came to life then a new window popped up on the screen containing a single, solitary file named Dead Line.

Adam opened it. He expected it to be full of reams of information. Different files. Different operation logs from work carried out by the Regulators over the years. There was none of that. Just one simple .TXT file.

"Is it broken?" Jack asked.

Adam shook his head. "Shouldn't be."

"Why the hell did it take so long to copy?"

"Damned if I know." Adam was already opening the file.

When it opened, there was a list of names. Adam began to scan through them.

"Who do you think these are?" he asked. None of the names so far were ringing any bells. There weren't many. His laptop began to whine as the fan kicked in. Some memory-intensive process was happening. Then the text file disappeared.

"What did you do?" Jack asked.

"I don't know." Adam pulled down the lid of the laptop, looking to where the drive had been connected. It was still flush in the slot. "Doesn't look like a loose connection."

"Useless," Jack scolded, probably only half meaning it. "Get it back up."

Adam opened a new browser window. The drive wasn't showing. "Ah shit," he said, guessing what had happened.

"What did you do?"

"I don't think it was me." Another window opened. This one was looking for any sign the drive was connected. It was. But the data was gone. "Fucking thing is self-deleting."

"What good is that to us then?"

"Hold on." Adam had a plan. He unhooked the now worthless drive before reaching into the glove compartment for the second one. "You want to get your camera phone ready?"

"Gotcha." Jack reached into his pocket, picking up on what Adam wanted to do.

"Get it filming, not a photo. That way you know it's running before it comes on."

"Yeah, will do." Jack was tapping at the screen of his phone. "Go for it."

Adam breathed in, then held his breath as he connected the second drive. The browser window returned. The same file name as before. He didn't hesitate. Double-clicked on it and waited. The file opened. The names appeared. The laptop began to whine again. Seconds later, it was gone.

"You'd better have got that," Adam said exhaling.

"I got it, chill your beans," Jack laughed, showing Adam his phone. There it was; a video of the names. All of them on the screen. "I'll send you a copy."

The two of them looked at the list. The document didn't say who the people were. Adam knew though. These were the In Statera. The people culpable for whatever happened when the Dead Line was tripped. Most of the names meant nothing to him. One stood out.

"Jesus Christ," he sighed.

"What?"

"The name."

"Which one."

"John Norman."

"I don't know him."

"You should. He just became the prime minister." There was a moment as they processed it before Adam asked, "What do we do with this?"

"We need to strengthen our hand. Tell Thea. It's just you and me versus the British government otherwise."

"It feels like a fair fight."

"All the same."

"Fine. I think we should bring Marshall in as well."

"From the *Inquirer*? Why?"

"Because if anyone is going to be able to work behind the scenes and piece together whatever it was Nathan Nelmes was onto, it's either going to be him or someone who works for him."

"Do you think we can trust him?"

"I don't know. But I do know I trust him more than I trust Five not to screw us."

"Thea's different."

"She might be, but she still does things by the book. More so than us, anyway."

"Fine. You tell Marshall. I'll speak with Thea."

Adam could tell that Jack liked the situation about as much as he did. Neither of them had ever expected it would come to this.

42

"Good evening. Britain faces the gravest threat to its security in over eighty years. We stand on the precipice of a war with a seemingly invisible enemy that wishes to strike at us at times and places of their choosing."

"Well, that's dramatic," Jane tutted as she watched the broadcast of the new prime minister making his emergency address to the nation.

"Never before have we faced an enemy like this. Never before has someone been so brazen as to believe that they can attack the very foundations of our democracy, to take the lives of those elected to serve you, the people. Never before have we had to react in the ways we are going to."

Thea tensed at that. There had been no briefing ahead of Norman's speech. No one knew what was coming. Not a single leak. He had taken few meetings and with a select number of people. She had wondered if his mind had been made up on his course of action long before this speech was written.

"Under Article 15 of the European Convention on Human Rights, I have sought to notify the courts that oversee your liberty, your very freedom, that due to the very real threat to our nation, I will be suspending normal parliamentary operations. I have informed the King that Parliament will be prorogued with a provisional return date of April of next year, at which point a general election will be called."

"That's nearly ten months. That's unheard of," Jane said. "That'll never fly."

As if he was answering her, Norman went on. "The King, the Cabinet and most importantly, the Leader of the Opposition have all agreed on this framework, reluctantly. We aim to conclude the necessary operations required to end this madness that has gripped our country for the last few years and end it decisively. When this is all done, we will return it to you, the rightful owners of our great nation, to once again elect your Parliament. A Parliament of the people. Free from outside interference. Free to return Britain to its rightful position as a global leader. We're about to undergo a major surgery. We need to cut this cancer out. It will be strange for me, as a politician, to not face the rigours of parliamentary process. But for you, the people, the change will be minimal. Your life will be allowed to carry on as it should do, until the storm passes. Then, together, we will rejoice in the return of our sovereignty."

Norman nodded at the camera as he ended his speech and the feed was cut.

"Well, holy shit," Jane said. "We live in an elective dictatorship now."

"Is it that bad?" Thea asked. She wasn't really sure she understood half of what had just been said.

"Parliament has never been suspended. Not like this. We've prorogued it. We've had longer sessions without elections.

We've never had a government operating without oversight for this long."

"Is it even legal then?"

"Damned if I know. I guess someone has told them that it is. And I can imagine that any sort of challenge to it will take longer than ten months to bear any fruit. Promise of an election at the end. If it ends."

"If it ends?"

"Well, why do this? To what end?"

"What did Jack say? That the people behind all this need to make some course corrections. That the country had got away from them. The power that they enjoyed had been diluted. Norman's job is to stop Parliament doing anything drastic for a year. In that time, they'll buy up who they need to, set up whatever systems they need so they can control more MPs and so on. Get rid of some of the more idealistic ones. This is them putting their hand back on the wheel."

"Is it bad?"

"Only if you like your constitutional democracy free from corruption."

"Fair enough."

* * * *

Thea had considered not going back to her flat. Obviously, there was something to be said for being somewhere that no one expected her to be. But there was also something to be said for sticking two fingers up at those who wanted her dead. Showing them that she wouldn't be cowed. She also believed that it was unlikely that Pegg and Cartwright would make another move so soon. They'd be worried about any potential exposure from their last attempt. Now they would be regrouping. Biding their time and concocting a plan that would continue to keep eyes off them. Both she and Jane figured that would take them a little bit of time. So maybe tonight she'd be able to sleep.

It was only when she approached her flat and saw the living room light on that she realised that wasn't going to be likely. She regretted not taking up Jane's offer to supply her with a firearm. Thea was firearms-accredited but she hated using them. Hated having them on her. It made her feel more vulnerable. You were more likely to be in a gunfight if you had a gun. Right now, she wondered if it would at least be a little comforting. At least whoever had turned the light on wanted her, or anyone else, to know they were there. That had to count for something.

The door was still locked when she got to it. The windows at the front of the house looked secure. She took a deep breath and entered.

"Hello?" she called out.

No response. Not great.

She walked through the hallway, into her living room. Jack Quinn was sitting on her sofa.

"Evening."

"I should have known," Thea shrugged. "How are you?"

"Shit."

"I figured. I'm sorry."

"It is what it is. We all knew the risks. David and Lowri especially. Probably wrote the risk assessment for it."

"All the same."

"All the same." Jack looked sad. There was no escaping it. His shoulders were sunken. The bravado and arrogance that usually accompanied him were gone. Thea saw before her a man who was sick of it all.

"What now?" she asked.

"Now we go after them all."

"You know who they are?"

"I have a list. I need you to furnish me with the details of everyone on it. Obviously I've not got access to the sort of database I once did. Once we've got it, we'll do the rest."

"Define 'the rest'."

"No. You don't want me to do that. You just need me to do it."

"Don't patronise me, Jack. Don't pretend that I don't know what's happening. Don't pretend that you not saying it makes the blindest bit of difference to my conscience or my implication. You think I'm stupid? You think a judge hearing our case would be stupid enough to believe your tacit omission of what you're going to do means I'm innocent? Stop trying to fucking protect everyone by shouldering it all and get to the fucking point. This isn't just your fight. We're all in it. I had to fucking kill a guy in this flat this morning."

"Oh."

"Yeah, fucking oh. So cut the crap and tell me what you're going to do."

"I'm going to find them. I'm going to make them tell me what they've done. Then I'm going to kill them. All of them."

"How many of them are there?"

"Thirteen."

"A baker's dozen."

"Shouldn't take me too long."

"I am glad that you're efficient in the areas of torturing and killing."

"It's a skillset you never really lose."

"Shame for you."

"It really is." Jack looked at her. "Why are you so angry at me?"

"You think I'm angry at you? I'm angry at a hell of a lot of things right now. Not everything begins and ends with Jack Quinn."

"Yeah, but me specifically. Right here, right now, why are you angry at me?"

"Because you came in here talking as if hurting these people and killing these people doesn't matter."

"Does it?"

"It should do."

"But does it?"

"Yes. It matters to me. I hate it. This isn't how the world is supposed to work."

"What do we do then?"

"Put them on trial. Send them to jail. Strip their assets."

"That last one might hurt them," Jack agreed. "How do you propose we do it?"

"With due process."

"Got any evidence you'd like to submit to the CPS?"

Thea shook her head.

"Would you trust them to stand before a judge if you did?"

"Yes," Thea lied. Jack said nothing. Thea knew that he had seen through her. In truth she'd not really tried to be convincing. "Fuck's sake, why can't anyone just play by the rules?"

"They play by the rules. The problem is that they write them. Make them up as they go along. That's what this is now. Stop anyone playing the game whilst they get their deck in order."

"And I'm trying to work out if that's so bad," Thea explained.

"Maybe there's a deeper discussion about sovereignty that we could go into, if they hadn't left a trail of bodies to cover up what they're doing. But this is where we are. They pushed too hard. Now we need to stop them."

Jack was right. Of course he was. Nathan Nelmes had died and he didn't deserve to. The people working at the *Daily Inquirer* had died and didn't deserve to. They were innocents in all of this. Just doing their jobs or trying to find the truth. They'd paid with their lives and the law had no way of finding those responsible.

"What if we could put them on trial?" Thea asked desperately. "What if we found the evidence. Now we have their names, we can dedicate resources to this. We've uncovered the people working against us at Five. We're on the front foot. We can stop them."

"One of them is John Norman. Think you might have heard that he just got a promotion."

"Ah, shit the bed. Let me get my laptop." Thea sighed. She had no fight left in her. No energy to even be remotely surprised that, actually, the person who was at the top of all of this was now the prime minister. After what she had heard earlier, it made perfect sense.

It took only a matter of minutes for Thea to have her laptop up and running and working through the list of names. A pattern emerged very quickly.

"They're dead."

"Not all of them," Jack said. Three remained. The others had all died. Recently as well. None in circumstances that the authorities would call suspicious, but they wouldn't have been looking at them as a group.

"What's the succession plan?" Jack added.

"How do you mean?"

"Well, this group has existed for generations. People in the families have continued the tradition. Stands to reason that the torch would have been passed in some if not all of these cases. Sons and daughters would have been prepared for this moment, to assume the mantle."

Thea was already scrawling through more data. "Looks like someone thought about that. At least to a degree. Two of the men died in the same plane crash alongside their families. Wiped them out. Another saw his only son jailed for his part in a Ponzi scheme, then took his own life. I mean, if someone wanted to send a message to anyone else thinking about taking over the family business…"

"Then I would assume anyone left decided not to get involved. Jesus. This doesn't make any sense though. This was supposed to be the In Statera wrestling back control."

"Looks like someone is wrestling control from them."

"John Norman."

"He certainly looks to be the man," Thea agreed, even if she was still uncertain.

"What?" Jack must have heard the hesitancy in her voice.

"I don't know. I don't feel it's safe to assume anything anymore. Norman might be calling the shots. But what about the other two? What if he's trying to buy himself time? Make one last desperate grab."

"We're already down one PM. I don't think these people are idealists in the sense that they'd nobly sacrifice themselves for the greater good. This was always about greed. Either Norman thinks he can win this battle with whoever is taking them out, or he's in on it. Same with the other two. We need to know."

Thea brought up the remaining names. "John Norman's not someone you're going to be able to ask easily. That leaves you with either Alistair Ramsey or Victor Clarke. Ramsey is a former communications magnate. His family made their money in radios and telegrams in the first half of the twentieth century. Now he collects a pretty penny earning interest and waiting to die in the House of Lords."

"Of course he does. What about Clarke?"

"Clarke is more of an enigma."

"How do you mean?"

"His presence is there. Worked in finance and technology. Made his money in the seventies and eighties. Plenty of articles on him." Thea pulled up a couple of magazine-style interviews with a tall, thin man with a shaped goatee that got greyer as his hairline slipped backwards and the articles got more recent. "But before that, there's little. His family history isn't there like the others. He's only ever done a handful of media as well. There're two or three interviews with him at best."

"The cuckoo in the nest."

"You think?"

"He doesn't fit the profile of the others. Of what we know the In Statera to be. He feels false. He's the one I want."

"And when you get him?"

"We'll get acquainted. See how he wants this thing to end. It's his choice."

Thea didn't ask what the choices were. She didn't imagine Clarke was going to enjoy them. "I suppose it's pointless asking you if you want me to tag along."

"You don't want to be where I am," Jack shook his head. She was a little relieved.

"In that case, I'm going to talk to Norman."

"To Norman?"

"I reckon I'm owed a favour." Thea thought about Jane putting her in harm's way. It was a bit of a reach, but if anything was going to prove that Jane really was on their side, she figured a security briefing on the ongoing threat with the new PM was something she could argue for at the very least.

"Hell of a favour."

"I took a hell of a risk. Apparently."

"You sound less than impressed."

"I am. But I'll get over it."

43

Jane hadn't liked Thea's request. She'd outright refused at first. Even when Thea pointed out that Jane had in fact almost got her killed, Jane resisted, but less so. In the end, she'd put the request in for a briefing. More out of politeness than expectation, Thea assumed. But within an hour, the request had been granted. Jane had been surprised. Thea less so. If Norman was in on this, he knew who they were. He wouldn't want to pass up the opportunity to see them. To find out what they knew.

"Then it's going to be a mistake to see him," Jane had said when Thea explained her theory. "We can't tell him what we know, or we risk giving the game away. We can't tell him a pack of lies either, because that would be bloody obvious and again, we'd tip our hand."

"We best find somewhere bang in the middle then."

* * * *

Thea didn't find many situations intimidating. Meeting the prime minister at the Houses of Parliament was one of the few exceptions. As they cleared security, the buildings loomed up around her, enclosing her in the courtyard as they walked to the entrance they had been designated. There were more checks before they were allowed entry into the building itself. It felt more secure than Glasshouse Seven had. But then this place didn't rely on being hidden to survive. This was the very face of British democracy.

They were met by a civil servant who quickly took them up a stairwell away from any of the main areas, heading up to the second floor of the building. The top floor. The ceilings were high and the building immaculately decorated. Panelling ran along the lower half of the walls, whitewashed paint the upper. Dark wooden benches filled the gaps between the doors to each room, allowing anyone who had to wait before entering to rest easily should they need to. There were no windows in the corridor; panel lights above them lit their way. He pointed out where the Speaker's House and Black Rod were situated, both at either ends of the corridor. They headed in the direction of the Speaker's House, stopping just short. The civil servant beckoned for them to take a seat on the wooden benches either side of a thick-looking oak door. Then he was gone and Thea and Jane were alone in the building.

"I expected it to be busier," Thea said.

"Normally we don't come here," Jane replied. "Most of the business gets done at Number 10. I guess he's got a few bits and bobs to do in the House today. Show some face to the cameras and all that. Given that he's effectively closed down democratic scrutiny, I assume he's been told that he needs to be seen to be doing the job."

"I can teach him a thing or two about not being seen."

Jack's voice made them both jump. Thea stood up, getting into his face.

"What the fuck are you doing here?"

"Taking a meeting with the prime minister."

"How the hell did you get in? Jesus. There are cameras everywhere. Your face is going to be setting off all sorts of alarms."

"Then we best get moving." He hammered on the door. From inside came a confused-sounding "Hello".

"Sounds like he's in," Jack said, opening the door before Thea could stop him.

* * * *

"What the hell is going on?"

Norman was standing. He'd have pressed a panic button by now. The moment the door had opened, in fact. Which meant there was no time for hesitation.

Jack stepped forward, feeling Thea and Jane watching him as he did so. Neither of them had reacted yet. He was banking on the fact they wouldn't. They knew the stakes and now they were here, confronted with a simple choice, he had gambled that they would side with him. All the same, he had to make it look convincing. For their sakes. He placed one hand on the scruff of Norman's jacket. Jane made a noise, somewhere between a yelp and a shout but Jack ignored her. He reached into his pocket, pulling out a packet of gum.

"See this?" he pushed the gum up towards Norman's face so there could be no doubt that he could quite clearly see it. "This isn't gum. It's cyanide. One word out of you, I shove one of these into your mouth and make your chew it. You'll be dead in seconds."

It didn't matter that it was a lie. Jack saw the fear in Norman's face. Fear meant he believed him.

"What the hell are you doing?" Thea asked angrily, which was good.

"Me and Mr Norman are going to go for a little ride. You guys are welcome to join me, or you can stay here. I'll deal with our problem."

"How, Jack?" Thea asked.

Jack ignored her. He took out his phone. The number was ready on speed dial. "We're a go," he said as the line was picked up. Adam was on the other end. He didn't need to reply. He just had to do his part.

"Don't do anything stupid," Jane warned, even though she wasn't doing anything to stop Jack.

"Probably a bit late for that," Jack shrugged.

He pushed Norman towards the door, opening it himself as they reached it.

"Not a word," he warned him again, placing his arm firmly on Norman's as they stepped out into the corridor.

"You'll be dead in seconds," Norman said. If it was meant to come out as a threat, then any malice or energy was lost and the words sounded flat and lacking in belief.

"So will you," Jack replied.

"Wait." Jack turned his head. Thea shook hers. "Fuck's sake. I'm coming with you."

"You sure?"

"Someone needs to be the voice of reason."

Jack didn't have an objection to that. It might serve to keep Norman quiet, if he felt he had an ally. "We need to move," Jack said.

They stepped out into the corridor. Mercifully, it was still deserted.

"This way," Jack forced Norman to face the direction he wanted him to go, towards Black Rod's chamber.

Norman shook as he walked, Jack could feel the man's arm quivering in his grip. He wondered if the prime minister was going to faint. Walking together already looked conspicuous, carrying him on his shoulder would look even worse.

"There's a door leading to a staircase just before we reach the end," Jack leaned into Norman's ear. "When we get there, take it."

"To the roof?" Norman's voice quivered.

"To the roof," Jack echoed.

The world slowed down as they walked. Every step took forever. Was this what it was like walking on the moon? Trying so hard to get somewhere, but seeming to take forever? Jack listened for the noise of footsteps coming, of armed police looking to intercept them. There had to be cameras in the corridor. People had to be wondering what was going on, seeing the three of them marching like this. There was no way that alarms weren't being triggered, either physically, or in people's heads.

"Quicker," Jack urged, pushing Norman forward, forcing him into a semi-trot.

They were nearly there now. Twenty yards at most. Then ten.

"Stop!" a voice called out from behind them.

"Run," Jack pushed Norman once more. He didn't look back. Whoever it was couldn't shoot. The prime minister was too close to them. He hoped Thea had the sense to keep up.

Norman reached the door first. Jack grabbed him, stopping him from opening it himself. He spun Norman around so that his body was now between Jack and the voice of whoever had called to them. He didn't look back. He didn't need to. It was armed police.

"Stop or I'll fire." More hollow instructions that would never be followed through.

Jack ignored them. He pulled Thea past him and through the door first, then stepped in himself, dragging Norman through like a rag doll last.

A set of stairs greeted them. Thea was already running up them, Jack followed, keeping Norman behind him.

"Don't go through when you open the door until you know it's time," Jack called to Thea.

"How will I know it's time?" she called back.

"You'll know," he replied.

Thea reached the door and slammed into it, letting it burst open. She crouched down to one knee. Jack stumbled up behind her.

"What are we doing up here?" Thea asked.

Before Jack could answer, the door below them crashed open.

"Stay where you are!" came the voice again. Jack saw shadowy figures racing up the stairs, dressed in smart suits, guns drawn.

"Help!" Norman squealed.

Come on! Jack urged Adam silently. He didn't want to spend the rest of his life in jail.

The figures were getting closer.

Time was running out.

Where was he?

A loud clatter rang out over their heads as a dark-grey helicopter swooped up from the Thames, over the roof.

"Go!" Jack shouted over the sound.

Thea ran out of the door, Jack came behind her, hauling Norman along with him. Norman struggled to keep up, stumbling and tripping as the downdraught whipped dirt and debris from the roof, forcing them to shield their eyes.

The helicopter spun around sharply in front of them, then circled behind them, putting itself between them and the door they'd just come out of. The side door opened as it settled just feet above the roof. Jack saw Adam hanging out of the door, his hand extended to help them in.

Thea got there first, Adam grabbing her forearm and pulling her in. Seconds later Jack was bundling Norman in as he clambered up himself, arms grabbing at him, helping him up as he went. He wasn't sure if it was Thea or Adam. It didn't matter. The door slid shut behind them.

"Get the hell out of here!" Adam shouted to the pilot.

Jack felt the aircraft lurch violently upwards, then the nose pitched down as the engines roared and it began its escape.

"That was a fucking terrible plan," Adam grinned.

Jack sighed. It was. But it had worked. The initial danger had now passed. No one was shooting at a helicopter with the prime minister in it. They were safe. For now.

44

"Get out of your clothes," Adam turned and snapped at Norman.

"What?" the prime minister looked lost as he slumped against one of the seats in the rear cabin of the helicopter.

"Take off your clothes," Adam reaffirmed. He didn't want to have to force the issue, but he would have to if Norman didn't start complying quickly.

Norman stared back at him open-mouthed. There was a whine from the engines of the helicopter, then it pitched right, throwing the occupants in the back towards the door, until each of them managed to grab hold of something to stabilise them. The jolt seemed to shake something in Norman, making him more compliant. He reached up and began to remove his tie, before shedding his jacket.

"This is your plan?" Thea shouted over the noise of the engines. "Kidnap the prime fucking minister?"

"It's the only choice," Adam heard Jack calling back.

"Now what are you going to do with him?"

Norman was taking his trousers off now. "Everything," Adam reminded him, before handing him a grey tracksuit top and bottoms to put on.

"He has a choice. Change his mind, or don't."

Norman was completely stripped of his old clothes now. Adam bundled them up and slid open the side door, throwing the clothes out of the aircraft as it skipped over the Thames, barely at rooftop height. He slammed the door quickly shut before the pilot banked to that side.

"Where are you taking me?" whimpered Norman. Adam got the feeling that any resistance he had was minimal and fading fast. Had they already made their point? "You won't get away with this," he sneered, pulling the jersey over his head, as if countering the thought in Adam's head.

"I don't need to get away with it," Jack replied. "It just needs to happen."

The helicopter banked sharply once more, away from the Thames, now to the south. Adam saw London City Airport peeling past his window as they turned over Woolwich.

"Flight time about five minutes," the pilot called from the cockpit. His name was Gary Keppler. He'd flown for the Regulators for a number of years and had been the first name Adam had thought of when he had been thinking of who to approach. He was loyal, which was always a good starting point. He was also a little bit crazy. Not in an unhinged manner, but he wasn't averse to taking risks and proving his own worth, which Adam also knew would help in finding someone capable of executing the job they were planning. Adam had told Gary the plan from the off; it was only right that he knew what he was getting himself into. He hadn't batted an eyelid. "When do we take off?" was all he'd asked. Now he was guiding them over south-east London towards their planned landing site.

"Any sign of anyone following?" Adam asked.

"Not yet, but we're bound to be being watched. They know where we are. I'll drop in hard and fast on the descent, give us the biggest possible head start," Gary reported.

The eyes in the sky certainly worried Adam. The transponder on the helicopter had been turned off seconds before they veered towards the Palace of Westminster, and even with their low altitude, there was no doubt that they would be being picked up on radar, or on the screens of any of the monitoring AWACS flights that often took residence over the North Sea and would now be being re-tasked to turn away from the east. If they were able to guide people into the spot where they were landing, then getting away might just become impossible.

He knew this wasn't the time for doubt. They were committed now. No going back. If they got this wrong, he would never see his family again, and what's more, they'd share his shame. His girls would grow up only knowing him as a traitor to his country. Their lives would forever be scarred.

For one fleeting moment he wanted to shout at the pilot to put the chopper down right there and let him out. He wanted to go home, to shut the door, and pull the curtains. To hold Laura in his arms and promise her that this was it. This was the last time he was going to be a Regulator. That he was done playing cowboys and it was time to come home and be the father and husband he knew they deserved.

He looked at Norman. Maybe the prime minister sensed something changing in Adam. He seemed to be staring hard into Adam's eyes, silently pleading for help.

What would happen if he helped him? Would all be forgiven? Maybe. Maybe not.

He looked to Thea and then to Jack. Jack was focused. His face hadn't changed since he'd been hauled into the helicopter. A menacing snarl simmered around the edges of his mouth, threatening at any time to break out into a full-blown scowl if anyone pushed a button he didn't like. Adam had seen it a thousand times. It was Jack's growl. The look he adopted when there was someone around that he wanted to keep in line. Adam wondered if he would be directing it at him if he knew how much he was wavering.

Then there was Thea. If Jack was simmering, she was close to boiling point. There had always been an anger about Thea. He couldn't even begin to imagine what she was thinking about the scene that had unfolded. Thea Watts had always been someone who had done things by the book. Kidnapping the prime minister was not something he could ever have imagined her condoning.

Yet here she was. Angry about everything. Furious in fact, of that there was no doubt. But she hadn't stopped Jack. She hadn't raised the alarm. She had joined in instead. If she could find a way to make this right in her head, then surely he could as well.

45

The helicopter lurched, the engines whining once more. They were coming to the end of the route now. Jack looked out of the side of the chopper and saw Stratford below. They spun around the outside of the London Stadium, heading north, before taking another sharp turn to their right, into the apartment blocks that had once housed Olympic athletes. Jack saw people staring through the windows as they flew past, heading back towards the river. They banked over Stratford International and then Stratford Station, the helicopter slowing, dipping lower and lower, over the railway itself. It followed the course of the tracks, leaving it only when they forked east and west. The helicopter accelerated, fifty feet above the road below. Then they were over the Isle of Dogs. The skyscrapers of Canary Wharf reached up around them, hiding them from the AWACS. Every now and then Jack saw the lights of police cars that raced below. Most of them would be trying to predict where they were going to land. Trying to be the ones to get there first and pen them in. None of them knew they didn't have a chance. That they would be long gone before anyone got to them. If everything went according to plan.

The helicopter slowed to a near hover just past Glengall Bridge, edging closer to Millwall Outer Dock. On the northern perimeter land that had been cleared for a development that had been stymied by planning permissions over and over again. An ideal landing site. The pilot turned the chopper towards it. Their altitude lowered. Jack looked out north in the direction from which the police would have to come. They were closing in already. He could see cars racing through the narrow streets of the Isle of Dogs. Down the A1206 towards them. Penning them in on the island.

The pilot extended the wheels as the first car reached the perimeter of the building site. Armed officers were scampering out and they still weren't down.

Then they weren't going down anymore. They were rising fast, back into the air as high as they could. The nose tipped down and they accelerated away, back between the buildings, ascending all the time. Jack knew it wouldn't last. Just another ruse. Another misdirection. He also knew that the next time they dropped, they'd be dropping quickly and for the last time.

His stomach lurched upwards as it began. He looked at Norman and saw the man gripping the chair. Panic in his eyes. He didn't know what was going on. Probably thought they were crashing. In a way they were. The landing was going to be hard. And it was going to hurt.

They dropped. A split second before they hit there was a roar from the engines as the pilot did everything he could to slow the landing. Then there was the thud. Metal cracked. The helicopter bounced. Jack felt the back-end rotating, kicking out behind them. Now it was his turn to grab hold of something. He heard someone gasp. Then a grunt and shout from the cockpit. The noise of the engines grew louder. The helicopter wobbled. If it tipped over, they were done for. They needed to get it down properly and get it down now.

The next hit wasn't as hard. A combination of the skill of the pilot and the momentum being eaten up by the first attempt. The cabin shuddered and the engines began powering down. Jack was already up from his seat.

"Out! Out!" he hollered, grabbing at Norman, dragging him from where he sat, out through the door.

The chopper had landed in a small storage yard. A line of metal containers faced them, stacked two high and at least twenty containers across. Jack knew the number of the one he wanted: 014. He frogmarched Norman without looking back. He knew the others would be following.

Container 014 looked like all the others. There was no special lock. No keypad or fingerprint sensor. Just a run-of-the-mill padlock. Nothing that made it stand out. Jack had a key for it, of course. All Regulators did. This was one of their safe rooms. Somewhere that they could disappear into when the heat was on and kidnapping the prime minister certainly brought a fair degree of that. The padlock slipped free. Jack heaved the bar that operated the container door upwards and it swung open.

"In."

Norman went in first, pushed by the rest of them, every one eager to find the solace of the container. Jack was last, closing the door behind him. The container was completely empty. Nothing inside it. Nowhere to go.

"You think you can hide out in here?" Norman asked.

A metallic twang rang out in answer as the locking mechanism put itself back in place.

"Sure," Jack replied.

Norman went to say something else but was stopped by the sound of an explosion. The whole container roared as the sound echoed inside it as charges that had been placed in the chopper ignited.

"Let's go," Jack said.

"Where?" asked Thea, which on the face of it seemed a fair question.

Adam was already answering it. He knelt down at the far end of the container, his hand searching for something to grab. Then he had found it. He pulled. The bottom of the container lifted up, the hinges sitting in an innocuous-looking seam that ran the whole way round. If someone didn't know to look for it, they would easily miss it. At least for a while. When it was raised, it revealed a hatch in the ground.

"Down here," Adam answered.

"Where does it go?" Thea asked, but it wasn't a question that needed answering to make her go through; she was already making her way to the hatch.

"It gets us out of here." Jack replied as the sound of sirens grew louder. "Now let's move before anyone decides to make too much noise."

Adam went first, then Norman. Thea and the pilot followed, before Jack made his way down, closing the hatch behind them. Once more, the sound of some mechanism placing everything back the way it was before they entered could be heard above them. They were alone in a tunnel that led down below London and ultimately to the epicentre of the Regulators' movement.

46

Stories had been told to Thea about how the Regulators did their business. About the systems that they had in place. The cases that they built. The prisons where they housed the guilty. At the centre of it all was the court where judgments were passed. The epicentre of every decision that they made. Lives had been ended in this room. Or at least, the life they could have had. Freedom was taken. Retribution was delivered. Standing in it for the first time, it seemed even more awe-inspiring. A perfect circle with walls that towered above head height, reaching up to where the Vehm passed judgment from their gantry. It took her mind to the Roman colosseums of the past, where an emperor's thumb would signal your fate or fortune. To stand in the middle of this pit – for that's what it truly was – and look upwards felt humbling. She knew that was intentional. How much bravado had leapt up from where she stood now and crashed with futility against the walls. There was no changing the minds of the people who rained down judgment on their prey here. Like with the emperors of old, when you were in their den, there was only ever one way out.

"Creeps me out still," Adam said as they stood there.

"How can you ever think this is the way to do things?" Thea replied, keeping her voice low, as if someone might be listening above them.

"I don't see we have much of a choice really." He looked at where Norman sat slumped against the wall.

"We should have," Thea replied. Adam just raised his eyebrows in response.

"Shall we crack on?" Jack walked into the space. He'd secured the perimeter with the help of the pilot who had then been sent on his way. To where, Thea didn't know. Clearly he didn't fancy hanging around whilst they interrogated the prime minister. She wasn't sure she did either, but she couldn't find it in her to leave. Something was telling her to see this through.

"You know they're going to be right behind you?" Norman called. "They're coming."

"You reckon?" Jack said nonchalantly. He carried on before Norman could reply. "See, I don't. Not really. That site has been picked for a reason. It's not overlooked. So even if people see a chopper come down, they don't see us. And when the police do get there, we're long gone."

"They'll find where you went." Norman tried a sneer, but it came out half-hearted.

"Let's ask the expert. Ms Watts. As a former police officer, what do you do when you arrive on scene? Set a perimeter. Search the area. Look for witnesses, right?"

"Right," Thea agreed, not wanting to offer too much. Clearly Jack had a narrative he was getting into here.

"And what's the best sort of witness?"

"Someone close by," Norman called out. "Someone who saw what happened."

"Jesus, it's a good job you never went up for a real election," Adam sighed. Norman shot him a confused glance.

"A camera," Thea corrected him.

"Yeah. Obviously a storage centre like that will have lots and lots of cameras. Cameras at the entrances and exits. Cameras pointing at the containers themselves. They're the first thing you go through."

"They are," Thea agreed.

"Of course, there are blind spots. Places people can sneak out. Somewhere like that can't expect wall-to-wall coverage. It has to protect its investment, however, and that's the containers. So, the cameras point at that. They capture everything that goes in and out. Now, say a helicopter lands in the car park. You might see that pass through a camera, but if it lands in a blind spot, you're not going to see the people get out. Not going to see them make their escape."

"But we went in the containers," Norman blurted out. This time Thea sighed. Adam was right. It was a good job he hadn't run for an election.

"We did," Jack said thoughtfully. "Walked right into them. Clear as day. Thing is, the cameras never saw that. They saw a chopper come down and land just out of shot. Then an explosion. No one ever went near the containers. So why start looking there?"

"I don't understand." The penny hadn't dropped.

"They manipulated the footage," Thea hissed at him.

"They? How?"

"Amazing what you can do with AI these days. Real-time video editing. Wipe out anything that looks like a person. We'll have simply disappeared. They'll check the wreckage when it cools down. Someone will say we must have burned up in the crash. When that doesn't work, they'll widen the perimeter. Then eventually they'll assume we've got lucky. Found a route out that they didn't think of. They'll scratch their heads; they'll shrug their shoulders. But not one of them is going to think that the footage is manipulated. Not in time, anyway. They'll see what they need to see and they'll act on it and they won't come anywhere near this place." Jack walked towards where John Norman sat on the floor, bending down so his face was in the prime minister's. "So, Mr Norman, when this conversation begins, I want you to think of two things. First up, how long you want this conversation to last. And secondly, how long you think you can last."

Norman stuttered as if he had something to say, but all that came out was air and any remnants of bluster he had.

"Good," Jack said. "Shall we crack on?"

He turned to Adam who stepped forward. "We'll get to the point. We know you're part of the In Statera. We know that the plan is for you to circumvent the democratic process for the next year or so that your group can put in place whatever apparatus is needed to extort or coerce as many officials as you need to continue to make this country sing to your tune. Let's not even begin to pretend otherwise."

Norman said nothing. At least he wasn't going to fob them off.

"We also know that there're only three of you left," Adam went on. That brought a reaction from Norman.

"What?" He moved back against the wall as fear took over, his eyes darting from Jack to Adam as if he thought they were responsible. That was interesting.

"They didn't do it," Thea pointed out.

"Could have done," Adam retorted, looking at Norman as he did so.

"I'd have enjoyed it," Jack added.

Thea shook her head and sighed. Machismo was clearly going to be the order of the day here. "You'd have both been black-sited the moment you took out the first one. Don't forget where you got the information about what happened to them." She could play at that game too. It was all right Norman feeling scared of them, but she needed him to know that she was in charge still. That the rule of law still had some sway, even down here inside the underground court of the Vehm.

"That would have been interesting," Jack turned to her and smiled.

"It's not the point either. Point is, someone's killing them. And if I were a betting man, my money would be on you," Adam said.

"It does make sense," Jack turned back to Norman. "Complete power grab. You've got the top job now, why do you need the rest of them? You can make yourself the top dog of the country and the In Statera. What a prize."

"I couldn't. It's not possible," Norman stammered. Thea knew he was telling the truth. There was a panic in his voice. This news had scared him more than being kidnapped. More than being brought to a secret facility by two vigilantes and a rogue Security Service agent. She stepped past Jack, looking straight at Norman.

"How is it not possible?"

"We don't know who each other are. We never knew. That's half the point. Plausible deniability. The other half is so that we don't start screwing each other over. We keep our distance so that it never becomes personal. It's not worth the risk. We destroy lives, after all. Why open ourselves up to that? We stay in the background. For the most part anyway."

"You do know that staying in the background usually precludes you from doing jobs like being the actual fucking prime minister, right?" Adam laughed.

"All right," Norman sneered. "Fair point. That was a risk. One I think I've got away with. Or did. The whole ruse to take control of government for a year – it wasn't my idea. It was one of the others. But I saw an opportunity. They needed a stooge, so I suggested myself. I thought, who better to be at the top of the table than me? I suggested that the In Statera had enough dirt to ensure that I would do as I was told for a year and then retire."

"You weren't worried about them coming after you afterwards?"

"That's not what we do. If the course doesn't need correcting, we don't act. We only do things when things are going awry."

"Looks like someone thought something was going awry. They decided to clear house completely."

"It can't be, though," Norman shook his head. "There's no way one of our own turned on us. Who are left?"

Adam looked at Jack and Thea. Thea knew the other two would be wondering the same thing. Should they share that information with Norman? What were the risks of him knowing who the other In Statera were? Thea knew that they couldn't. The less he knew, the less powerful he could be.

"Alistair Ramsey and Victor Clarke," Jack said, looking back at Norman.

"Jesus, Jack," Thea whispered, shaking her head. Why the hell had he done that? Didn't he know the risk this guy posed?

"Ramsey? The old bastard in the Lords. Well, I would never have guessed. He certainly can't have been calling those sorts of shots, can he? The sod can barely keep his eyes open for more than five minutes at a time. Spends most of the sessions napping. I don't know Clarke, other than reputation. But why would he come after everyone?"

"Why would anyone set up a covert group to mould the world how they see fit?" Adam asked.

"Yeah, why?" Thea meant to only think it, but it just slipped sarcastically out. Jack and Adam turned to look at her. She didn't react. It was a fair point.

"So you reckon it's Clarke?" Jack asked.

"It has to be," Norman was back to pleading. This time for it was his innocence. Even if he wasn't saying it directly.

"Not Ramsey."

"No."

"Not you?"

"God, no."

Jack sucked his teeth. "Adam?"

"Could be," Adam said noncommittally.

"Might not be," Jack pointed out.

"Shall we take him with us for now?"

"Take him where?" Thea asked.

"Somewhere safe. Till we can work this all out."

"Have you got anywhere?"

Jack pulled a face. "Not really. No."

There was something about the way that he said it that told her he was asking her for a favour. The sort of favour you might ask if you'd forgotten your wallet and it's your round. *You get these, mate, I'll get them next time we're out.* Only it wasn't drinks. It was the illegal detention of the most powerful person in British democracy.

"Oh, for fuck's sake."

47

Jane had shared Thea's dislike of the request, although her expression of disgust had lasted a little longer than just four words.

"We should never have got ourselves involved with this," she lamented when she had released enough vitriol to calm down.

"I don't really think we had a choice," Thea replied.

Jane grumbled and muttered something to herself that Thea couldn't make out over the phone. "I suppose I can find somewhere," she said finally.

They ended the call with the promise that Jane would be in touch when she had a site. In the meantime, she warned that they needed to get out of London as quickly as possible. Roadblocks were already being set up on the main routes and all air traffic had been grounded. The search for the prime minister was unprecedented in its scale. "Your face and name are everywhere. Quinn's and Morgan's to boot."

"That'll make life interesting," Adam said when she reported it to them.

"It was always going to happen," Jack replied. "Hopefully we can get far enough outside of any cordon before we head surface side."

"How big are these tunnels?" Thea asked, trying to wrap her head around the scale. She already thought what she'd seen was impressive enough, but clearly there was even more to come.

"There's a whole city's worth of stuff going on under London. Victorian projects that fell into obscurity. Cold War projects that the government will never admit to, just in case they ever need to get them rolling again. Even stuff that the Vehm put together themselves. Access routes between things that already existed. It's a playground down here and very few people know how big it really is. If anyone."

"How far out can you get us?"

"Other side of the North Circular, but we're still going to be well within the M25. I imagine that we're going to have to take a very scenic route. We could do with intel on where they're setting up roadblocks, see if we can't plot our way around them. They can't cover every road."

"Would we not be better heading south? I mean, we disappeared this side of the river. Surely that will play into their thinking. Is there a secret tunnel under the river you could use or something?"

"If we head back towards the city, yeah. We can find a route south of the river."

There was something in Adam's voice that sounded as if he didn't like the idea of heading back into the city.

"You think there's a chance we might run into someone underground?" Thea guessed.

"I wouldn't want to rule it out. If they're taking this seriously…"

"Which they are," Jack interjected.

"Which they are," Adam nodded. "Someone knows what tunnels are down here. They'll be looking in them. Might not be police. Military. Security Services. Who knows?"

"If we're top side sooner, we have a better chance," Jack added. "There's a safe house that we can access from the tunnel. It has a van and, more importantly, it has a drone. We can put that up, send it out ahead and ensure the road is clear."

"What happens if someone spots the drone? They're going to lock that area down quickly."

"Then we'll get out quickly. Look, all of these plans come with really massive fucking drawbacks. They're all shit. I'm not asking you to buy into it as an absolute. It's going to require a little bit of luck and a lot of patience to get to the other side. You need to stay the course, Thea. This is what we've committed to now. You chose to come along on this trip, so you're going to have to play it our way. It's not time to sit around second-guessing, we've got to get our skates on."

It felt like a dressing-down. Thea's first reaction was to blurt out some sort of angry response. The words were forming but she managed to stifle them. On this one, Jack was right. They might have set the ball rolling, but she had chosen to join them. Picking at the plan meant slowing things down. Allowing the net to tighten.

"Whatever," she said, one last petulant remark to show she wasn't happy, but she'd play ball.

"You know you're all screwed," Norman said from where he'd been sitting listening to the exchange.

"Maybe so, mate," Jack went over to him, hauling him off the ground as he spoke. "But you're screwed worst."

* * * *

They jogged the length of the tunnel. Norman wasn't the most cooperative, dragging his heels as they went, his complaints echoing against the tunnel until Jack firmly pointed out that he could "shut the hell up and stay conscious, or be carried and not."

From there on, there was silence, except for the sound of their footsteps on the concrete. The tunnel was supposed to be taking them north, out of the immediate area. They passed under a ladder that led up to what looked like a hatch. Thea asked if they could take it but Adam said they were still too near to the original site. It took another half an hour at a steady pace to get to where they wanted to be. This time there was a door on one side of the tunnel. Jack keyed in a code to the electronic keypad that deactivated the lock, then they were through, following a tight spiral staircase up to another door. Adam went through first, then Norman, then Thea. She stepped out into the hallway of what looked like a Victorian terraced house. Looking back, she saw that the door sat under the stairs as if leading to a larder or storage space. Jack eased out after her, shutting the door behind him. She heard the thud of an electronic lock as it closed.

"This is weird," she shook her head.

"Just a bit," Adam agreed, smiling as he said it.

Norman was looking around, his mouth open. He was struggling to believe it as well. "How on earth is this possible?"

"Vehm has been around a long, long time and it's got a lot of money," Jack replied, stepping into the galley kitchen which ran along the back portion of the building.

"All the same," Norman said. "This is absurd."

Jack wasn't listening now. He'd opened one of the drawers in the kitchen, moving the contents around till he found what he was after. Keys.

"No time for a cuppa I'm afraid," he said shutting the drawer.

A door took them from the kitchen into the small yard. At the far end was a brick garage. Jack unlocked the door to the garage with the set of keys and they trooped in. A van waited for them, just as had been promised. Jack pressed the key fob and the doors unlocked.

"Get our friend comfy in the back," he said. I'll have a look for the drone.

Thea and Adam secured Norman in the rear of the van. Two bench seats ran along either side. Norman sat nearest the driver's cab, his right hand cuffed to a ring that jutted out of the adjoining wall between the two sections. He said nothing by way of complaint. Perhaps even he was beginning to realise the seriousness of his situation and had resigned himself to his fate.

They heard the noise from the roof of the van. Jack clambering up on to it. Thea wondered for a moment what he was doing. Before she could ask Adam, Jack jumped down and peered in.

"Drone's on the roof. Good to go. You guys ready?"

"You driving?" Adam asked.

"You're flying then," Jack replied, handing him a remote control with a small TV screen attached. "Keep me posted."

"What route are we taking?"

"Figure we head north. Should take us through Chingford, Epping, that sort of way. See if you can find a clear route. Once we're outside the M25 we can start thinking about how we get to wherever we're leaving our friend here."

"Good luck with that," Norman said sardonically.

Adam ignored him. "Sounds good." Jack shut the door behind them and they settled in.

* * * *

The drive was slow and steady. Adam launched the drone
once they were out of the garage. The noise of the engine of
the van masked it enough that it wouldn't attract the
attention of anyone in the area. The last thing they needed
was the van being linked to a drone launch. Not today. That
would be the sort of thing that aroused suspicion. Thea
wasn't a fan of not being able to see where they were going
but having no windows to look out of also meant no one
could look in and she figured that was a fair compromise.
All the same, the longer the journey went on, the more
tension she felt growing inside her. She didn't like not
knowing what was happening and even Adam's
commentary from the drone did little to reassure her,
especially when it did spot police activity in the area. The
first time had been a roadblock that the drone had spotted
about half a mile ahead. Thea was certain that the drone
would be seen and that the area would be closed down
immediately. That they wouldn't be able to escape. But it
wasn't. Adam was able to find a new route and Jack was
able to keep them well off the radar of those looking for the
PM. Everything seemed to be working in their favour. Until
it wasn't.

"I think we've got a problem," Jack called through the slot
between the cabins.

"What's up?"

"I'm not certain, but I think we're being followed."

48

Adam circled the drone back towards the van, letting it skim over their heads at about a hundred feet. The car they were looking for was a black saloon car. Jack said it was about four car lengths back.

"Where did you first see it?" Thea asked as Adam concentrated on piloting.

"Somewhere around Buckhurst Hill," Jack replied. "If it's coincidental, he's taking a very weird route."

Adam found the car. He watched it while Jack took them through a couple of side streets, altering his course. The saloon didn't turn at first, but then did, taking a parallel road, just out of line of sight. Gambling on an intercept point.

"Jack, do me a favour, pull a U-turn when you get the chance."

"Got it," came the reply. Seconds later they were turning right hard, then reversing, before completing the turn and heading in the same direction. Adam watched the target car. It carried on until it reached the next turning. The grid-like pattern of the residential streets they were on served to allow them to take calculated risks. They turned again, following the van.

"They're tracking us."

"How?" Jack asked. "Another drone?"

Adam tilted the drone's camera on its gimble, up from the ground and its bird's eye view to the sky around them. He rotated it, looking at the skyline. There was nothing in sight. "I can't see anything. Doesn't mean they're not higher up."

"You sure they're tracking?"

"They didn't miss a beat on that turn."

"Shit."

"Did we miss something on Norman?" Adam asked, working his way through the possibilities.

Thea's phone rang. She looked at him, her face dropping as the thought dawned on her at the same time it did him.

"Fuck. Sorry," she said looking at the display. "It's Jane."

"Answer it," Adam replied insistently. "Don't give anything away."

"What?"

"Just answer the phone."

Thea answered. Adam could hear snippets of Jane's side of the conversation. The woman spoke loudly. Perhaps they didn't need to be bugging the phone. You could probably hear her from a couple of offices down. When the call was over, Thea turned to Adam.

"She wants us to head to a site just outside of Luton. Near the airport. We used it as a processing site for people brought into the country who shouldn't have been."

"Fine. Jack, Luton. Best way you can."

"You want to go there with them following us? I mean, if they're into my phone, they probably heard all of that."

"I know. The last thing we want to do is let them know that we're on to them. Right now, they're sitting pretty. Waiting."

"Waiting?"

"If they wanted to bring us in as we are, they could have done that by now. But no-one is coming for us. There's no net closing. This is a tail. They want to see where we go, then they're coming in."

"Why?"

"We'll ask them when the chance arises."

"We need to warn Jane. Find some way to get word to her."

"We can do that," Jack called back from the cab. "It's sorted. But for now, let's string these idiots along. They think they're hunting us. Couldn't be further from the truth."

Thea looked less inclined to agree, but she sat down anyway.

"All unravelling before your eyes, isn't it?" Norman sneered at her. That was enough reason for Adam to elbow him in the gut. Norman wheezed and bent over.

"Shut the fuck up. Stupid wannabe dictator prick," he said, feeling much better for it.

Jack continued to take them on an indirect route north. They knew that passing the M25 would be the hardest part of their journey. Roadblocks had been set up at every junction. Where traffic wasn't attempting to join the motorway but merely going over or under it, it was being funnelled to select routes. Roads had been blocked. Access restricted.

But it wasn't just roads that could take them past the makeshift barrier the police had created. There were other routes that slipped under or over the motorway. Unofficial routes. Places where people weren't meant to go. Places the police simply didn't have the manpower to watch. That was what Jack was aiming for.

When construction of the M25 began in the seventies, it gouged through great swathes of the English countryside. Through fields, hamlets, woods and more. Even over ancient Roman roads. It was one of these that Jack was heading for. An old Roman road near Theydon Bois that was now used as an access road for local businesses. In places, it was little more than a dirt track kept going only by walkers. But importantly, where it met the M25, the route had been preserved. A tunnel linked both sides. The reason for that privilege wasn't clear from the map. There were no businesses on the north side that needed the access. Maybe it had just been to placate some local historical society who had demanded the right to be able to retrace the Roman road. It didn't matter. It was there. And it was unguarded.

"Going to be a police roadblock a little north of where we get off," Adam warned. "Let's hope they don't decide to move it down." He didn't think it likely. The main access to what had once been the Roman road was now part of a small industrial estate. There would be a multitude of vehicles going in and out of there. The police didn't have the resources to be dealing with that level of disruption as well. "Traffic is building. We might have to wait."

"What about our friends?" Thea asked.

Adam nosed the drone back around, keeping well away from the road they were using so as not to be spotted. "They're still a little way back. Keeping their distance," he noted.

"Well, fingers crossed," Jack said.

Adam heard the engine throttling down as the van slowed. The drone showed it approaching the queue of traffic. They weren't quite at the yard yet. Jack clearly didn't want to drive along the line of traffic and cut the line. Anything that drew attention to them was something to avoid.

"They're going to work out what we're doing," Thea said quietly. "There's no way they think we're going through the checkpoint."

"Does it matter if they do?" Adam asked. Nothing about what their tail had done so far suggested they were looking to intercept them.

"If they want us in the hands of the police, they might."

"They could have had them closing in on us before now. They want to see where we go. Who else is in on this."

"We still need to find a way to warn Jane."

"I'm working on it," Jack called from the front.

"How?"

"I've sent her some flowers."

"What?"

"Well, I figure that the line between you two is being intercepted. That probably means all calls are being monitored. But web traffic can be a little harder to intercept, at least quickly. And if you're getting something through a video link, say from a home doorbell system, that's usually encrypted. I would imagine in Jane Astley's case, it's heavily encrypted, what with her being a spy and all that."

"You put a message in with the flowers," Thea said.

"With instructions to the florist to ring the doorbell and repeat the message. Now, if said florist is on the payroll of the In Statera, stands to reason I've fucked us all. But I took a punt on that one."

"You really do think outside the box sometimes."

"Traffic's clearing. Hold on back there. Got a feeling it'll get bumpy," Jack said, brushing off the compliment, and the van moved off.

* * * *

"Hello?"

The delivery driver looked a little nervous as they peered into the camera. It was the first thing that made Jane uncomfortable. The second was the appearance of a bunch of flowers. No one should be sending her flowers.

"Hello," she replied, trying to keep from sounding standoffish but knowing that she hadn't.

"Uh, I've got a delivery for Jane Astley."

"You can leave them on the doorstep please," Jane said, making a note that she should send a team over to have a look at them, rather than handle them herself. She didn't expect there to be a bomb or anything in there, but God knows what they could be coated in. She didn't see any gloves or anything on the delivery driver's hands, but that didn't mean he wasn't wearing some sort of protection.

"I've got to read the note, apparently." The poor guy looked flustered. This clearly wasn't what he normally had to do as part of the job.

"Read the note?" she replied, but he took it as an invitation to do as he was told.

"Roses are red, violets are blue, we're being followed, tailed by two. Love Taj." He looked up at the camera again. "Are you a spy or something?"

"Yeah mate, MI5, obviously," she scoffed, which seemed to do the trick, as the driver laughed.

"Okay," he said, bending down and placing the flowers on the doorstep. "Have a nice day."

The line went dead. Jane took a second to deduce that Taj stood for Thea, Adam and Jack. They were being followed. More pertinently, they didn't reach out to her directly, which meant that they thought their communications had been compromised. There was no way to get a message back to them, so they would be continuing with their plan to meet at the location. It was on her to be ready.

49

The game of cat and mouse continued as the van moved through Essex and into Hertfordshire. They only reached Bedfordshire when they arrived at the airport, the perimeter fence on the eastern side of the runway serving as the county line as well. They drove north, around the edge of the town, finally reaching their destination, a small outbuilding that stood a hundred metres back from the main road down a dirt track.

"I hope your mate came up with something good," Adam said as they got closer. The drone had long run out of battery. Adam had crash-landed it in a field some miles back. A nice new toy for anyone who found it and was resourceful enough to put it back together.

"Jane has her ways," Thea replied, thinking back to how she'd left her out to dry with Pegg and Cartwright. She was certain that it would be them in the car behind. Or people working for them.

The van bumbled its way up the dirt track towards the outbuilding. The sun was setting now and as they exited the vehicle the light was fading as red streaks of cloud sliced into a deepening purple sky.

"Enjoy it, can't imagine you're getting more of these," Adam said to Norman as he helped him out. Norman, for once, didn't have a comeback.

Jack was out of the front of the van now and he made his way around to where the others were looking back the way they'd come.

"You think they're far behind?" he asked.

Adam shook his head. "Nah. Dumped the car by now I would think. Coming in on foot."

"Yeah," Jack agreed. He turned towards the building. It was two storeys tall but looked at best one room wide. Some sort of storage building, built from brick and timber long ago. Functional in a different time. Now, a useful place to hold someone till the cavalry arrived. "Let's get ourselves checked in."

The door to the building was thick and made of metal. It needed a good shove to get it open, but at least it was unlocked.

"Someone's expecting us, I guess," Adam said as he stepped in and looked around. There weren't actually two storeys. Just the one. He could see remnants of the timbers jutting out of the walls where the second storey would have been, long since removed. Someone behind him found a light switch and four spotlights from the ceiling of the building lit them up. There was nothing in there. No chairs, no tables, just an empty space.

"Spartan," Jack muttered.

"Standing room only I'm afraid, but you've been sat on your arse all day. Probably do you some good," Adam smiled as he spoke to Norman. The man looked as if he'd finally accepted what was happening now.

"Where the fuck is Jane?" Thea asked.

"Probably waiting somewhere nearby. We gave her the heads-up after all. If she's got a masterplan to deal with our friends out there, chances are the best thing to do is sit tight," Jack said. It sounded like good advice.

The rumble of a low, fast helicopter appearing out of what felt like nowhere told them otherwise.

"Who the hell is that?" Jack was already moving towards the door, his pistol in his hand. He took up a position against the frame, pulling it open and looking out as the thumping of rotor blades almost directly overhead was joined by the sound of another helicopter roaring past.

Adam joined him quickly at the door, forgetting about Norman for a second. "This going to be Jane's plan?" he called back to Thea over the din.

"I hope not," Thea was right next to him, but she was shouting also.

"Someone keep an eye on him; I'm going out there," Jack said opening the door further. Adam saw in the field ahead of them the dark silhouette of a Chinook touching down in the field just yards away.

"Mate, get back in here," he pulled at Jack, trying to rein him back in but Jack was already out of the door. A burst of automatic gun fire came from near the helicopter. It missed, too high by a clear distance. Jack fired a couple of shots back into the darkness.

"Jack!" Thea called.

"It's not worth it!" Adam added.

Jack ducked and scurried back towards them.

"What the hell did she do?" he shouted as the door slammed.

"I don't know." Thea's response was equally fraught.

"Now you're going to see what happens when you cross the line." Norman was standing up straight again.

"I should put a bullet in you now." Jack turned and raised his gun at Norman, the prime minister stepping backwards as he did so.

"Jack!" Adam shouted as Jack marched forward. He rested his gun inches from Norman's face and stood there impassively. "Don't."

Jack didn't move. Adam saw a look on his face that he knew all too well. Emotionless. Impassive. Letting the moment become less than it actually was. Adam's kills had been necessity. Only when they'd shot first. And he had never killed someone up close and personal. Jack, on the other hand. Different story. One that stretched way back to before he'd ever met Adam. One that would be with him forever. No matter how much Jack might want to tell himself otherwise.

The second helicopter rattled overhead, looking for a landing spot no doubt.

"None of us get out of this with him dead." Thea was pleading now.

Jack said nothing. He just stared straight into the eyes of Norman who cowered before him.

There was a hammering at the door. Someone barked at them to "Open up!" their words somehow defeating both the metal door and the sound of the two helicopters.

"Let's play this out, Jack," Adam had edged forward. Now he placed a hand on his friend's shoulder.

Jack's nostrils flared once, then he exhaled, stepping back, the gun pointing at the floor.

"Open the door," he said, still looking at Norman, but addressing the others.

Thea was the one who heaved it open. Then there were soldiers pouring in quickly. Adam found himself face down on the mud, his hands and ankles being secured with thick cable ties. Voices shouted. Someone said they'd secured the principle. But there were no shots. No one put a bullet in the back of his head. No one slit his throat. He risked a look upwards. Thea was being hauled from the floor. Her wrists and ankles had also been tied and two soldiers were carrying her. Then he was being lifted. Grabbed under the armpits. Carried out into the darkening night, awaiting his fate.

50

It had taken three of them to carry Jack. Two under his arms, one to lift his feet. A question of size. He was simply too tall to be moved like the others. They were taken out in front of the building and deposited kneeling outside in a line. The two choppers' engines were off, but the fans inside still made a hell of a noise as the rotors slowed their cycle. Jack looked around for signs of anyone in charge. He wanted to try and get a handle on what or who they were dealing with here.

A set of headlights turned up the driveway to where they were. Then another. And another. And another. A convoy of four black Land Rovers. They raced effortlessly over the humps and bumps, skidding to a halt yards away from where they had been lined up. Two men in suits, well built, short hair, obviously close protection officers, exited the first. They stood their ground, waiting. Only one got out of each of the second and third vehicles. Both stepped to the rear passenger doors. Out of the first he saw Jane Astley. She moved out of the way as the driver shut the door, hovering in position, looking back to the third vehicle, waiting for the passenger. The door opened and a man in his late sixties stepped out. He wasn't tall but he looked sturdy. Definitely strong for his age and continuing to keep in shape, despite the best efforts of Mother Nature and the fine living that his immaculate suit denoted. He had thick grey curls that were cut short. Jack would have been able to tell by the way he walked that they had been shorter before. Buzz cut. Ex-military. But he knew that already from seeing the man's face. This was Jonathan Hargreaves. The Home Secretary. Former Brigadier General in the British Army. He'd served with distinction in the Falklands. Had been loved by his men. Known for his down-to-earth, affable nature. A rarity in top brass. Even rarer in politicians. He looked over at the three prisoners. His face gave nothing away. Then he strode to Jane, stopping to mutter a short order, before heading into the building.

Jane looked at them and walked towards them.

"I'm going to rip her fucking throat out," Thea hissed.

Jane stopped just short, as if she'd heard the threat. Or maybe she could see the murderous intent in Thea's eyes. "Give it a minute," she said calmly.

The three of them said nothing in reply. What could they say? They'd been caught with a kidnapped prime minister. Jack turned his head away and looked straight ahead, zoning out of what was going on. Waiting until he was needed again.

* * * *

It took more than a minute. Nearly quarter of an hour passed before the door to the building was opened and Hargreaves walked imperiously out. He whispered something in Jane's ear and then turned to the three of them.

"Get them on their feet. I need them walking," he ordered. One of the soldiers who had been guarding them stepped over, walking behind each of them and cutting their ankle ties before hauling them up. When he was standing, Jack moved around on the spot, circling his ankle, letting the blood get back to where it was supposed to be.

"Come," Hargreaves said bluntly, turning and heading back into the building.

The three of them didn't have much choice in the matter. Each was escorted by a soldier through the door and deposited inside the room. Norman had been released from his cuffs and was sitting on a small stool that someone had found for him. Two soldiers were flanking him, but Hargreaves dismissed them with a nod of his head. They stepped out of the room. Jack watched them as they went. He saw Jane standing behind by the exit. The door was shut and the six of them were alone.

"Well, this has been quite an evening," Hargreaves remarked.

Jack didn't quite know what to say. What to expect. No one else seemed to either. It was clear that, even if Norman was the PM, Hargreaves had control in here. It seemed best to keep quiet and let him say what he wanted.

Thea clearly didn't agree.

"Fuck you," she snarled at Jane. "I can't believe I even entertained the idea that you were using me as bait. How could I have been so stupid?"

"You'd do yourself a favour if you stopped being so stupid now," Hargreaves scolded. "If it wasn't for your colleague here, you would be facing a life with very few choices. I think you could limit them to running, imprisonment or death. None of which I'm sure you'd have enjoyed. Needless to say, your actions today will have consequences. Your career, as you know it, is FUBAR."

Once a soldier, always a soldier, Jack thought to himself as he heard Hargreaves using the acronym for 'Fucked Up Beyond All Recognition'.

"To be honest, we could use that term a lot in here," Hargreaves went on, walking slowly around the room as he did. "The big problem I've got is that I've got a high-ranking member of the Security Service coming to me telling me that the PM is in some sort of secret society that wants to lop the head of our democratic beast. And to be honest, I find that a little hard to wrap my head around. It's all rather far-fetched, isn't it?"

"Indeed," Norman agreed.

"I mean, underground groups going around doing as they see fit with no oversight? It's just not plausible. It's not something that happens in our country. Maybe in America. Where everyone thinks they could be a cowboy and a statesman at the same time. Here, however, we have rules, we have organisations and we stick to them. No, I simply don't believe it. I don't believe that there are secret organisations out there." He walked around behind the three of them, stepping between Adam and Jack and placing a hand on each of their shoulders. "What do you think, gentlemen? Does that sound like nonsense?"

"No, sir," Jack replied. "Sounds plausible to me."

"Do you have proof?" Hargreaves asked, his hands coming away as he resumed his circling.

"Yes, sir," Jack replied. He saw Thea give him a confused look.

"Really?"

"Yes, sir. Mr Morgan here is a member of such a group. As was I once. You've a number of other members detained at the moment."

Norman pulled a face as he listened, tilting his head. "I'm sorry, what?" he said.

"Quite true," Hargreaves said thoughtfully, nodding as he rubbed his chin with his hand. It was almost theatrical. Jack could see where he was going with it. "I suppose any doubts that I had should be at least alleviated by the fact that we know that such groups exist. We spend a hell of a lot of money going after them. Did quite well at it, in fact. But that still leaves a little bit of a problem for me. You see, you're Regulators. We know you are. You admit it. I'm supposed to believe that the man in charge of the country is something else. A man in it for his own ends and the ends of those who helped to get him there. And I see absolutely no proof that he is. Some list that could have been typed up anywhere. What an absolute nonsense. The courts can't be making a decision based on that, can they? Where would that leave us?"

"Sir, with all due respect, that's why we took that decision for you," Jack answered once more.

"Hmm. Not too sure that's the way things should be done, is it? You were a soldier once, weren't you, Quinn?"

"Yes, sir."

"You followed orders."

"No, sir. That's why I'm not a soldier anymore."

"I know, I read your file on the way over. I have to say, I agree with you there. The army got itself in some muddles. But those moments were always individuals over organisation."

"With all due respect, sir, again, the organisation wasn't interested when I brought it up."

"Would it have changed anything if it had?"

"It would, sir. It would have changed the army. It would have brought the perpetrators to justice. And what I've come to learn is that sometimes you can't get justice. Either because the system doesn't want it or can't give it. In this case, justice can't be given. That means we're dealing with it."

Hargreaves sighed. "You were. You're not now. I am." He looked at Norman. "John, is any of this true?"

"Of course not. I've bloody told you. It's a fabrication," sighed Norman from where he was still sat.

"Of course," Hargreaves looked down. "How could it be anything else? But by whom?"

"I don't know," Norman said indignantly. "The Regulators or the Vehm. Russia even. I haven't the foggiest. But I will find out."

"I am certain you will," Hargreaves agreed. "And that's what bothers me. Because what happens when you do?"

"What do you mean?"

"Well, this prorogation thing we're doing. It's all because we're in a time of turmoil. There's no doubt what these fools have done exacerbates that. Proves the point almost, doesn't it?"

"That's why we eliminated the Regulators," Norman pointed out. "We knew they were dangerous, so we dealt with them."

"Well, you clearly didn't," Hargreaves snorted. "I mean, look. This is all happening after the fact. They still got to you. Determined bleeders, I'll give them that. So now, you're justified. But you didn't need justification. And I did my own research, naturally. Of course, I found nothing to support their claim that you were in on this," Hargreaves said.

"Obviously," another sneer from Norman.

"Alistair Ramsey was the same. I couldn't find a shred of evidence on him. It's like the whole thing was absolutely fabricated. Which made it all the more bizarre when he confessed everything to me less than an hour ago."

"What?" Norman croaked.

Hargreaves exhaled. "If that's true, stands to reason that your involvement could be true too. Which means I have an impossible choice. Let you go, as I have no evidence, no proof. You would be free to return to the office of prime minister and take this country down a very, very dangerous road. One that you know I was long opposed to. Or I remove you."

"Remove me? You can't just remove me. I'm the prime bloody minister."

"And I think you're also a fucking charlatan and an enemy of the state," Hargreaves roared, cowing Norman. Jack felt the hairs on the back of his neck stand up. "So, no, you will not be the prime bloody minister. Someone else will. Someone that the people of this country choose in a free and fair election. All knowledge of your crimes of course will be forgotten. Your record will remain. Your name honoured. But you will not and cannot serve this country."

Norman rushed to compose himself. "Then let's talk deals."

"A deal? Amazing how quickly the mask slips when the tables are turned, isn't it?"

"What choice do I have?" Norman growled. "You've bought into it, doesn't matter what I say now, does it?"

"It doesn't matter because it's true," Hargreaves pointed out.

"Fine. Believe what you must. My resignation for my freedom. How about that?"

Hargreaves hummed. "That could be acceptable. But it would need to happen today. It would need to happen now. An instant resignation, a call for a general election."

"I can do that."

Hargreaves' eyes narrowed. "I really hoped it hadn't been true."

He turned and circled back around the three prisoners. He stopped behind Jack, who felt him working at the cable tie around his wrists. Then, with a quick snap, his hands were free. Hargreaves came back around to his side, reaching into his pocket and removing a pistol.

"Here," he passed it to Jack. "I commandeered it from one of the soldiers. You can finish it now."

"Sir?"

Hargreaves nodded at Norman and stepped away. Jack looked at him, then at the pistol, then at Norman, whose mouth hung open like a broken overhead locker on a plane.

Jack passed the gun back to Hargreaves. "Sorry, sir. I don't believe in people having their cake and eating it."

Hargreaves took the gun back without hesitation, pocketing it. Jack realised he must have been expecting this reaction. Had it all been a test? Hargreaves answered that for him.

"I appreciate the candour and, of course, you are right. It's unfair of me to ask you to do that. But out of interest, what were you going to do with him?"

"I honestly hadn't got that far ahead. I'm a soldier, sir. Not a judge. Not a politician."

"A soldier would follow orders."

"Then I guess I'm not that either."

"No, I guess you're not. You're a Regulator."

Jack didn't argue this time.

51

"What the fuck just happened?" Thea asked as she and Jane clambered into one of the waiting Land Rovers.

"I think I took a gamble and won." Jane was smiling as she replied, which suggested that it really had been a gamble. Thea didn't know whether to thank her or not.

"You like risking it with my life and liberty, don't you?"

"It's a rare indulgence, so I make the most of it when the opportunity arises."

Thea laughed and shook her head. It might take her some time to process just exactly how risky Jane's plan had been. But it had worked and it wouldn't have been without risk to Jane. She had put her head on the line by contacting Hargreaves and telling him what had happened. Protocol would have been to go after the PM, to get him back. But she'd opted for the riskier approach. She had accepted that Norman needed to be stopped. Now the bigger problem wasn't theirs. For that alone, Thea probably owed Jane a couple of drinks.

"Why Hargreaves?" she had to know. The Home Secretary was a man of the military. A man of order and process. He'd have been low down on any list Thea had come up with.

"Dumb luck, really." Jane shrugged. "Caught him on the radio the other morning, bellyaching about how he wasn't a fan of the planned government shut-down. How it was undemocratic. The press expected him to resign sooner rather than later in protest. I guess I kept him in a job."

"At least someone has one."

"You'll be fine," Jane soothed. "Let the dust settle. See where the cards land. If things do go awry, Hargreaves is going to be a hell of a character reference in our circles."

"Yeah," Thea said, not really believing it. The Land Rover pulled off and she looked out of the window. Hargreaves and Norman still hadn't come out of the building. She wondered what deal was being negotiated and who it would benefit.

* * * *

They were taken back to London. The Home Office had its headquarters on Marsham Street, just a couple of blocks away from MI5. Thea figured that she could walk back and pack up her belongings afterwards. Hargreaves made them wait individually, ready for a debrief. A selection of aides kept pestering her to see if she wanted any refreshments. Thea thought they were more likely just interested in what she was doing at the time. Interrupting her train of thought. An hour later, she was called for.

She was surprised to see that she wouldn't be alone. Hargreaves had taken up a place at the head of the table.

Jane sat to one side, which wasn't completely surprising, although Thea had felt certain their separation had been in preparation for individual debriefs. On the other side were the bigger surprises. Jack and Adam. Thea had been certain that they wouldn't even have been given a debrief, let alone whatever this was. She nodded as she sat at the oval table, accepting the offer of a glass of water from the aide.

"Let's get started shall we?" Hargreaves edged forward in his chair as he spoke. "John Norman will cooperate from here on in with whatever we chose. He is no longer a member of the In Statera. Nor is he prime minister. At least once his resignation is accepted. Ill health, I hear. A period of recuperation out of the public eye. All the best for him. He cut a deal, the details of which will only ever be between myself and him," Hargreaves admitted. "It's better for everyone that way. No more bloody scandal. This country has seen enough."

"What about Ramsey?" Jane asked.

Hargreaves let out a derisory snort. "The bloke is completely cuckoo. Early dementia they reckon. No idea how he's still turning up for the House. He'll be shuffling around asking the Lord Speaker for a nice pot of tea before too long I shouldn't wonder. An easy out for all of us. And before you worry about succession plans, we're covertly monitoring all of his children to ensure that there's no legacy going on there. It is, after all, the best we can do. But they'll be on their own."

"Only they won't. There's still Victor Clarke." Adam spoke now. He looked happier in this setting. Sitting at a table, discussing the facts and coming up with a plan.

"There's still Victor Clarke. Yes. He's the reason I called you all here. You see, no one seems to know where he is. In fact, he's such a reclusive man, I've yet to find anyone who's ever come face to face with him."

"What?" Thea said it at the same time as the others in a chorus of confusion.

"Best guess, he's a totem. A red herring that we'd exhaust ourselves looking for."

"Or a false identity for someone who doesn't want to be found," Jane said.

"How can he not exist? There are photos of the guy. Interviews."

"All of which lead nowhere. We have his birth certificate. We have his bank accounts. His company filings. Hell, we even have his passport, which strangely enough for a billionaire businessman, has never been used to leave the country. He is a fabrication."

"I don't buy it," Adam shook his head. "Someone created him. I doubt it was any of the others. That doesn't make sense. Why have a false identity to throw us off? That name was on a list with the rest of them for a reason."

"And the rest of them were getting killed off," Jack added. "We can't ignore that fact. We're down to the last three In

Statera. Now, stands to good reason that whoever was cleaning house is one of the three alive. It could be Norman or Ramsey. No escaping that fact. They wouldn't know that Clarke wasn't real. So that could be why he remains. But let's look at how they're approaching this operationally. Ramsey, he's out of the picture, if what you say is true. He won't have the wherewithal to pull this sort of thing off. So that leaves Norman and whoever's behind Clarke. Now, we know Norman was making a play to be the PM. Stands to reason that he might feel vulnerable. What if the rest of his group decide he's gone too far? Maybe he needs to take them out first? And it would make sense that Clarke is left standing, because Clarke doesn't exist. But Norman wasn't worried about that. In fact, he needed the rest of them around him. His plan was a realignment. Get things back to how they were."

"If we believe him," Thea interrupted, because if the truth be known, she wouldn't believe Norman in the slightest.

"Fair point," Jack nodded, before turning and looking at Hargreaves. "I suppose you'll find a way to know for sure on that one. In the meantime, you need to find a way to know for sure that it's not Clarke. Or whoever is Clarke."

"I don't understand why Clarke, whoever, would do it?" Jane asked.

"Because he's a purist. The In Statera works on making small changes. It doesn't get involved until it has to. Norman has broken that golden rule and gone big. Whoever Clarke is has decided enough is enough. The whole sorry thing has failed and the rest of them need to go. Time for a new era."

Hargreaves raised an eyebrow. "It's possible."

"We've been saying they've been cleaning house for a long time. The question always had to be why. Norman doesn't make sense. He is the PM but there's no real aspirational aspect to that. It's more like him stepping down to the factory floor. Taking one for the team. They control prime ministers. They don't need to be one," Jack added. "We just need to find out who Clarke really is. There has to be someone who's talked to him. He's got this media presence. He's done interviews and things like that. We need to find someone who's spoken to him."

"The *Inquirer*." Adam was pulling his phone out already. "I'm sure they did a piece with him once. That's why they went in there. Fifty quid says the journalist who did the interview with him is one of the ones they took out and that anyone else who's ever spoken to him has met some abrupt end. Stands to reason Nathan Nelmes did a piece as well."

"Shock and awe as a distraction technique," Jack sighed.

Thea took her phone out, searching for the article. When she found it, she looked at Adam.

"I'll take your bet," she said.

"What do you mean?"

"The journalist who did the piece on Clarke. It wasn't Nelmes. It was Aidan Marshall."

52

They'd argued back and forth over Marshall's involvement. Ultimately there was nothing in the way of proof. Only the coincidences that linked Nathan Nelmes, the shooting at the *Inquirer* and Victor Clarke. But as Jack had said when summing up, "There's no such thing as coincidence."

They'd settled on visiting him. Just Jack and Adam. Asking for more information on Clarke and seeing where that got them. Adam had seemed happy with the compromise. Jack already knew that he was going to kill Aidan Marshall. This was the man who had put in motion the plot that had destroyed his son's life. There was little doubt of that in his mind as the two of them drove out of London towards Marshall's home in Woking.

Little was said on the journey. Whether Adam knew what Jack had in mind, he wasn't sure. But there was a definite tension between them. The two of them pulling in a different direction. One wanting answers. The other, retribution.

Marshall's home wasn't overly grand. A larger-than-average detached house with a pebble driveway. Out front, two silver saloon cars were parked up. "I thought he lived alone," Adam said as they stopped.

"He does," Jack replied, making sure both his pistols had one in the chamber.

"You really think it's coming to that?" Adam asked.

"You don't?"

* * * *

If Aidan had any sense of the danger that he was in when he opened the door, he didn't show it. In fact, he seemed completely unsurprised to see the two of them. Which all but confirmed Jack's suspicions.

"Adam," he stepped forward, embracing the Regulator warmly. "Good to see you. I was wondering if I ever would again. And the famous Jack Quinn," he turned his attention to Jack, who gave a stern enough look to ensure that Aidan knew that a hug wasn't on offer. "A pleasure to meet you at last."

Jack took the hand that was offered and shook it. That was as friendly as it was likely to get.

"Come in, gentlemen, please." Aidan walked them into the house. If the outside looked traditional, the inside was anything but. Large open spaces. Bright walls and contrasting furniture. Huge glass panels where once there had been rear walls opened out onto a perfectly manicured and landscaped garden.

"Drink?" Aidan asked.

"We'll pass, I reckon," Adam replied.

"I thought you might. So, let's forgo the whole dance we need to do before we get to the thrust of why you're here. You think you've figured it all out." Marshall turned to a well-stocked shelf of drinks behind him. He took an expensive-looking bottle of whisky and poured a glass as he spoke.

"That you're Victor Clarke. That you're in the In Statera. And that you've been the one killing people. That's what we've figured," Adam replied.

Aidan nodded. "All of those things are true." He took a small sip of the whisky. "I'm intrigued, though, to see if you know why?"

"Because you're a cunt who wants to rule the world. Or as close to it." Jack's bluntness didn't draw much in the way of reaction. Aidan took another sip and pulled his lips tight, which could easily have been from the strength of the alcohol rather than Jack's words.

"That's disappointing. Really. I mean, Jack, no offence, I figured you'd go for the base reaction, but Adam, I thought you'd have talked him into something a little more sophisticated."

"Sophistication, is it? Well, I mean, your house is sophisticated. Your business empire. Maybe even the way you've arranged your position within the In Statera. But there's not a lot of sophistication when it comes to killing people. I'd say all of that was pretty low brow stuff if I'm honest. Tabloid, not broadsheet," Adam said dismissively.

Aidan laughed. "I like that. But no. What I did was sophisticated. And it took a lot of time, a lot of effort and, sadly, a lot of blood, sweat and tears. Those were the unavoidable consequences of war. And this was a war."

"Against who? Democracy?"

"No!" For the first time Aidan sounded slightly rattled, his voice sounding a little shriller as he defended the accusation. "That's the one thing I always sought to uphold. You see, this is where your position blinds you to what I've done. You ever see the meme, with the guy in the Nazi uniform asking: 'Are we the baddies?'"

"What's a meme?" Jack asked.

"He's not going to know what a meme is," Adam added.

"A meme. An internet joke. A picture usually."

"I've no idea. What is it?"

"It doesn't matter what it is. The point is that you are the people in that picture."

"We're a meme?" Jack was genuinely confused and it helped that his confusion was stopping Aidan pontificating.

"Forget the meme. The Regulators and the Vehm. You hold yourself up as moral. As the good guys. Well, news flash, you're not. You're as bad as the In Statera. Both of you. Equally horrific sides of the same coin."

"I respectfully disagree," Adam pointed out.

"Think about it. A well-funded group, run by rich people who make decisions about what's right or wrong for the country, then outsources the dirty work to private contractors. You tell me, is that the In Statera or the Vehm?"

"The Vehm always respected the laws of the land. That's where the difference lies." Adam was doing the arguing here and Jack was content to let him. This sort of theoretical stuff wasn't his cup of tea. He was waiting for the action which he felt sure was soon to come. Aidan was making this speech to stall, to get something ready. Of that, he was certain.

"Only that's not true. The laws of this land say everyone is entitled to a trial in front of his or her peers. The Vehm bypassed that. It's a fundamental right of everyone. They might dress it up as getting into the cracks that justice can't reach, or whatever motivational slogan they use on their Monday morning mail blast. But in reality, they just want to call the shots. Just like the In Statera. I find both things reprehensible, so I made it my life's work to destroy them. And now, I have." He raised his glass in salute, then knocked it all back.

"How did you even end up in the In Statera?" Jack wanted to know. That part of the story didn't make sense to him.

"When I was younger, I was a bloody good journalist. One of the best. It meant I found things out that perhaps I really shouldn't have. In 2006, I interviewed a gentleman named Cecil Roscoe, some well-to-do antiques dealer. He was a horrific human being. Racist. Homophobic. Misogynistic. Hated the proles, as he called them. But he liked me. And not just because I knew a little bit about antiques." His tone and raised eyebrows meant they knew exactly what he meant.

"I thought you said he was homophobic?" Adam said.

"Self-loathing is nothing new. And that man loathed himself almost as much as he loved himself. He was a real mess of a human being. Very complicated. But I knew there was something going on there. The more he tried to impress me, the more he told me about his so-called power and influence over the world. He dropped hints that there were things that he could make happen on a political level. I thought he had the ear of some MPs, so imagine my surprise when he started to let on that he was part of a secret society. I thought it sounded like a bloody good story, so I followed it. I did whatever I needed to in order to gain his confidence. As I said, blood, sweat and tears went into this. When I found out what he really was, I was appalled."

"Why didn't you expose him? You had the power. You had the story."

"I had no proof. The same as you don't. And admittedly, here is where the three of us become one and the same. I knew that they needed stopping and the only way I could do that was from the inside. Unfortunately for Roscoe, his health began to fail not long after he told me."

"I bet it did," Adam added the flourish and Aidan smiled.

"It was so unexpected. He deteriorated quite quickly without ever having an heir apparent in place. I promised him that I would keep his life's work alive and take up that mantle, but he was reluctant. How could a lowly journalist be in the In Statera? I was his bit of rough, not a man who could be trusted to rule the country. And he was right, of course. He was far too sound of mind to agree to that. But all that needed was a slight change in tack. His mental faculties had to be affected, not just his physical ones. With the right medication and repeated lies over a sustained period of time, by the time he shuffled off this mortal coil, dear old Roscoe was incredibly close to Victor Clarke, a businessman of great esteem. He was more than happy to hand over the reins to him."

"How did it all work? The In Statera were supposedly unaware of each other. How could you take his place?"

Aidan reached under the counter he was propped against and pulled up a black briefcase. "In the modern world it's all very simple. We have this." He opened the case and turned it to face them. It looked as if it had a laptop embedded inside it. "As secure a system as they could muster. It requires biometric data to be accessed, and this…" He reached inside his pocket and removed a round golden disc. Larger than a coin but intricately designed showing a set of scales set in perfect balance, with an eye in each. Crossed swords lay underneath, whilst other flourishes of pageantry were embossed elsewhere. Unicorns, lions. Symbols of who knows what.

"Is that your participation medal?" Jack quipped.

"Very good. No, in the olden days this was the identifier. They did the whole cloaked meeting thing. I suppose at the very beginning they all knew who each other was. But as time passed and the mantle moved to future generations, withholding their identity must have seemed advantageous. I imagine if you follow the history of the In Statera deeply enough, there will be some moment of betrayal somewhere that caused everyone to decide it was best to remain incognito. Now it's more hi-tech. You place it into a custom-made reader and, along with your biometrics and triple lock passcodes, you're in."

"Nice to see the old traditions being kept alive," Adam nodded.

"Anyway, once I was in I tried to find out who the others were, so I could remove them. It was always the plan. The problem was, as I tried to maintain my cover, I came across the Vehm and their private police force, so I had to add them to my list. An already complicated plan got more complicated. It took time. It took cunning. And finally, I realised my best option was to set the two sides against each other in open warfare. You could destroy each other for me. I exposed In Statera operations where I could. Pulled off operations that risked their cover. You nearly were on to us at one point, but you… you, Jack Quinn… bottled it."

"Me?"

"Yes. You let the police have their way instead. Handed over a suspect to that Watts woman you're so fond of."

"You are fond of her," Adam agreed. "You should look into that."

"Behave," Jack warned.

Aidan's face snarled a little at the interruption. Jack could tell they were ruining his moment. He had done all of this; why were they so calm and uninterested? He was going to crack at some point. Which was what they wanted.

"You were behind the plot to blow up a nuke in London?"

"It would have got everyone's attention, wouldn't it? Sadly, when things went pear-shaped, someone else in the group made the smart decision to kill off Bowen. The true story never had the chance to get out. I had to bide my time. Then I got lucky. The paedophile ring coming out fell into my lap. And what was better, Adam, was you bringing the story to Nathan. It was perfect. The In Statera were seething. They needed revenge. The Dead Line, as they called it, had been crossed and they went to war. I could have waited and watched but I wanted one last thing. I had heard the rumour that there was a list of names out there, held by the Vehm, of who was in the In Statera."

"There was. How did you find out?"

"Nick Poole. A useful asset, I must confess."

"I would love to catch up with Nick. Remember me to him when you see him next," Jack said. He hadn't forgotten Poole. He hadn't forgotten what he'd done to his son.

"To have you two slug it out to the death would be absolutely fine by me," Aidan smiled.

"Not for him."

"Probably not. But afterwards, I'll have one loose end, not two."

"You seem awfully confident about walking out of here," Adam pointed out.

"I aim to walk out of here, gentlemen. It's your choice whether you do or not. And you do have that choice. It's the only one where you get satisfaction, though, Jack."

"Keep talking," Jack growled. His patience was wearing thin now. Story time was nearly over.

"Nathan Nelmes of course was desperate to follow the lead for me. And he did it brilliantly. Found me the list."

"You killed him?"

"I had him killed. Then to cover any crossover I had my systems purged during the raid. Smoke and mirrors and all that."

"You used my son to cover up Nathan letting you know about the list?"

"Poole used your son. I didn't know the details of his plan. It wasn't one I'd have gone with, but he insisted that if we wanted you back on the map, and we did, then we'd need to do something drastic."

"Why did you want me? I was out."

"You weren't, Jack. You never are. You thwarted me with Bowen. You came back into the fold and helped me after that, whether you knew it or not. You started a war. But I couldn't tell what you were going to do after that war started taking casualties. What would you do when David died? What would you do when Adam was behind bars or dead? I couldn't risk you going on the warpath. Going rogue, especially. I needed you constrained and visible on the field of play. And here you are."

"And your grand plan was what, exactly? Because you've just talked for five minutes and I'm clear as mud."

"I wanted the In Statera gone. I wanted the Vehm gone. I wanted the Regulators gone." Aidan stepped forward, his voice rising to a shout as he reached the end of his speech. "I wanted rich fucking arseholes hiding behind anonymity to no longer be able to call the shots when it comes to justice and law in this country. I wanted you all wiped off the face of the earth because this isn't democracy. This isn't fair on the people. What you do is wrong and it has to end. It has ended. I destroyed it all. And I don't care what you two do to me, now, because if you so much as try anything, we all die."

53

Adam watched Aidan. His mood had changed dramatically in the last few moments. His eyes had widened, his breathing had visibly quickened. He was a man at the end of the road. He'd seen it enough times before.

"We don't need it to end that way," he said, his palms up and forward trying to calm Aidan, whilst wondering just how it was that they were all going to die. He took a step forward.

"Don't come any closer," Aidan warned him. "If you do, it's over."

Aidan wasn't holding anything. There was no sign of wires on his body. No explosive vest attached to him under his shirt. The briefcase could easily have been a bomb. Adam and Jack were about seven metres back from the briefcase. No guarantee of a kill although the injuries would be at the very least severe. Lung damage. Ear drum damage. The sort of thing that *could* kill you, but might not. But there was no sign of a detonator on Aidan. He wasn't the person in control. Someone else was. If Aidan was incapacitated by Jack and Adam, which would seem very likely, then they would want a failsafe. It meant someone watching.

"Who else is here?" Adam asked, keeping his palms facing Aidan.

"Don't worry about that. Just know that if you do want the chance to live and fight another day, you need to let me walk out of here first."

Adam looked at Jack, who cast his eyes to the sky. Adam knew what he meant. He remembered David and Lowri. A drone.

"Okay," Adam agreed, shrugging his shoulders and lowering his arms. "Guessing you've got a drone up there. We can work with that. We can let you go, but what proof do we have that we walk out of here as well?"

He didn't actually expect an answer. He was buying time.

"You don't," Aidan smiled, his voice lowering again as he felt the control heading back his way. "I'm afraid you are completely out of options here. You either stop me from leaving and we all die, or you let me go and you might live."

"I mean, the noble thing to do would be to take one for the team and wipe you out with us," Adam said conversationally. He looked at Jack. "That work for you?"

"I dunno, mate. I've got a bit of a thing to tend to with Nick Poole. Personal issues."

"You see, I said you were base in nature," Aidan smiled again. "But it's what might save you. As I said, I have no love for Poole."

"I'm not so sure about that," Adam replied. "You see I reckon you do have a connection with Poole. Otherwise, he'd have blown us all to kingdom come by now."

Aidan's eyes widened slightly and his nostrils flared as Adam caught him in the lie. "Really?"

"Yeah. I think you would have told him you were going in hard on him when you spoke to us. Forewarned him that you were going to have to badmouth him, but that it wasn't personal and that he had a role with you for life. Because let's face it, Nick Poole has burnt all his bridges, so the only way really he gets to keep living like he does is if it's for you."

"He could fuck off to Russia or something. I bet they'd give him a warm welcome. Or bleed him dry of everything he knows, then make him a cup of their famous tea," Jack suggested.

"I don't think he'd be into that. If he's scarpering off somewhere, it'll be a nice warm country, where you can buy a new identity for pennies on the pound. Guarantee he's got it sorted though. Plane ticket in hand as we speak," Adam countered.

"If you think you're rattling me, you're very much mistaken," Aidan sighed.

"Nah. Not rattling, pal, just buying a couple of moments," Adam smiled.

"For what?"

Above them there was a small '*crump*' sound as something exploded. Then as Aidan began to ask, "What the hell happened?" flaming metal fragments crashed into the garden and onto the roof of the house.

"Your drone's fucked it, mate," Jack stated as Adam's earpiece relayed the confirmation from the army captain who had been listening in the whole time and liaising with his team.

They stood for a second, Aidan open-mouthed, Jack and Adam smiling. Then Aidan ran. As he did so, Poole appeared in the garden, assault rifle in his hands. He fired into the room at distance. Jack and Adam scrambled for cover.

"I want Poole," Jack called over the sound of breaking glass and bullets.

"Then I'll deal with Marshall."

Jack returned fire first and Adam broke from where they'd hidden, running in the direction Aidan had gone. It was back the way they'd come, towards the door. It was open when Adam got there. Aidan was already getting into his car. Adam launched himself into the doorway, propping himself against the frame of the door. He took a breath and fired. The whole clip. Into the front of the car where Aidan was climbing. It lurched forward, spinning its wheels on the gravel. Adam ran down the steps, releasing the empty clip, his other hand bringing the next one up as he did so. Before he'd levelled the gun again, the car veered right, swerving, then fishtailing on the gravel as the powerful rear wheels bit. It was facing away from the gate now, the front window towards the house. Adam could see a clear shot. He fired. Another clip gone in seconds. The engine whined then slowed to an idle. The front window was gone. Shards hanging where the last bits hadn't been separated from the frame. He dropped the clip, reached for his last one, sliding it into the gun.

Aidan was leaning back in the driver's seat when Adam approached. He couldn't see his hands, so he kept the gun trained on the man's face. The first sign of movement, he was ending it.

"I should have thought of that," Aidan gasped. He was hurt bad. He wasn't going to make it. Even if Adam called for help. Which he wasn't going to do.

"Everyone has all the answers until they don't."

"I was so close," Aidan croaked.

"Closer," Adam admitted. Aside from the loose ends, Aidan Marshall had achieved everything he set out to do. The In Statera, the Vehm, the Regulators. All gone.

"That's good then," Aidan shuffled in his seat as if he could ease the pain. "I did well."

"No, you didn't." Adam lowered his gun as Aidan Marshall's eyes rolled upwards.

54

Poole fired another burst into the room as he approached. Jack could do nothing to slow him. He was one on one with a guy with a machine gun. He was completely outgunned and right now, outflanked. He fired back. Two shots. A token gesture. He had to conserve his ammo. Poole answered with another volley that told Jack it was less of a concern for his opponent.

Jack heard the crunch of glass as Poole reached the threshold of the house. There wasn't much ground left to cover now. He needed to think of a way out of this quickly. He looked for something, anything, to give him an edge. The sound of glass breaking stopped. Poole was in the room. Jack shuffled around the corner of the kitchen island. The bottle of whisky Aidan had been drinking had fallen to the floor and smashed. A waste of good spirits.

Jack looked at the shelf where it had originally been taken from. More whisky. Vodka. Rum. Tequila. All expensive-looking. Which usually meant more kick than your regular supermarket varieties. Which also meant more flammable.

Time was running out. He let out a groan of pain. Something he hoped was convincing. Then he ripped the sleeve from his jersey. The sort of thing he'd do if he was stemming blood flow. Poole would have heard all of it. He would have known his prey was wounded. He would be readying himself for the kill. With a little bit of luck, he'd be savouring the moment.

Jack lunged for the shelf, grabbing at what he hoped was the right bottle. Poole saw him and fired. Jack got back down just in time. His fingers fumbled with the lid. A stopper. No unscrewing. No fiddling with a cork. God bless excess. As soon as it was out, he was forcing the fabric of his sleeve in, down to the remaining spirit. He glanced over his shoulder to his left. Poole loomed large at the other end of the kitchen island. Jack ducked back. More gunshots, chewing chunks of marble or whatever the hell the island was made of. Spitting them out so they flicked at Jack as he took the flare from his pocket. He slammed it into the floor, the red flame spitting, the smell rushing up his nose. The fabric was already there, the flames licking. He held the two together. *Why the hell not?* he thought. More chance of it doing what it was meant to.

He stood, spinning as he did, presenting himself to Poole. The gun came up as Jack's arm came forward. The barrel of the gun had almost found its mark as Poole realised what was happening. He tried to move out of the way, but his momentum was going one way and Jack had locked on. The bottle and flare left his hand, his arm whipping them forward with all the power he could muster. Flames and sparks swirling together as it arced end over end towards its target. The bottle crashed into Poole, shattering against the butt of the gun that he'd brought up to deflect it with. To protect himself. In the end it did the opposite. The spirit exploded out, some of it already alight, the rest of it igniting in the maelstrom of flare and fire. It rained down on Poole who screamed in pain, spinning and beating at his body, trying to put the flames out.

Jack hadn't ducked. He hadn't wasted a second. His right hand had carried on downwards, back to his hip. Back to his holster. He reached his pistol then brought it back up. Whilst Poole danced with the burning liquid, Jack took aim. No wasted time. No final one-liner. Three shots. All at his head. All hit their target. Poole dropped to the floor dead, the fire still eating away at his flesh.

"You all right?" Adam called from out in the hallway.

"All good," Jack shouted back; he turned and saw Adam in the doorway. "That worked well."

"Best plan we've had in a long time."

"Low bar."

55

It was cold down by the banks of the Thames that night. Jack looked at Southwark Bridge from the bench where he sat. The dome of St Paul's Cathedral crept up behind it. People walked past him. Some had got their jackets back out from wherever they'd been storing them over the summer. Others still hadn't conceded that summer was over. They wore their T-shirts and their short sleeves as if clinging to hope that even as September ticked around and the nights grew longer, that there was some last vestige of summer left. Jack hoped there wasn't. This summer had been hot enough. Whatever way you looked at it.

A figure approached.

"They say the country's a lot safer now," Thea said as she sat down next to him.

"Sitting next to me seems to be a dangerous place," Jack warned.

"Then maybe I should keep this brief." Thea was smiling at him when he turned his head. "How are you?"

"I've lived," he replied.

"I can see."

"You?"

"I'm good."

They sat looking at each other for a moment. Jack couldn't help but feel happy to see her. Really happy.

"Are you working?" she asked.

He shook his head. "No, not yet. I don't need to. Not for a while anyway, till I figure out what I want to do."

"You want to be a Regulator, Jack," she said softly.

Jack said nothing.

"It's different now," Thea went on. "After it was all done, Hargreaves brought them in. The Regulators, the Vehm. There's a new world out there. It's no longer us versus them. People are cooperating now. We're working together. Governments and private enterprise, on their own, they can't do everything. Same as in any walk of life. But coming together, working with each other, we might just save this world, Jack."

"We?" That surprised him.

"I'm now the liaison between the Regulators and the UK government. Unofficial, of course. My job doesn't exist because this relationship doesn't exist."

"The Regulators, the Vehm, they were supposed to hold governments to account. How does that work now?"

Thea put a hand on his shoulder. "Come and find out."

"Maybe," he replied. "First, though, I need to take care of some personal issues."

* * * *

Jack hadn't realised how much he had missed being able to go into somewhere without worrying about who was looking for him, until the first time he'd gone to watch vigil over Calum after it was all over. Hargreaves had worked hard to ensure that Jack's record was scrubbed clean. The same with everyone else. For that, Jack figured he probably owed the guy something. But then, hadn't he already done enough?

He paused outside the room his son was in. Isobel had left as he arrived. They'd said a quick hello. Isobel had said she was glad he was there. That nothing much had changed. The doctors were hopeful. But that there still wasn't much more than a 60:40 chance in Calum's favour. And even if the 60 won, his life was over. There were crimes he'd committed that he would have to answer for. Hargreaves had promised something would be worked out, but that the murder of innocents couldn't go unanswered. Jack understood that, but as he stood looking at his son, he couldn't help but feel that he'd received something his son deserved. A second chance.

Jack opened the door and stepped into the room. The sound of Calum breathing through the ventilator cut through him with every breath. He felt the tears in his eyes. This was on him. There was no escaping it. Not only the fact that Calum had been used as bait, but everything that had driven Calum to be this vulnerable. To be this scarred from the way Jack had failed him as a father. As a human being. He hadn't done what was needed and now he needed to find a way to fix it.

He sat down, taking his son's hand. It felt small. Like it had done when he was a boy. Calum might have been a man now. He might have bulked up, but to Jack he would always be his son. His kid. The child he loved with all his heart but just hadn't been able to show it properly. Why the fuck hadn't he been able to show it properly?

He bowed his head and placed Calum's hand against it. "I'm sorry," he sobbed. "I'm so sorry, son."

He cried. He didn't know how long for. It felt like hours. When it was over he didn't feel the usual release that crying brought. His wretchedness and despair lived on. They hadn't gone away. Calum was still going to prison. His boy, the kid who had been bullied, who had been so alone that he'd been manipulated into an act of unspeakable evil. If he survived this, prison would kill him. And it would do it slowly, cruelly.

"I wish I could have saved you," Jack sniffed. "I would do anything to save you."

Jack looked at Calum once more. He couldn't let him go to prison. Not Calum. It would be a death sentence. And Isobel and Kat. They would have to watch their son, their brother, dying in slow motion before them.

He needed an answer. A way out of this. But there was only one looming in his mind. One he couldn't bring himself to do, but one he knew he had to do. It had to be him. It had to be quick. He had to save his son from this.

"I'm sorry," Jack bowed his head. Inside, he felt nothing but agony as his soul tore itself in two over the fate of his son. To survive the night and live a life of misery until he died, or for Jack to end it and save him. He needed to have a plan. A way to make this right. He remembered what Emmie had said to him. That he'd avenged Calum. Won the victory against those that had hurt him. But that it had got him nowhere. It hadn't helped. Her words hung in his head.

Jack wept as he made the decision. The hardest decision of his life. The one he would carry with him forever, but that he knew was right.

THE END

The Regulators will return in 2025.

Authors Notes

I'm going to start with the apology. Dead Line took a lot longer to write than I ever dreamed of. There are multiple reasons for this.

Firstly, the writing process took place in a period of my life when there was a lot of personal upheaval. I started the first draft in spring 2019. By summer we were in the process of moving house. Add in a young family and a full time job and let's just say things were crazy. By the time 2020 came around and it looked like I was about to get a big chunk of time to write my book, the whole world went through what I will simply call "a thing."

I know for some writers this meant they had a lot more time on their hands. For me, I was lucky enough to find extra work that I could do from home, especially as my wife was furloughed for a long time. This kept the roof over our head, but coupled with the way things were, it wasn't a good head space for me to be writing in and Dead Line fell by the way side. When I did finally come back to it and complete it, the final story was bloated, slow and ultimately not what I wanted to put out there.

I had lost my belief and mojo at that point. I decided to embark on a new writing adventure and finished another book, *Dead Men Don't Pay*, which will be out this summer. Doing something different gave me creative scope to find myself again. By the time I returned to Dead Line at the back end of 2023 I was hungry. I was ready. And I tore into it. The result is something I am immensely proud of and now I'm sitting on about three Regulators ideas trying to work out which one comes next in the universe.

There is no excerpt from the next Regulators at the end of this book as there was the last two times. Just a promise that they will return. And they're going to keep coming back for years to come. I'm having the best time writing them again. I can't wait to show you where they're going next. But we will have to wait. Just not as long as last time.

Thank you so much to everyone for your patience. Thank you to all those who have supported me along the way. My wife, kids, family, friends. The team at the U.K. Crime Book Club. All the absolutely fantastic authors I've got to meet over the last few years doing Pub Quizzes, live events and podcasts. This community is a special place and now I really feel a part of it.

Thanks again,

Ben.

Printed in Great Britain
by Amazon